ALIENATION

ALSO BY THE AUTHOR

THE STARSTRUCK SAGA

Starstruck

Alienation

Traveler

Celestial

Starbound

Earthstuck

Inalienable

AIX MARKS THE SPOT

NOVELLAS AND SHORT STORIES

Miss Planet Earth (Pew! Pew! - The Quest for More Pew!)

The Horrible Habits of Humans (Pew! Pew! - Bite My Shiny Metal Pew!)

Miss Planet Earth and the Amulet of Beb Sha Na

Head over Heels (Starstruck Halloween Short)

Lasers and Tiaras (Starstruck Short)

Study Night at the Museum (Unbound: Stories of Transformation, Love, And Monsters)

BOOK TWO OF THE STARSTRUCK SAGA

ALIENATION

S.E. ANDERSON

BOLIDE

ALIENATION

First published in 2017 by Bolide Publishing Limited

Bolidepublishing.com

ISBN: 978-1-912996-33-9

FOR MY FAMILY
SUGAR ON IT!

ONE

THE ART OF SPACE TRAVEL AND HUMAN REPAIR

THE UNIVERSE WAS A COLD, DARK, AND empty place.

And I loved it.

I drifted in perfect silence, my legs dangling, useless, in the void below, my senses a mere whisper in the back of my head. Everything was pure in the quiet: there was no worry, no stress, nothing to get wrapped up about.

It was amazing.

The darkness extended forever, though it seemed to have some depth. Unlike a cave or a pitch-black room, this kind of darkness had no end.

So it was a little weird I could see my hands. Strange, perhaps, but I wasn't worried. Nothing worried me.

There was no up or down; no left, no right; just eternity. And while I knew it was cold, the temperature didn't bother me. It could have been warm; I didn't care.

ALIENATION

For a minute, I thought I must be dead. What did death feel like, anyway?

And then the stars came out.

They blinked into existence, one by one, little holes pocked with pins on a distant black fabric. I reached out as if to touch them, but they were too far away, so very far away. Even so, I felt the heat radiating from them, the warmth that pulsed as they pulsed. They were so beautiful. I wanted to pick them up, pluck them off their celestial shelf, and bury them in my chest, keep their warmth forever.

Once again, I wondered where I was. I remembered feeling intense pain, like someone had tried to force me through a slivered crack in a window, yet all that was left was a dull, vague ache, like a long-forgotten memory bobbing slowly to the surface. I felt my chest with my hands. It was still there, intact. I was fine.

And it didn't matter, anyway.

The stars almost looked like diamonds. They didn't twinkle like the stars watching over Earth. I wondered why they didn't twinkle like they were supposed to. Twinkle, twinkle.

"Is she … singing?" The voice was angelic, the most beautiful voice I had ever heard. Ethereal. It wrapped me in a sweet, heavenly blanket, lifting me higher in space and filling me with a deep sense of satisfaction. My bliss grew tenfold. The pretty lights around me made me grin.

"Um … she might be?" another voice answered, just as beautiful, if not more so. It was deeper, resonating in a timbre that took my breath away. I turned, swaying awkwardly in the emptiness, searching for the sound. I listened without hearing, letting the voices wash over me. The pain I thought I remembered was a lie. There was nothing but beauty here.

"Has this happened to her before?" the higher voice asked. A woman, I realized, wondering why I hadn't noticed before. I could find no sign from where the voice came, but I was in no rush to find out.

"I can't remember if we've jumped Terrans this far," the other one replied, worried. "Who knows what we're meant to expect?"

"If her brain's fried, just remember it was your fault; you were steering."

"I thought you were."

"No. Your friend, you drive." The voice, though still beautiful, sounded harsh.

"Really?" There was a pause. "We should have a system for jumping friends."

"Yeah, like we have a lot of those."

And as she stopped talking, so the angel left. I reached out for it, letting out a small moan. I begged for the voice to return, to warm me once again.

It was getting cold now.

There was a quiet sigh in the distance—neither melodious nor divine. I realized my arms felt heavy. Were the stars rising? No, I was falling, slowly at first, so slow I didn't notice until it was too late. The stars rushed past me in a dizzying ballet, going faster and faster.

ALIENATION

My world shattered, my universe ending. The tightness in my chest grew, and I could do nothing to stop it. I drew wildly at the space around me, wanting to scream, but the pain clutched my windpipe and kept me silent.

"You're saying I screwed up, huh?" the male replied, almost savagely, but beneath it I heard fear—the same fear in my chest. His voice sent a tremor through my universe. "What should I do? Do I wake her up, or do I—"

"Better not," the other voice said, and I wondered how I ever have found it angelic. It was harsh, gruff; crude. "Don't mess with her. She should be fine once it washes over."

"Are you sure? These people can die in their sleep, you know. Combusting spontaneously, just like that! Poof, they're gone."

"Urban legends, surely."

"It's no joke," the man assured her. "I need to make sure she's okay. I don't want her to—"

"Fine. Your guest, your responsibility. You mess up her brain, it is not my fault. Clear?"

The voices went silent, and the world returned to normal. The stars slowed, and I bobbed amidst them but the sense of peace was gone. I worried about where I'd gone and what I was doing here. My legs and arms, still dangling beneath me, hurt from their own weight, and it annoyed me that my chest still felt constricted.

And then, suddenly, there was a chill. The cold hit my muscles, making them contract and spasm. The space around me melted. The stars didn't race; they disappeared as if to say they were done with me.

I stifled a scream as the universe crumbled around me. The world was bleak and black, then gone, and then nothing at all.

I threw out my hands to grab the void, to clutch at everything, anything, and found warm flesh. Bouncy, springy skin. I grabbed onto what I assumed, and hoped, was a hand. My anchor to reality. My mind finally pieced itself together, the thoughts flying and reassembling until it all made sense again.

Like rising to the surface after being underwater too long, I floated upward. My eyes pushed themselves open to reveal a gray ceiling and a face with a hand clutching it from forehead to chin, from cheek to cheek.

"She's opened her eyes," the voice muttered from under my hand. I pulled it back quickly. My face, which I realized was damp, felt hot—was I blushing? But the man smiled, unperturbed by my facial groping. The next step was to figure out who he was, and what he was doing there.

The woman put her face in front of mine, her halo of bright hair fanning out from her sharp, olive-toned features. Red, pink, blue, and purple strands fell away from her face, the deep, gray eyes scanning me just as intensely as I scanned her.

"Doesn't look too screwed up," the woman muttered. She snapped her fingers next to my ears then threw up a stiff index finger and brought it back and forth across my line of vision. The man looked annoyed, practically glowering, but if he had anything to say to her, he kept his mouth shut.

"Reactions seem normal enough, but I don't have much of a baseline to go with. This appears to be the norm for lower cognitive life forms. Wait until the word processing boots up and you can have a normal conversation with her. Might take a while but count yourself lucky: she has all her limbs."

I turned my head to the side and let out the contents of my stomach. My throat burned, but I was more focused on how the vomit sloshed and hit his shoes. My eyes and nose felt clogged and hot. Instantly, there were hands on my neck, but they were there to hold my hair, gently, as I sat up and retched once again.

Ugh, gross. I felt rung out, hungover. Not only that, but I was pretty embarrassed.

It wasn't the woman holding my hair but the man. He stared at me with a worry so intense I could barely process it.

Was I dying? Sure felt like I was. He looked at me like I had minutes left to live.

I opened my mouth, but before I could utter a sound, it snapped shut. I tried again, taking a deep breath before forcing my jaw open, but the sound leaving my vocal cords didn't resemble words in the slightest. Instead, a prolonged squawk left my throat, my body's awful attempt to take up birdsong. The sound was loud, unstoppable, and most certainly pungent.

The woman let out a snort. The man glared at her, shutting her up. "Not a word," he ordered.

When he turned back, I coaxed my jaw into moving at my command. My lips danced before they managed to let out a sound.

"Hey," I croaked.

"Hey, Sally." A smile spread across his face. "Are you all right? You can hear me okay?"

"Pressure," I said, forcing a yawn to pop the bubbles in my ears. It didn't do much to help. The world was becoming clearer, and their names floated back to the surface. I was not a fan of the real world lagging.

"Zander?" I sputtered, and his eyes lit up.

Zander, the man I hadn't seen in two years, who had returned in the middle of the night to take me to the stars, the man I had hit with my car, the man who had blown up my workplace, the man not of this earth. Or, my Earth, anyway.

I'm pretty sure we weren't in Kansas anymore. Well, not Kansas, but our solar system probably wasn't anywhere near here.

He had promised to come back and made good on that promise, even if it did come a little late. I wanted to be angry about that, angry at how he had abandoned me to deal with the aftermath of the plant's explosion by myself.

But for him, so he claimed, only a week had passed since leaving Earth, a side effect of his kind of space travel.

ALIENATION

As for me, I promised myself I wouldn't mention any of that. I wouldn't let anything ruin this trip, the one I had been waiting for since seeing the stars as a child for the first time. If this was my only shot at leaving my planet, I sure wasn't going to ruin it.

I took his arm, and he helped me up, my legs wobbly and weak. I narrowly avoided the puddle of vomit on the floor. I felt empty and drained, but my muscles were slowly coming back to me.

"Are you well?" the woman asked, perched on the impossibly high windowsill above us, giving me only a second of her gaze. The large window was the only one in the room, and she was staring at the world beyond it, as if she were a sentry, keeping watch, keeping us safe from the shadows. She almost looked comfortable up there; how she had gotten on the sill, I had absolutely no idea, but it was likely she was doing it just to show off.

It sounded like something Blayde would do.

Blayde, the living weapon, an amazingly dangerous military panoply in the form of a petite, muscular woman. Not human, though she sure looked it. I had no idea what she was, seeing as how she and her brother hadn't told me about their planet of origin or anything.

Not that it would have meant anything to me if they had.

"I'm fine, I think, thank you." I pretended I didn't know that Blayde didn't care about my well-being. I regretted speaking almost instantly. The words rang like cymbals in my ears, crushingly loud, every syllable a blow to my eardrums.

She was colder now, despite only having been gone for a week. Was that normal? I had thought Blayde was warming up to me when we brought down Grisham. She had allowed me to come along on this trip, and I was under the impression that was massive coming from her. But it seemed whatever I had done to deserve merit in her eyes had washed away in her week with the Killians. I guess liking me a tiny bit wasn't the same as wanting me to tag along.

I tried to take a step on my own, shaking off Zander's hand. My feet shuffled zombie-like on the cold stone floor, legs shaking as I put weight on them. Finally, though, I stood on my own, and I was proud of that, but now my mind was free to worry about other things, and it mainly focused on what I was doing here.

"What happened?" I asked, teetering on my still weak limbs.

Blayde shrugged. "You blacked out." It was obvious from her tone she didn't care.

"Nothing bad or anything," Zander was quick to say, his face all smiles and nods. "Your body reacted a little differently to the jump than expected. There's nothing to worry about. The first time can be a little traumatic for some. It's not a very pleasant process, having your body reduced to atoms and sent to the other side of the universe in less than an instant."

"Oh, okay." I smiled sheepishly at my crutch. "I can see why that's problematic … for some."

I gave him my best attempt at a reassuring grin. The look on Zander's face said he didn't buy it.

ALIENATION

"You sure you're all right?" he asked.

"Positive."

To prove it, I distanced myself from his grasp and managed a few tentative steps. I really was fine, it seemed. What a relief.

I wondered why the floor felt so cold, even though my Chucks. And then I wondered where in the universe we could be, and the cold faded. I had more interesting things to think about.

"You see?" I cracked a real smile this time, the excitement pulsing through me. "Totally fine. Nothing to worry about. So, where are we?"

At first glance, the answer was simple: we were in someone's garage. The room looked somewhere between a barn loft and a cathedral with vaulted ceilings and the one large window high on the wall. The floors looked like they were made of stone and the rafters of wood; nothing seemed otherworldly in the slightest. We could have been anywhere in the U.S.

A large tarp covered a vehicle in the middle of the room, something bigger than a car but smaller than a truck. Larger in sheer bulk, maybe, but it sat on the floor rather low, only reaching my hip. I had an incredible urge to rip off the tarp, go *aha,* and discover a spaceship. But we were technically trespassing, and I should probably limit what I touched.

No matter how exciting those things were.

I was relieved my duffel bag had arrived in one piece. I knelt and rifled through it while waiting for someone to answer me, feeling odd and out of place and not sure when it was polite to repeat myself, like when I was a kid and invited to a friend's house for the first time. I pretended to focus on my bag to stifle the awkwardness.

Still, it was awkward.

"Not quite sure yet," Blayde said excitedly, slipping down from her perch. "The reason we have so little light is because there's a huge billboard blocking most of the window. That isn't sunlight in here: It's artificial UV, pumped in to make this place seem more natural in exchange for stealing their view. Great for the owner, sucks for us. We're going to have to go out."

"Hold on, what?" I jumped to my feet, wide-eyed.

"Which part has got your head in a twist?" Blayde made the sweetest, most patronizing smile a face could make. "Was it the UV light thing? Or the problem of being a real estate owner in a universe where anyone can pop into your home?"

"Go back to the part where you don't know where the hell we are."

"Oh, yeah, that." She shrugged. "Zander didn't tell you? Universal lottery. We jump and see where the solar winds blow us. Destination: anywhere."

"So we could be anywhere in the … entire universe?"

"Yup."

"So the air out there might be poisonous and destroy our lungs and burn off our faces."

"It could." She shrugged again. "But it won't. Back me up here, Zander."

ALIENATION

"Jumping may be random, but we never arrive anywhere where the atmosphere hates us. That would be awful."

"Okay, great," I said. "Coming from people who can't die … totally reassuring."

"Blayde and I can survive pretty much anything, but it doesn't mean we like breathing sulfuric acid."

This was, after all, the deal I had struck to see a different corner of the universe. We can jump somewhere at random, then back to the starting point, but further than that and we can never go back. Dangerous, but it wasn't every day I got to leave the planct, and it wasn't as if Zander hadn't explained the situation before.

Well, two whole years ago.

"Not to mention, I'm a fantastic driver," Zander said, running a hand through his hair. Blayde let out a loud snort.

"Oh please," she said. "Until ten minutes ago, you thought I was the one doing the steering. We arrived safely through wishing and praying. A whole lot of praying. Thankfully that hasn't done any of us in yet."

"It's a good thing I remember how to get back to Earth, then."

She turned her attention to the wall, drawing her hands over it like she were caressing a body. Her hands were gentle and delicate, running over cracks and crevasses, searching for something. Her eyes were focused, determined.

Zander watched her, somewhat excitedly, as if wanting to join her, and with a start, I realized I was holding him back.

"So, um," I said, trying to break the silence. I was determined not to be the third wheel on this interstellar trip. "How do we get out of here? I don't see a door."

"It's probably hiding," Zander replied. "It's what happens when you max-up your privacy settings."

"So how do we … where can we find it? Can we find it?"

"You have to coax it out," Blayde grunted, but it was invitation enough. We joined her by the wall. I ran my hands over the stone-like interior, trying to find anything out of place, though not sure exactly what I was looking for.

I wondered again what the walls were made of; it felt like stone but was wrong, somehow, like it was artificial. My mind shouted Alien Tech on repeat. I took a long sniff, taking in the scent of damp stone. It smelled like the musty cellar of an old English home.

There were no drafts to follow for a clue to the door's whereabouts, but the noise—or rather, the loud buzz—coming from the outside seemed louder at one end of the room. Blayde paused and inspected that side more intently.

Her strange methods of searching for an exit had to be the culmination of years of experience in finding herself in tight spots. Her fingers tapped the walls as if she were playing the piano; her right foot came down more forcefully on the floor than her left, leaving a slight pause for her to listen.

My eyes caught the tarp again. I left Blayde to her search and snuck over to it, determined to peek. I lifted a corner to see the fender of a bright red sports car. At least, it looked like a sports car. I was disappointed. I had expected something a little more futuristic.

I jumped when someone touched my elbow. Zander crouched beside me, taking the tarp from my hand and letting it fall back in place. "We're trespassing, remember?"

I nodded, feeling like I had been lectured by a teacher. A bit embarrassing, but Zander was still smiling; no hard feelings.

"I barfed in the corner."

"We should probably clean that up."

"Ah, here," Blayde said from across the room. She ran her hand along the wall, and an arch lit up in the dust. A bright blue light glowed from inside the stone itself. Within seconds, a door materialized as if it had been there all along.

"What the …?" I stammered, and Blayde smirked.

"They don't have this on your backwater planet, do they?" She sniggered. Zander rolled his eyes.

"Security. The door only exists when you need it," he explained, "and Blayde, calm down, will you? Be polite. We're all—"

"Yeah, yeah, rainbows and sunshine," she muttered. "Anyway, ready?"

I wondered if giant bees inhabited the world outside. Maybe we'd get stung to death by killer bees in a strange twist of fate. Part of me wanted the door to stay safely shut forever.

But the rest of me wanted to see the world beyond. That's why I had come along, after all; I wanted to see the universe, if only for one short day. To quench my astrolust. A brief trip with my best friend, who happened to be a space-hopping alien.

Life had stopped making sense the second I hit him with my car.

Blayde and Zander were ecstatic, their faces radiant with joy and excitement, though they did not voice this aloud. After a long look shared with her brother, Blayde ceremoniously took out her laser pointer, adjusted a small dial on its short handle, and pointed the tip at the crack between the door and its frame. She severed the lock with surgical precision, a motion she had obviously performed many times before.

She threw the door open, and my heart skipped as I prepared to lay eyes on my very first alien planet.

TWO

A WHOLE NEW WORLD,
A WHOLE FANTASTICALLY UNSETTLING VIEW

HERE'S A LIST OF THINGS I EXPECTED TO SEE outside the door: a city from the future, full of squid-like beings; an alien hillside, grass growing red from soil that had never been stepped on by humankind. Maybe an apocalyptic wasteland, who knew?

What I didn't expect was somebody's living room.

It looked like any old living room, with warm, orange sofas and odd-brown wallpaper. It was lit, however, by fluorescent lights, basking the space in an air of office dullness. The smell of old shoes turned my nose.

What I expected to see even less of were five bald men—if they even were men—in black suits, waiting in a row, glaring at us. Not tailored suits, but tight body suits like what a diver would wear. The men bore almost identical expressions of pure concentration.

Oh, and they were pointing guns at us.

I should have mentioned that first.

"Oh, sorry." I said it like I had waltzed into the wrong room in a house and not just jumped across the galaxy to land in their living room. Not quite sure where that reflex came from, but it was a terrible idea.

They responded with gunfire.

The sound was like being inside a continuous clap of thunder. The blasts, loud and all at once, made my ears burst with pain. I was ripped backward, my feet coming out from under me as something red hot whizzed by my ear.

Great, first futuristic thing I lay eyes on, and it's a laser bullet-thing trying to kill me.

Zander shielded me as Blayde slammed the door shut with a flash of her hand against the wall. All that was left was the stone wall—at least, I thought it was stone.

The wall of fire continued for a few seconds—*bam bam bam bam bam*—then slowly subsided. I doubted it was because they were out of ammo.

"There's no escape!" said a voice, booming through our small garage. It was a strange accent, but it was clear and in audible English.

I balked. None of it was English; it couldn't be. Whatever translator Zander had given me, back when he and I were saving Earth from the not-so-passive-after-all Killians, still worked. And it was really pulling its weight.

"Come out with your hands or other appendages high in the air or away from any garment of clothing, if you are a garment-wearing being!"

ALIENATION

"You okay?" Zander glanced me over from top to bottom. I brushed him off, breathing heavily. No, panting. I had gone from calm to panic in a half-second flat, but that was the least of my worries.

I hadn't been hit, thank goodness, but Blayde had collapsed to the floor. Not the best way to start our trip to an alien world.

"Is she …" I asked, but I already knew the answer. The bloody hole smack dab in the middle of her forehead confirmed my fears.

"Dead, yeah." Zander prodded her limp shoulder with his index finger. "Don't worry, she won't be for long. They used condensed plasma instead of metal bullets, so it's a quick fix."

"Yeah, okay, not worrying." I wanted to throw up again, but the contents of my stomach were already sitting on the other side of the garage.

"You are surrounded. Surrender now, and your deaths will be quick!"

"Zander, what the hell is going on?"

"I have to be totally honest here." He leaned against the space that had once been a door, placing his ear against the fake stone. "I have only the slightest of ideas."

I wanted to roll my eyes, but my energy went into de-escalating my racing heart, preventing this panic from growing into a full-blown attack. I'd had quite a few of them in the years since my brother's accident and then during the incident at the plant, but no way was I going to have one now. I had my pills with me. My mood was stable, but none of that took the dead body at my feet, or the confused alien at my side, into account.

I took deep breaths and focused on counting beats, all the while incapable of taking my eyes off Blayde's. The last time I had seen them so empty and devoid of life had been on Earth. The day the plant blew up and Matt died and Zander and Blayde had left me behind.

It was an accident; everything was an accident. I forced myself to look away. *She'll always be okay.*

"Well, what is it?" I asked between terrified breaths.

"What is what?"

"Your idea."

"Oh, that." He nodded slowly, keeping one ear pressed against the wall. "I don't think they like us trespassing."

"Well, I gathered that much," I stammered. "What else? Come on, man, deduce something here!"

"You deduce!"

"I don't even know where we are. Were those guys aliens?"

"Probably?"

"Why do they look human?"

Zander lifted his eyebrows and gave me a knowing look. I inhaled sharply. "Fine, I guess people can be both."

"Exactly." He smiled, the nicest human-looking alien I knew, then went back to listening to the wall.

"So, are they immortal space jumpers too?" I asked.

ALIENATION

"Now isn't really the best of times for alien genealogy, Sally."

"But can they jump in here?"

"I doubt it. I have yet to meet anyone other than Blayde and I who can do that."

"Oh." A breath. "Oh! Are you saying you're the only ones in the entire universe who are—"

"If you do not turn yourselves over this instant, we will be forced to take drastic measures."

"Sally, not the time. We'll have this conversation when we're not in imminent danger."

"Your deaths could take longer than anticipated, and your families will be stuck filling out the forms for the rest of their lives."

"You're not really in any danger, though, are you?"

"Sally!"

"And then their children will waste their lives filling out those death forms. You would not want that, we suppose."

Zander's sentence was punctuated by a sharp inhale—not mine, surprisingly. Blayde's eyes brightened, and she sprang to her feet, wiping the blood from her forehead in one fluid motion. She looked as if she had returned from a bathroom break and was ready to get back to the game.

"Why are you yelling at the Terran?" asked Blayde. "I thought you said that wasn't allowed?"

Zander glared at her with murder in his gaze. He begrudgingly stepped aside to let her have access to the door, though it was evident he wanted to kill her himself.

It astounded me how quickly someone like her could recover from … well, death. One minute she was on the floor, a hole through her noggin, and now she was brushing it off like it was nothing more than a minor setback. Like a mosquito bite, more annoying than deadly.

"If you two stop squabbling for one minute, we'd be a lot further along," she said. "Maybe we should call this place quits and head back to Earth."

"No!" Zander and I shouted.

Blayde lifted her eyebrows, setting her eyes on her brother. "Oh, come on," she said. "It's not safe for Sally here. You realize that, right?"

"When have armed security guards ever stopped us from doing anything? I mean, anything? They're nothing. An inconvenience."

"I'm more worried about who they work for," she said. "What if they recognized us? Huh? What then?"

"No one would believe them."

"Well, I'd rather go somewhere else, if that's okay with you. If you still insist on your silly little date night with Sally, you can pick a better planet to have it on."

"It's not a date, sis. It's a thank you for helping us save her entire planet. Or don't you remember that?"

"You'd think her planet not being incinerated by angry Killians looking for their lost kin would be enough thanks," she grumbled. Zander ignored her, pointing at the door instead.

ALIENATION

"That buzzing we heard earlier, it's a silent alarm. I think we're in some rich guy's safe room. His car's probably a rare valuable he wants to keep safe from thieves."

"The car Sally threw up on?"

"Next to it, Blayde, next to it!" I stammered, finally able to get a word in. My heart was calming down, the attack averted. But the physical threat from the men outside was far from over.

"Semantics," she scoffed. "Right. Well, if you must insist on staying, we should get out of here. Now. Before they …" She sniffed the air, and her shoulders dropped with annoyance. "Before they try and gas us out. Great. Zander, hold your breath. Sally … try not to die."

"What?" I sniffed the air and smelled nothing out of the ordinary then stopped myself. That would probably kill me quicker.

"Out the window, hurry!" She punched her hand against the wall where the door commands had been, sending sparks of blue light scattering across the stone. "That should give us some time."

"Did you just lock us in a room with deadly gas?" asked Zander.

"Yes, and I'm dying to make a fart joke." She shrugged. "Come on, no way we were getting past them with Sally in tow."

With that, she flickered out of existence, making herself useful on the windowsill. It was too high for me to climb, but then again, I didn't have their helpful gifts.

Zander clutched my hand. "You trust me?"

"I still do," I said, taking it. "Well, I think."

A blink and we were on the windowsill. Jumping short distances, where Zander had a visual reference for our destination, didn't seem to affect me the way that one, awful interstellar trip had. I shuddered at the thought, and Zander picked up my hair, possibly thinking I would be sick again.

"I'm all right," I said quickly.

"Yeah, you don't have to keep reminding us," Blayde said, not taking her eyes off the window where she fiddled with a lock. Zander dropped my hair, brushing it gently off my shoulder. The feeling of his fingers on my skin sent prickles of electricity up my spine, leaving the path he had touched etched on the surface.

Even if the hand he had been holding was now clammy with sweat.

"Careful out here," she said and threw the window open a notch.

The smell of burnt fuel hit my nose like a literal punch to the face. The runway stench was magnified a few hundred times, singeing my nostrils and making my nose hair curl. I stumbled back from the window, reeling.

My knees gave out as a coughing fit overwhelmed me. My breath was short, the air coming in small gasps. For a split-second, I was convinced the planet had no air and I had run through the small amount I had brought with me.

ALIENATION

"Smog," said Blayde, sniffing. "Probably not good for your health, Sal gal, but better than deadly gas."

"Sal gal?" I coughed, and Zander ripped the window wide open.

"We have to try," he said. I nodded slowly.

Blayde stepped onto the windowsill and took a left into the odd yellow haze. There must have been a ledge. I followed her out, Zander taking the lead. The air was hazy, thick with smog, and I threw my arm over my nose to block out the horrible, overwhelming stench. Blayde's form was barely visible in the haze but was surrounded by a halo of light.

I stepped toward her, and just like that, my breath was gone. Light blinded me from all around—above, below—overwhelming my already saturated senses. It was as if I had stepped out of a cave and into the brightest, hottest day of the year. What I thought was a wall was indeed a billboard, hiding the secret window from view. And I was perched on a ledge, miles above ground.

Now if there's anything you know about me by this point, it's that I'm absolutely terrified of heights. I hate them with a vengeance. I would hunt down and murder heights if I ever got the chance. But this was an alien planet, and I forced myself not to flee in terror. A room where I died of poisoned gas would be much better than facing those dreaded, hated heights.

The buildings reached for the pitch-black sky, massive edifices towering over us from all around, merging together to form a single block on either side of the road. It was more like a wall than a skyscraper.

The world fell away from the doorstep, setting us who knows how high in the air. Above us—darkness. Below us—more darkness. Everything between was a strip of vibrant yellow and dazzling lights. Advertisements and moving billboards hovered in the middle of nowhere, proclaiming bright neon drinks and snacks I had never heard of and would probably never get the chance to try.

Not that I was sure I wanted to—the ads were vivid and blaring. Just looking at them made my stomach turn.

A car roared as it came out of nowhere, whipping my hair into my face as it passed at breakneck speed. The street was full of them. Every small dot was a car, making the road ten times wider than I'd expected. The cars themselves had no wheels, fulfilling any hovercraft fantasy I'd conjured. Streetlights bobbed like buoys on the sea of nothingness, shifting through colors that only the drivers could understand.

I couldn't help but think this was absolutely the coolest thing I had ever seen.

The cars were flying. Flying. This wasn't like the movies, no matter how awesome The Fifth Element was. Nothing compared to seeing them in person. My jaw hung to the floor as I took it all in: the roar of the city, the lights burning my retinas, the cars straight out of a science fiction film.

ALIENATION

I inched closer to the ledge, gripping the side of the billboard to keep vertigo from settling in, feeling a little like Leeloo, only with a whole lot more clothes on. No matter—vertigo would come whether I wanted it to or not. My vision tunneled even as I trembled in awe of the world before me. The amazing, vivid, racing world.

And it was *real*. I rubbed my hands over my eyes and forced them to blink. No, the city hadn't decided to up and leave after I opened them again. It was still here.

Even if this turned out to be a dream, this right here, right now, was the most real thing I had ever seen.

Everything Zander had ever told me burst into reality. It hit me like a fish being flung at my face. At first, disbelief that this was happening, followed by the certainty that I could not be imagining the smell. My heart didn't so much skip as plunge into my gut. It was like standing in a fishbowl, only instead of fish, cars whizzed past my face.

"You okay?" asked Zander, calmly. The proximity of his voice startled me, and I turned my head from the fall to face him. His gravity-defying hair wafted in the wind created by the cars rushing by.

"You don't have to keep asking me that, you know."

"You stopped moving," he said, nonchalantly, "and there are men with guns that will break into the safe any second now."

"Oh, right, I did," I said through trembling lips, and turned back to the task at hand. Which seemed, much to my dismay, to follow Blayde down this tiny ledge and around the corner of the building. "It's just … so much to take in," I replied, lie after lie.

"Are you crying?"

"It's the fumes?" I wiped my eyes with the corner of my sleeve.

And yet, despite the pain in my chest as I wheezed, despite the terror of being so high up, despite the tears of awe mixing with tears of pain, I was the happiest I had been in years.

And also the most terrified. Because, you know, potentially dying was on the table.

"Then let's keep moving. Not too far now, okay?"

I nodded, and took a tentative step forward. A gust of wind flew against my face, and I stifled a scream. It was as if I were already falling. One misstep, and I would plummet to the bottom of this foreign city. No one would find my body, down in the deep, deep dark.

"Keep your hand firmly against the wall, and don't look down. Okay?"

I didn't even care where the voice came from. I reached for the wall, looked up and away, and walked forward on trembling feet.

"Faster than that, Sally."

I put my sleeve over my mouth and stared straight ahead; the flashing advertisements, the orbs of the street lights, glowing as they hovered in the air, somehow stable in all this movement. The blur of cars that raced through the air so quickly they could win a Formula 1 race without even entering.

ALIENATION

This all clashed horribly with the sky, which was as dark as a bowl of black ink and twice as deep, like velvet. It was almost an eternity of blackness, a deep hole that could suck you in if you came too close. A darkness so intense—a starless, moonless darkness that stretched over the city like a sheet, suffocating its inhabitants. The air itself was constraining.

It was, in itself, an oxymoron—being both claustrophobic and agoraphobic at once. It pressed down on me despite the width of the avenues and the massive buildings that were spread out.

We rounded the corner and there was Blayde, halfway inside a window. She grinned at me, more at ease in this world, in this crazy danger, than I could ever be.

She offered her hand, and I took it without hesitation. Silently, she lowered me to the floor—this window wasn't so high off the ground—and reached back outside for her brother.

"We've been here before, haven't we?" Zander asked, halfway through the window, pointing at the world beyond.

"Definitely familiar," she replied.

"Yup, I'm sure we've been here before. I recognize these buildings."

"It's been a while, though. The cars are much nicer."

She leaned an unnatural distance off the ledge, her agile body perfectly balanced on the stoop. I wanted to fling out a hand to grab her before she fell, but Blayde seemed comfortable hanging over the abyss. Legolas himself would be impressed. I wanted to ask what her elf eyes saw.

I tore myself away from the sight and froze. We were in another silent room, devoid of people, like the garage. The walls were coated with a dark black substance with glowing blue rings on the floor shimmering to an unnatural degree. Above the rings, stuff floated.

I didn't know how else to describe it. It was just … junk. There was a block of metal sitting in the middle of the air, minding its own business. A dark, leather biker jacket. A plumbus. Something red and very fluffy, which looked maybe like it was alive.

"So, um, where are we?" I asked, looking at Zander for answers. I would have looked to Blayde, but seeing her leaning out the window turned my stomach. Stunningly beautiful view or not, it was a long way down from that ledge.

"Sally," he said, indicating the outside world. "Welcome to the capital planet of the Fushin system, the gem of the Alliance, the city that never sleeps, the world of a million lights. The planet city of Da-Duhui."

THREE

IN WHICH ZANDER IS AN ACTUAL FASHION THIEF

DA-DUHUI.

This alien place had a name, a word I could throw into my mind to classify everything I saw, to make sense of it. Da-Duhui: a city light-years away from my home.

Blayde decided this was the best time to close the window. Instantly, the air in the room shuddered and took a breath, as if a filter had been turned on. I inhaled, relishing in the freshness.

She jumped down to the floor in a classy superhero landing then looked up to check her handiwork. Five pairs of feet raced past the window, a string of muffled words trailing them. "Are we ... are we safe here?" I asked.

Blayde shrugged. "Sure, so long as we don't touch anything else."

"And *where* are we?"

S.E.ANDERSON

"Da-Duhui." She cocked her head. "Are you in shock? You realize we *just* had this conversation?"

"I got that bit"—I glanced around—"but what is this place?"

"Museum? Art gallery? Could go either way. Try not to touch anything. There are probably more alarms here than there were in that last room."

"You *have* been here before?"

"M'yeah." She pulled a tattered book from her inside pocket, her journal. She flipped through the pages, brows knitting together and casting lines on her forehead. Her lips turned to form into a small frown. It was an expression I was beginning to think was permanently baked into her features.

"I'm pretty sure we have," said Zander, forcing concentration, staring back in time and bringing up the memories locked in his mind. "I have no idea when, but it was recently enough that I recognize it. I know it was a good trip, though."

"I've got two lines in the journal." Blayde jammed her finger at the page as if to squash a bug. *"Visited Da-Duhui. Avoid for a while. Don't eat the pizza.* And that's it, so not much to go on."

Zander rubbed his temples, squeezing his eyes shut.

"Hopefully some memory will surface," he said, suddenly back to his usual cheerful self. "How long ago was it?"

"Before Ja'karon. Now *that* was a good time. We should have taken Sally there."

31

ALIENATION

"You were almost eaten by a swamp-beast, and you tried to sell me into marriage with the Earth King. Yeah, that was fun."

"Don't be so dramatic." She grinned, slamming her journal shut. "He obviously liked you. And I didn't get any complaints at the time. Anyway, it was much more interesting than Da-Duhui, where the only thing I cared enough to write about is their bad food."

"Interesting? This place is plenty interesting," said Zander. "And most of all, it's safe. There's no drama. Just a good, classic alien city to show Sally. Harmless."

Blayde let out a snort, making me wonder just how harmless it really was. If her idea of fun was narrowly avoiding death, I wanted to stay away from the places she gave five stars to on Yelp.

"We just escaped deadly fumes and a gun squad, Zander," she said.

"But the upper levels are really nice."

"If we can get Sally there in one piece, yes."

"Which we will."

"All this for dinner away from Earth?" Blayde looked at me now, squinting in doubt. "You get much better food on her planet. I think. Honestly, I wasn't around long enough to check."

"This isn't about the food, Blayde!"

"Then again," I said, "if you mentioned to stay away for a while, that's probably for a reason, right? Should I ask … ?"

"Ask all you want, but I don't have an answer." Blayde stuffed her journal into the inside pocket of her red leather jacket. "You can't expect me to remember everything. My mind has much more important things to focus on."

"But it *is* safe, right?" My eyes glanced at the window the security guards had run past. Had they seen our faces? Would they come looking for us? "You keep arguing about it, so how safe can it really be?"

The siblings exchanged long looks. Blayde communicated with her eyebrows alone, raising and dropping them as she shifted through a wide range of expressions. Zander seemed to understand her, sort of; after a minute of watching her emote a variety of eyebrow poses, he sighed and broke eye contact.

"As safe as it possibly could be," he answered. "Crime rate is null on the higher levels, but you don't have to worry about that. We'll make sure nothing happens to you. I promise."

"What Zander means to say," Blayde interjected, "is that this is a fun trip and definitely not business. There's nothing to worry about."

"Remind me, what would a business trip for you two involve?" I asked. Blayde rolled her eyes. Typical. Well, I hadn't known her all that long, certainly not enough to know what typical was, but it seemed familiar enough.

"Let's find something fun to do." Zander rubbed his hands together with that smug grin on his face that meant exciting things were about to happen. The kind of grin that stretched too wide for his face. He looked like a kid in a candy store.

ALIENATION

"First of all, let's stop standing around this place, okay?" said Blayde. "It gives me the creeps."

"Something gives you the creeps?" I trotted after her as she walked toward the room's only exit. "You? The immortal, intergalactic space ... what are you exactly? Travel blogger? A cop? An assassin?"

She shot me a glare. "I have a bad vibe, that's all. Give me a break, will you?"

"Sorry, I just ..."

"Run, run, run, run, run!" shouted Zander, snapping my sentence in half, flashing past us in a whirl of black leather. His hand caught mine and tugged, and, suddenly, I was running after him, an alarm ringing in my ears.

And, unlike the invisible swarm of bees that never was from the garage, this wasn't the silent type. It sounded like a fire truck on steroids. I wanted to throw my hands over my ears to protect them from the shrill whine, but Zander gripped my hand, rushing me forward. My feet stung as they hit the floor, faster than I ever wanted to run. My breath was ragged, burning through my mouth and throat.

"What the hell did you do?" I stammered, right as a chunk of ceiling exploded above us. "Shit! What was that?"

"Don't look back!"

He didn't need to tell me twice. I had only been on this planet five minutes, and already, two separate factions were shooting at us.

The hallway didn't fit the dark surroundings of the museum-like room. Here, the floor looked like wood but was harder to run on, and the walls were covered with a washed-out tapestry. None of the sleek, futuristic walls from the first room or the old, musty concrete from the garage.

"Did you—is that the coat that was on display?" I shouted over the siren, my feet pounding on the floor. His hand tightened as we sped up. "Why are you wearing it?"

"It's mine!"

"Is that how things work? You take it, so it's yours?"

"No, it is mine! They took it from me first!"

"Seriously?"

"I can't remember who or when, but I'm sure!"

We spun around a corner and almost tumbled down a set of stairs. I staggered as the step I took forward landed on the floor of the landing below. Zander had jumped us forward without warning.

There were a series of rapid thumps, and a form crashed to the floor in front of me, a chunk of brown banister landing beside him. I screamed as I took in the blue skin and the wrinkles around the massive head. Zander helped himself to the creature's gun and tugged me forward. I stepped over the alien, launching into another run.

Feet thundered on the wooden stairs far in front of us. Zander opened the closest door and rushed us inside. Blayde thrust it shut behind us, her breathing calm and composed. The only thing out of place was a smear of blue gel on her cheek.

Pretty sure that wasn't shampoo.

"Zander." She stormed at him, arms akimbo. "What the veesh did you do?"

"Isn't it awesome?" He twirled for us to take it all in, displaying the jacket like a peacock spreading his tail feathers. It was battle-worn, the kind a biker would wear. No patches or pins, just plain, old black leather, singed on one sleeve, brown in spots from age and use. No mythical treasure, no secret hoard of magic, just an old, battered leather jacket.

"If there were an award for the stupidest move in history, you would be the guest of honor every year. Actually, multiple times per year."

Zander's face fell. "Don't you recognize it?"

"Nope."

"Oh, Come on, it's my favorite jacket!"

"Was your favorite jacket. Which you forgot even existed then stole from a display case." Blayde ran her hands through her hair and closed her eyes. "What was the point of me getting us out of the frying pan if you go and throw us in a fire? We're even deeper into the block now than we were earlier."

"But it's *mine!*"

"You could have disabled the locks. Silenced the alarm. There are a million different ways to steal something from a … a … what was that place, a museum of illegally acquired items? Last I checked, Da-

Duhui was under Alliance control, and I doubt they'd have any jacket of yours displayed so nicely. They think you died centuries ago."

"Not sure what they think about me, but at least they'll see I'm well-dressed."

"Excuse me," came a voice from behind us, "but would you please tell me what you are doing in my bathroom?"

I turned around to stare at the mustard-colored couch, wondering where the voice had come from, until I realized the couch was not a couch but something alive. The thing before me was a big, sluggish looking mess of dark green skin and yellow pustules. The eyes were bulbous and reptilian, though the eyelids dropped pitifully, all the muscles on its face closely followed by bags. To top it off, it was completely bald, the scalp speckled like a toad's back. It took all my willpower to stop myself from gagging. The thing even smelled like a swamp.

"Shit." Blayde slapped herself in the face and grunted. "Zander, take him out."

"Why me?"

"Do I need to say 'please'? Or do you want me to list the reasons? Well, let's start with you getting us into this mess in the first place. That, and it's your turn. I took down the guys in the hallway. And I got us out of the safe. So?"

"May I have a say in any of this?" asked the slug, his voice low and raspy. "Do you know who I am? I assume you do, which is why you're here. What do you want? Riches? A way off the planet? You can ask, but you will have neither. You were dead the second you set your foot inside the doorway."

"Not now! Can't you see I'm busy here?" Blayde snapped, not taking her eyes of Zander. The slug looked shocked—if a slug could even look shocked. "What happened to you? You're on Earth for two minutes, and, suddenly, you're breaking every protocol we've ever established. They're in place for a reason, you idiot!"

"Can we argue about this later? There's a nude Oexasie sitting right in front of us."

"That guy's nude?" I stammered. What was the stance on modesty with other races? Especially one with no apparent arms or any other limbs?

And why was I worried about that when the stranger wanted us dead?

"Will any of you tell me what the *vrijalt* you're doing here?" the indecent Oexasie spat.

"Look, we're sorry. We're just passing through," said Zander. "Wrong house."

"Is that my coat?"

"No, it's mine!" Zander placed his hands on his hips and scowled at the Oexasie. "You can't even wear it." Zander's face flushed. "Please don't tell me you tried it on…"

"Guards!" the creature bellowed, and with that, we were on the move again.

"I'm ashamed of you, Zander," Blayde said as she dragged me unceremoniously down the hallway. She raised the weapons she had stolen from the last guards, aiming them at the new batch coming toward us. The guards crumpled to the floor without a sound. "Get back in the zone, or things will just get worse."

"Is that a threat?" Zander paused to glance her over, but she just rolled her eyes again.

"An observation. Down the stairs, now!"

The world flickered around me like channels changing on the TV screen. Jump, jump, jump. One after the other until we were standing in front of a door, which Blayde opened with a well-placed kick.

We were outside again, the overwhelming world rising in front of me. The smog didn't hit me as hard as the first time, but it still burned the inside of my nose and made my face feel grimy. This time, the ledge was wider, reaching out into the highway just waiting for cars to alight.

I struggled to suppress the cough clawing up my throat, all the while begging my body to not give up on me. I could see why Blayde didn't want me sharing their adventures. My entire body smarted, and I had only been running for a few minutes. After a combination of my reaction to the smog and vertigo, and to being on the run from people who thought we were robbing from them and then from people who we had actually robbed, I was exhausted to the core.

I needed to sit down or I would fall down.

Blayde strode forward on the platform and waved her arms high above her head. Within less than a minute, a flaming, red cab pulled up in front of her, alighting on the ledge. Literally flaming. As in the roof was on fire.

"Shit, this company's expensive," Zander muttered. "I didn't realize Flamers had branched out to other planets."

"They'd probably charge less if they didn't lose half their cars to flames," I pointed out. The whole thing was absurd to the point that I couldn't think of anything else to say.

"You don't know the half of it. Come on, don't dally, Sally," he said as he hustled into the taxi, laughing at his own terrible rhyme. Blayde shoved me forward. I tripped over the step and tumbled onto Zander's lap, but he was too busy talking with the cabbie to notice this, let alone my hands awkwardly pushing my body off his legs. I sat up straight, clutching my bag to my chest, trying not to think about the nothingness between the floor of the cab and the ground below.

But I did think about it, and there went my stomach, tying itself into tight knots I could have sold as a crocheted pillow.

"Scoot over." Blayde shoved me again.

"Wait, no!" But it was too late. Zander had slid behind me, and I was now the one next to the window. It was tinted against the glare of the street, but, even so, I could see out of it. And, boy, it was a long way down.

"Drive, drive, drive!" Zander shouted, and the taxi shot forward, shoving me back against the seat. My head hit the headrest so quickly I felt the wind gust out of me.

I saw stars I'm sure weren't actually there.

I looked out the window to see guards bursting out onto the platform, guns aimed high, but it was too late.

We had survived. But where we were going next, I didn't know.

The buildings flew past our windows too quickly to make out any details. I looked up to distract myself from looking down.

Being on the ledge hadn't done anything for my fear of heights. Already, the gleam of a new planet was wearing off, leaving room for vertigo to wiggle into my mind. My palms were so drenched in sweat I could have single-handedly rehydrated a desert.

Knowing the drop and a hovercar from my dreams were the only things keeping me from plunging to my death was enough to make anyone scream. Not to mention that Zander was wearing a stolen coat, no matter how many times he claimed it was his. I bit my lip, squeezing my duffel bag into my belly. The sweat from my palms stuck to the plastic straps.

"Which part of town are we in?" Zander asked the driver, his voice layered with what seemed to be a drunken slur. "I can't seem to remember." He laughed merrily, Blayde joining in with the same exaggerated giggling.

"Kurai—North," said the cabbie. He didn't seem at all perturbed that we were racing from what appeared to be gangsters with a museum of illegal things.

The driver turned back to look at me, and I almost squeaked. He was *human*. Or, at least, he looked human.

41

With dark skin and graying hair, he had the air of a well-read and well-traveled nerd.

"Where's the best place for local food in town?" Zander asked, leaning forward. He was quite literally buzzing, vibrating against me. I stayed with my back firmly pressed against the seat, my clammy hands clasped on my lap, and I stared straight ahead.

Don't look down. Don't look down.

"Um … if money's no object, you can't go wrong with the upper levels. I can drop you off on platform six. It's pretty popular with tourists."

"We're really going out for food?" I asked, as Zander sat back in his seat again. "Now?"

"Is there something wrong with that?"

"No, but …" But many things. We had just stolen a coat and run away from a slug guy. We had broken into someone's house—twice. "Did we come all this way for a snack?"

He grinned. "A snack? Maybe. If that's what you want."

"Erm, what do you guys actually do when you arrive on a new planet? Shop? Eat? Steal stuff and make a getaway in a local taxi?" I joked, but I guessed my fear crept into my words; something neither Zander nor Blayde could have missed. But if they picked up on it, they gave no sign.

Blayde leaned over to Zander to share another of their silent conversations, her brows rising and sinking fast enough that it had to be code. How she could speak so quietly and how he understood any of it, I would never know.

"First, a reminder, this is my coat. And to answer your question, sometimes all of that," Zander said meekly, "we're what you might call extreme tourists. We see everything worth seeing, enjoy the culture, maybe stay a night. Then we go on our way. It's fun."

"Right." I wanted to roll my eyes. "This is coming from the man who saved the planet quite a few times when he was on Earth. I wouldn't call that, or what we just did, extreme tourism."

"That was different," he muttered but gave no further explanation.

"I wasn't on Earth." Blayde laughed. "And when I'm around, things tend to be a lot more fun."

"I would call it 'more violent', but to each their own," I said.

"Ha! She's got you there, sis!"

"Though my little bro is right"—Blayde let out a small sigh of annoyance—"usually, we just see the sights. Nothing more. We're not around to save everyone every time, you know."

"So… you're just… vacationing?" I found that harder to believe than their jumping or their immortality. I had been at the power plant, seen them save an alien race. From which, I had gleaned that Zander and Blayde were running from an intergalactic vendetta, or something of the sort. Trying to see these two, well, heroes as anything on the same level as mere space tourists did not compute.

ALIENATION

But, then again, I had been part of their breaking and entering. And maybe assault and battery? Had they killed those guards?

"Pretty much." Blayde shrugged her shoulders as she leaned back in her seat. The speed of the hovercar didn't bother her in the slightest, whereas I was clutching onto anything I could just to stop myself from passing out.

"Wow," I replied, trying to hide my surprise. I failed miserably.

"I know, we're living the dream, right?" Blayde turned to plant her eyes on mine. My heart stalled. Her expression was both patronizing and threatening, and I shuddered, shifting back toward the taxi door.

Right next to the huge drop into nowhere.

Well, I was caught between a mile-high drop and an immortal alien vacationing-assassin-or-something, but, hey, I tried not to think about that. My stomach continued to knot itself, going from crochet ball to dense neutron star.

"I guess so," I mumbled. After all, it was my dream outside that window, my astrolust being satiated. I was finally off-planet Earth. Finally in space.

And I was in a taxi with a woman who was just a wee bit unhinged.

The taxi pitched in a steep climb, shoving us further into the backs of our seats. The city slid by us in flashing neon colors. I clutched my bag against my chest even

44

tighter, but, try as I might, I couldn't close my eyes. The view, though terrifying, mesmerized me.

It felt like I was taking off in the space shuttle. The entire frame rattled and shook, and I wondered how anyone enjoyed traveling this way. I stole a glance at my co-passengers, but neither Zander nor Blayde seemed the least bit uncomfortable. They seemed used to it. Hell, they seemed to *like* it. Smiling, chilling, chatting. When the car leveled out, I felt sweat rolling down my face, but they were just two people taking an everyday drive through the city.

I whipped my head away, but my eyes came face-to-face with the abyss, making me jump a foot off my seat, my body trembling. We had climbed much higher, way quicker than I had thought possible. I could see the tops of buildings now, and could no longer see the darkness of the bottom.

"What kind of payment do you take?" Zander asked as he leaned forward to speak to the driver.

"Anything Alliance," the driver muttered. He definitely deserved a massive tip for helping with our getaway, if aliens even took tips.

Zander checked his pockets, ecstatic to be wearing his favorite black jacket again. It looked remarkably like Blayde's, though it was more worn than hers. He pulled bill upon bill from his jacket, of every shape and size imaginable, chips of plastic and odd gems tumbling from his hands. It was like a personal, private collection of currency from around the universe in his pockets.

ALIENATION

"Alliance cash. Yeah!" He held out a bright blue bill, his level of excitement a little too high for just plain old money. "I guess our luck has finally turned."

Maybe it had. Maybe it hadn't. But as Platform Six came into view, I wondered if I had made a mistake coming along for the ride.

FOUR

CULTURE SHOCK AS AN OLYMPIC SPORT

PLATFORM SIX LOOMED OUT OF THE WINDOW, A wide plaza that protruded out into the highway, leading to an entrance between the buildings that was at least five stories high and just as wide. It was as if a monstrous giant had crashed his way through the walls, carving a path for people to walk and live away from the traffic. As we alighted, the shops lining the wide alley came into view, leading to the riches beyond.

Zander paid the driver, giving him a polite thank you as we tumbled out of the car. Well, I was the one doing the tumbling. My legs still shook from the ride, and probably from everything else I had been through, too. At least the air was more breathable up here.

"Well, I'll be staying here," said Blayde, sounding almost bored. "You two go and have fun, but that bar over is calling my name. Right over there, you hear it?"

ALIENATION

She pointed in the distance, at a small bar with a gigantic neon sign proclaiming it was the *"Home of the Beer of the Blade. Only for Warriors."* in eerie, fluorescent light.

"What exactly did we do last time?" She shook her head.

"Judging by the fact that no one has tried to kill us yet, I suspect it was quite a long time ago. No one seems to have recognized us, and I don't see any Wanted posters."

"True." Blayde nodded once. "In any case, keep a low profile. Don't get lost, and don't eat the pizza. I can hang onto the bag if you need." The last part seemed rather forced.

I turned around to see Zander mouthing a few words, stopping as he saw me. Blayde extended her hand, making a sound like a deflating balloon.

"Thanks." I handed her my bag, which she ripped from my grasp, then turned on her heels and left without another word. Honestly, I was glad to see her walk away. I would probably be murderous if I spent all day with her.

"Hold on, I'm going to talk to the driver," Zander said, but I wasn't listening anymore. No, I was too overwhelmed by the monster that was Platform Six. We were digging straight through the wall of buildings, the entrance a massive thoroughfare from the highway into the heart of the city. And we were evidently in the expensive part of town. The shops glistened with glamor, and everything radiated richness.

A car alighted beside me, and out stepped two birds, elegantly groomed and wearing silk shifts, with elaborate markings on their short beaks. Their legs were as long as I was tall, and spindly, making me wonder how they supported their body weight. The taller of the two gave me a shifty look.

"Macreneens don't like our eyes to linger."

I jumped. I hadn't noticed Zander's sudden appearance at my side.

"If we were on their home planet, they'd have you thrown out of the aviary for that transgression."

My face flushed. "I wasn't trying to be rude."

"It's okay. People are used to it here; it's such a melting pot. People often offend others without realizing it. They won't sweat the small stuff. They've learned to live with it. Purposeful culture insensitivity is a major offense, though. Anyway, come see!"

Before I could respond, he took my hand again, pulling me along toward the city.

"Hold up. Human here," I said, but I laughed as we ran. Zander was excited, and so was I. I was on a freaking alien world.

I thought he would take me to the massive passageway and into the heart of the block, but, no. He led me instead to the mural towering over the rest of the landing platform. The brightly colored orbs on the black ceramic background were dizzying in number and sizes.

A star map. A huge, overwhelming star map crafted in a glittering mosaic on the wall. Probably no more than street art for the people who lived here but jaw-dropping for a little human from Earth.

"We're here"—Zander hopped into the air to point at a specific star—"in the core of the Alliance. Earth's not even mapped, but your sun is. It's right about … here."

He pointed into the distance to a small, insignificant dot.

"The Alliance stretches all that way?" I took in the vastness of the mural.

Zander nodded. "You seem impressed, but they're small players when you think about it. I've seen civilizations spanning not just solar systems but entire galaxies. Plural. Some had cities with hundreds, if not thousands, of planets. These are just your closest neighbors, Sally. Say hi."

"Hi," I repeated, awkwardly. I was engrossed in the map, the hundreds of stars, the thousands of planets in this Alliance. It was surreal, seeing for myself the conglomeration of planets I had heard so much about but barely believed existed. It was more than my mind could process.

"They have the same name for it as we do?" I stared at the little orb Zander had pointed out, with the little word "Sun" staring back at me, overlaid on the art with hologrammed pixels that twinkled in the air.

"Nah, your brain is telling you what you want to see. I told you your translator's top-of-the-line."

"I didn't think it would still work after two years."

"Two years," he repeated. His face shifted from being excited, to a flicker of a frown, to his usual grin in the span of a second. "You're far from home, Sally. Same galaxy, at least. No worries there. Just a few light-years. Where do you want to go next?"

"What's this?" I asked, touching a large, silver orb sticking out of the wall.

"Sally, no!" Zander lunged at me, but it was too late. My fingers fluttered over the cold surface. A long, apple green man-thing appeared in front of the map. While it had the eyes and mouth of a regular human, it looked as if the rest of him had been squashed by a steamroller then reinflated to give him some depth. The thing was semi-transparent, and when it moved its mouth, I could see all the way through it.

"Mr. Gilmag." Zander shuddered. The weird green thing advanced like it had seen us, smiling with an unnaturally wide mouth.

"Hi, I'm Mr. Gilmag! The Da-Duhui tourism board would like to welcome you to Kurai," he said, in an obnoxiously chipper voice. "Please enjoy our outstanding locations for shopping and dining. I will be your guide on this journey of self-discovery."

"Off," Zander said. "Program execute? Program complete? Program terminated? Zing? Zap? End? Exit? Escape?"

"May I offer you a brief history of our city?" Mr. Gilmag ignored Zander's attempts to subdue him. "Ten thousand years ago, after the third galactic war, a treaty of nonaggression was signed between the planets of Pyrina, Da-Duhui, and Vorace. When a greater threat presented itself from beyond …"

"Just keep walking." Zander put an arm over my shoulders to steer me away from the eager animation. "He shouldn't be able to follow us past a certain radius."

"It can follow us?"

"And I can hear you," said the hologram, putting its hands on its hips. "It's rude to interrupt. I'm not sure what quadrant you were raised in, but—"

"Oh, my gosh, I'm so sorry."

I pulled myself from Zander's arm and gave the hologram an apologetic look, but the poor thing looked hurt. I wanted to walk forward and give it a hug.

"He's a program, Sally. He has no feelings. It's programmed to say that so you listen to the whole spiel."

"So what if I am?" Gilmag scoffed. "It doesn't mean I don't have feelings about—"

With that, Zander pushed me back, and we were out of its sphere of influence. Mr. Gilmag disappeared into computerized nothingness.

"What was that about?" I asked, staring at the place the green man had just been.

"A fresh attempt to catch the attention of Millionials," Zander said nonchalantly. "You coming?"

I tried to match his pace, but his exhilaration made him take wide strides. I had to trot to keep up.

"Oh, sorry." He slowed down. "Sally, first alien world, first time out of your solar system, let alone your own planet. What do you want to do first?"

"I don't know … Everything? How much time do we have?"

He caught me looking toward the bar where Blayde was probably making some new memories—or deleting them—and shrugged.

"Don't worry about her. She's been a bit jumpy since all this happened."

"Since you got separated?"

"Since I made a friend. It doesn't happen very often. Anyway, want to do food first? I'm not good at making decisions on an empty stomach."

"Heck, yes, how can I say no to food?" I laughed, wrapping my arm around his. It felt comfortable being around him once more, like nothing had changed in the past two years. Which, I guessed, for him, were just a few days. "Where are we going?"

"In a way, it's some kind of steakhouse? If you can call it that." Zander indicated that we should walk toward the grand entrance, and my heart leapt.

The passageway into the city was packed with people. I had assumed we'd take adventuring into the universe a little slower—that I would meet one race, then maybe another—but that was not the case. I couldn't even count how many different faces were here. There must have been thousands of different people, hundreds of different kinds of people, and humans were a minority.

ALIENATION

Though, I guessed, compared to the other races, we were a large group. But watching a reptilian couple-of-five crooning together reminded me that everyone and everything here was completely alien. No matter how many somewhat familiar faces I saw.

"Zander," I said, "there are *humans*."

"Distant cousins of yours," he said, leading me forward. "Humans are known for being prolific, though with relatively short lifespans. Basically like, um, rats."

"We're the rats of the universe?"

"Oh, no, of course not. Only in this arm of the galaxy."

Ouch, that hurt.

I was quickly distracted by the little ball of fluff on a leash dividing over and over again, a trail of tiny, fluffy balls following the original as its master took it for a walk.

Unless the ball was the master? It was hard to tell who was leading whom.

"Are there any robots?" I asked, pushing that information out of my mind. "Like, really cool robots? AI?"

"So many. At least one in each shop; the city couldn't run without them. Quite literally. There's an AI managing Da-Duhui, of course. The ICP."

"ICP?" I scoffed.

"What?"

"Come on, I see pee?"

"Oh, real mature, Sally." He laughed. "And, no, that joke doesn't work in every language."

"Works in mine. In any case, all this … it's amazing."

Now that we had passed through the tunnel lined with shops, everything ahead of us looked like a normal city. Well, normal by alien standards, I guessed. It didn't feel like we were miles above the planet's surface anymore.

Like a kid at Christmas, I ran from shop window to shop window, trying desperately to take in everything.

"Look at the technology here," Zander said. "Air conditioning air sprays. You know, to cool down the room or heat it up with one quick squirt." He pointed to the other side of the hall. "A clothing store with color changing cotton. Shoes that adjust themselves to the size of your foot; heels that reduce to nothing when your feet are painful. 3-D television—"

"Oh, we have that on Earth."

"They have holographic televisions on Earth?" His eyes widened. "Wow, a lot happened in two years. Your TV seemed 2-D to me."

"Optical illusions and 3-D glasses do the trick just fine." I shook my head. "Oh my gosh, I've seen holograms today."

Zander laughed again. How I had missed that laugh.

Zander was alive. It hadn't hit me until now. Two years of waiting, heartbreak, and doubt, and here he was, alive and just the same as he'd always been.

And yet, it was like he wasn't here.

Maybe it was me. Too much coming at me at once that even Zander himself felt surreal. I stopped in the middle of the street, unable to take another step forward, overwhelmed by everything around me. The shops, the inventions, the aliens, everything was a whirlwind of color and beauty so indescribable that it rendered me speechless. I felt small; I felt tiny. The immensity of the universe that I had gone so long not knowing about just exploded in my mind, turning my world head over heels. I could suddenly see. I was suddenly aware—of everything, of a cosmos my mind could not contain.

I was on another planet.

"So?" Zander said, walking ahead, his arms held out to each side. Whether it was an invitation to follow or just an excuse to showcase the return of his once-favorite coat, I couldn't tell. "What do you think?"

"This place …." I edged forward, trying not to stare at the kid with green webbed fingers who was obviously staring at me. "It's—"

"A lot to take in," he said quickly. "Take your time. It's not every day you get to see all this."

I struggled to breathe, but it wasn't panic that made me breathless; It was the enormity of where I was standing. Zander held out a hand and led me down the street, letting me take it all in.

"Ah, this is the place." He pointed at a warm and inviting looking restaurant. The doors were wide open into the street, as if calling to us, and I for sure wanted to go inside.

"Fancy restaurants always serve the exotic stuff. The type of food you eat if you have interesting tastes or an overflowing wallet. No, it's the snack bars and street vendors that have the classic foods, the ones teens and overworked employees eat during their lunch hour. The foods most intertwined with their culture."

"You seem to know a lot about food."

"Best way to understand a civilization. For example, if they serve vegetarian food across the whole planet, all roads indicate a culture that doesn't rely on other species for food. Either they revere animals, are prey to them, or they killed 'em off a long time ago … or maybe they're just kind to other beings. If you're somewhere else and see an anthropophaginian menu, make a run for it, Sally. They're cannibals."

"What can you deduce about Da-Duhui?"

"Well, they have pizza, so they know good food." Zander winked. "But as for the rest? We'll have to wait and see a menu."

"Wait, didn't Blayde tell us to avoid the pizza?"

He shrugged. "They may be bad, but at least they know what pizzas are. Always a good sign. You can trust a species that knows a good flatbread. There's an odd correlation between yeast and hospitality."

"The one-eyed tree," the sign above the door read. *"Come for the food, stay for the purple giant and its million holes."*

"What's that supposed to mean?"

"I have no idea. Probably a pun. You want to check out the menu?" He indicated a list that hung outside the door with a flick of his wrist.

A little sticker of Mr. Gilmag hung in their window. The city's office of commerce had given them some kind of award, but it was too small to read; probably a sign of good things inside, not that I wanted to trust my taste buds to Mr. Gilmag.

"Is this still technically street food?" I elbowed Zander softly in the ribs. Not that a hard jab would have hurt him. One of the perks of being immortal.

"Well, we're on a street." He waved his hands in a wide arc as if to prove that, yes, we were standing on such a street. "The taxi driver recommended it."

"I take it this is a high-end snack place?"

"Exactly," Zander said. "Good food, good quality, and a great idea of what to expect from the rest of the planet. Sound nice?"

"Space bistro? Sounds brilliant." My stomach growled in anticipation. Zander laughed, and the familiarity of that sound rushed back to me.

My two years had been an eternity. A time I didn't even want to think about, and at times, couldn't even bear. There was grief and breakdowns and time lost to hospitals, trying to heal my shattered mind. Weeks that seemed like one very long day, and days that seemed to drag on for weeks. It had taken me a long time to heal, and I wasn't even done yet.

Not that I would tell him that. I wasn't going to ruin our perfect evening by making him feel guilty for something beyond his control.

Zander ran his hand through his hair like he always used to, all casual-like, driving it home that it had only been a few days since he had last seen me. It wasn't like he would change that much in such a short amount of time. He probably never even missed me.

If his jacket was any indication, Zander could love something and lose it and forget about it just as easily. One day, I would be a memory to him, and the next, not even that.

At least tonight, Zander would be a memory that stayed with me for the rest of my short mortal life. The thought both warmed and chilled me, and I forced a smile as I walked into the restaurant.

FIVE

TURNED ON BY MYSTIC SPACE PIZZA

THE HOSTESS—A SMALL ROBOT WHO LOOKED LIKE a kitchen bin with a little green hat—led us to a booth by the window, spewed two menus out on the table, let out a cheery jingle, and drove away, leaving us overlooking the freakishly long drop outside. We must have gotten closer to the edge without knowing it.

We were higher now than when I had first seen the planet, and in a swankier part of town. But here, in this comfortable restaurant, the drop didn't scare me as much—not when there was a foot of reinforced glass between me and the fall. Still huge and daunting, it was now more intriguing than terrifying.

From one wall of buildings, I looked across to the other. I couldn't see the planet beyond. It all seemed to revolve around this one massive avenue. From here, it was as if the city planner had thrown up a mountain of design ideas, with the oldest buildings on the bottom and the newest ones on top, poorly stitching all his ideas together. Across from me were ultra-modern, or ultra-uber modern, fashionably designed buildings, while a long way down, the buildings were made of thick, re-enforced, and blocky concrete. It was like looking at a British trifle, with each layer looking and behaving completely differently.

I felt quite happy to be at the top.

A tall, domed structure with walls surrounding it sat even higher atop the neighboring building. Lights shone from behind the enclosure, as if a party of the most elaborate nature was taking place, a party that politicians and billionaires would be invited to and would be spoken about in the society columns of the local newspaper, maybe even the national one. And it wasn't much higher than we were.

I looked down as far as I could see, until the darkness of a world without ads and cars made it impossible to make out anything lower. Did anyone even live down there, in the darkness the lights couldn't reach?

"Any idea what you want to order?" asked Zander. His menu came to life in his hands. Letters and symbols hopped in the air before his face, lighting up in hues of blues and pinks.

"Let me look," I said, reaching for the heavy electronic contraption. As I opened it, holographic cartoons danced before my nose. I swatted them away to get to the actual list of food. This seemed to

ALIENATION

anger them, and they changed color violently in the margins.

"Zander?"

"Yeah?"

"Why is everything on the list pizza?"

I wasn't joking. Every single item was a variation of the word "pizza." There was pizza, pizza-pizza, and even pizzaaaaa. The list became more creative as I scrolled.

"Aw, your translator can't contextualize," he said, sadly.

"What?"

"You know how it works through brainwaves, right?" He closed his menu. "It's top-of-the-line because it doesn't need a repertoire of languages to translate to and from; it just tells you what foreign words mean to say."

"What does that have to do with the menu?"

"Well, since your brain doesn't have a point of reference for anything in there, it's telling you what you want to see. Apparently, you want to see pizza. Don't worry, I won't tell my sister your subconscious is trying to spite her."

I looked down at the menu again, wishing for images of the food to give me something to go by, but the dancing mascots were getting in a fight and the letters were crumbling in their wake. Half the words were gone by the time the one with the red hat had beat the one with the tentacles into submission.

"None of this is actually pizza?" I asked, desperate for clues for actual food. "Seeing as how we're supposed to avoid them."

"I have absolutely no idea," he said. "I just ask the servers for the specials and order whatever that is. I can't read these things."

The waiter appeared. I was sad to see he looked as human as I was, his skin a pale gray, blemish-less. I wondered if he was anyone else underneath it. Were skin wraps popular on planets where you could be anyone at all?

"What can I get you?" he asked, waving his hands in the air. A dozen or so of the mascots followed his fingers as they trailed by, much better behaved than the ones in my menu.

"What do you recommend?" asked Zander.

"Oh, our flatbreads. Those are absolutely killer," the man said, his eyes lingering on Zander. His index finger twisted the loose curl of hair that had fallen out of his ponytail. I guessed some things were the same across the entire galaxy, or at least in this arm of it—Zander wasn't just charming to the people of Earth. "They can be topped with pretty much anything you like: three different kinds of cheeses, bacon strips, pepperoni, onions, tomatoes, lettuce, platarum, and special sauce. Shall I get you that?"

"Aren't flatbreads just really thin pizzas?" Zander lifted an eyebrow. The waiter took this as a genuine interest in striking up a conversation and leaned a little closer.

"Um-hum," he replied. "A new hit food. They're bite-sized for our larger patrons, though substantially

ALIENATION

bigger for your average human. Not that that seems to be a problem for someone like you."

"Sorry, I'm not a pizza person." Zander shook his head as if it were something to be ashamed about, though he loved the pizzas we had on Earth. Maybe Blayde's warning had resonated with him, but I didn't have to listen. What they called pizza was probably something entirely different.

"Well, I am," I said, breaking the waiter out of his Zander-induced trance. "May I ask, though, when you say the pepperoni comes from—"

"Pigs. Raised on Veen and brought in fresh daily. Would you like to meet them? "

"The pigs?"

"Yes. What else?"

Pork. Pig pork. Though maybe what they called pigs and what I called pigs were different creatures entirely; I took that chance. I didn't want to meet my dinner before eating it.

"I'll have that flatbread, then."

"I'll have the …" Zander scanned the menu quickly, his eyes flying over the gadget, before jumping up and staring at me with wide, lemur-like eyes, asking quietly what on earth I had just done. Pizza? He blindly jammed his finger into the menu, squashing one of the animated characters, prompting the others to scream in horror at his hand. "The, um, this?"

The waiter left with our orders, a huge smile on his face as his head turned back for one last glance at

Zander. Our eyes met by accident, which led to an awkward connection. I pulled my gaze away and rested it on my friend instead.

I wanted to ask him what I had always wanted to ask, what two years of waiting had brought to the surface. The questions that had been swimming in my mind since the day he blew up my workplace and disappeared with it.

But I couldn't. I would not ruin this evening, for either of us.

Keep it together, Sally Webber!

"They always this flirty with you?" I asked instead. "The waiters, I mean?"

"He was flirting? Really?" Zander seemed surprised, though how he could not have seen it, I didn't know. He'd have to have been blind.

"Don't tell me you didn't notice the eyes he was giving you. He wasn't exactly subtle about it."

"No, I didn't notice."

He blushed, and I wanted to laugh. He could go from badass to bashful in five seconds flat.

"Never mind." I gave him a smile, a sort of mental *don't worry about it*, but his face was still an impressive shade of red, nonetheless. "Wait—they have pigs here? Tomatoes? Onions?"

"Why wouldn't there be?" He sipped his water.

"I guess I thought they would have something, I dunno, crazier. I mean, it's too much of a coincidence for them to have the same meat and veg as they do on Earth."

ALIENATION

"Why? If they have humans, isn't it a logical jump to think that everyone came from the same place, pepperoni and all?"

"Do we even know?"

"There are theories, but nothing's written in stone in the universe. Well, except maybe that huge stone tablet that predicts Blayde is going to go crazy and build a maze one day. It's a fun tourist attraction. But no matter. In any case, the general line of thought is that the human race originated somewhere else entirely then spread through the galaxy and lost touch with one another, oh, billions of years ago. Truth is, I think I know the place, but there are many different lines of thought. There's a few thousand following the cult of the Green Star, living on planet Cupios—last I checked—who believe the universe was seeded by the great Duster. They also believe that everything that happens is in reaction to their own sexual frustration and rejoice in that fact, which is why there are only a few of them. That, and the fact their practices involve putting things in bins and taking them back out again, repeatedly, and to very dull, monotonous chants. They're frequently referred to as Bin-Heads. They don't like that too much."

"What does this have to do with pigs?"

"Ah. Yeah, well, humans like pizzas, so they brought their pigs and cows and all that when they took to the stars. Makes sense, right?"

"You're saying cows are spread across the universe because their meat tastes good?"

"Yup, basically." Zander shrugged and drank some more water. "And cheese! Though there are entire planets of people who are lactose intolerant. And we're going to need something to drink, aren't we?"

Not space milk. "Um, sure."

He waved down the waiter, who rushed off to get us glasses of whatever Zander had ordered. But instead of returning to the conversation, he stared out the window, turning his gaze upward, toward the starless sky. Light pollution had wiped out any view of the universe, but that didn't stop him from squinting and staring.

There was a longing in his eyes. An urge to move, to go, to be out there in that darkness. It was almost as if he were tethered to the table, and that was the only reason he wasn't zooming toward the sky right now.

It was the same need I saw in him when he was stuck on Earth—the need to go, to move, to not be confined to just one rock. Part of him was permanently in that space. And he missed it.

Not that he would tell me anything about that.

"In any case," he said, "count it as a blessing. As much as I'd encourage you to try new foods, there's always the possibility you won't be able to process anything here. Whatever you eat, better eat carefully."

I grinned. "Aye aye, Captain."

"I take you halfway across the universe, and you order pizza?"

"Flatbread," I said.

"Same difference!"

"Pizzas that have been made halfway across the universe. That's the coolest thing I've ever done yet."

"I'm not sure you'll be as impressed as you expect."

"I'll think of them as being made from space pork. I'll be fine. Anyway, what's the plan for after dinner?"

"Well, I want to repay you for everything you did for me." Zander's smile seemed forced. Darkness crept into his tone but was quickly squashed out. "And Da-Duhui is the fashion capital of the Alliance, which is saying something since the last time I checked, there were over five hundred planets officially in the UPA. So, um, you want to go shopping?"

I almost spat out my drink. "Shopping?"

Zander didn't seem to know what had just happened; he looked as surprised as I felt. He squinted at me, tilting his head like a puppy.

"Why not?" he sputtered. "Technology. Clothing. Entertainment. Look, I can only offer you a short time away from your solar system, and it feels like nothing compared to the hospitality you showed me. Go ahead, splurge. Take a bit of the universe home with you."

"You are one courageous man. You hated buying clothes back on Earth, and those were for you. Are you sure you can manage shopping with me? Won't you get bored?"

"I've handled worse." He chuckled. "Remember, I've spent the last—ahem—eternity living with my sister. Imagine her in a shop. She'll wear clothes until they go rancid. I have to shove her into stores and not let her out until she's bought something that isn't made from rags."

"Then I would love to go shopping," I said, and he beamed.

The waiter returned with our food, huge steaming plates in hand. My mouth watered like someone had opened the floodgates. As he slipped them onto the table, I pondered how surreal this was. I didn't know what I expected; the plate in front of me was covered by a gorgeous pizza. The bread was darker than any crust I had ever seen, but everything else was spot-on familiar. The side of the plate was decorated with gray herbs that smelled like basil but looked like thyme. Rather than a side salad, there was a small pile of sliced blue, apple-like fruit with ultramarine skin and azure flesh. Beautifully alien.

Zander had ordered what looked like tempura, though each vegetable was larger than the size of my hand. Not that I recognized all the vegetables under the thick layer of bread. Some of them were round, some were star shaped, even triangular. The smell wafting off them was salty and sweet all at once.

"You know, it tastes better if you actually eat it," Zander suggested. "Taste buds are in your mouth, not your eyes."

"Good point."

He picked up one of the smaller veggies, the one shaped like star fruit, and popped it into his mouth, chewing away happily. For a minute, his tense exterior melted away and his muscles relaxed, pure bliss glowing behind his eyes.

I grabbed the first of my slices and pulled it away from the rest. The cheese wasn't stringy, and it came away easily. The smell was different, saltier somehow.

Any resemblance it had with pizzas back home ended the moment the juicy bite filled my mouth. My eyes closed as the sheer joy of the flavor overwhelmed me. It had a sweet, fruity quality to it, the taste so different, and, yet, so perfect. Little hints of sourness lingered in my mouth and tickled my tongue.

I needed more.

I gulped down the first slice then tackled the second one. Every bite was ecstasy.

Soon, they were all gone, leaving their tangy flavor in my mouth. I wiped my mouth down with a napkin, grabbed the excess sauce and gulped that down as well. How had that mess gotten there? I'd never been a messy eater, but I guess space pizza changes people.

I was out of breath. Zander stared at me, wide-eyed. He had only eaten a little of his basket since we had stopped talking. Just how fast had I scarfed down my food?

And why was I craving more?

"Sally?" Zander said, waving his hand in front of me. How many times had he called my name? I saw him through a fog, but I couldn't pull myself out of it.

"What?" I said, dazed, licking the leftover sauce from my fingers, pulling them through my mouth slowly, catching every last drop.

"Are you all right?"

"Never better. Stop asking!"

I would have smiled, only I was too busy trying to soak up the spots of sauce left on the napkin. I could have eaten the entire thing. Everything else seemed out of focus and unimportant. I needed that sauce more than anything else in the world.

Zander waved his hand again but not at me this time. He was trying to grab the waiter's attention, I think. Why did I care? The man fluttered to our table, sliding to Zander's side and beaming down.

"How was your meal?" he asked, all smiles. Zander's expression was cold and anxious.

"Delicious," I replied for him. "Absolutely sensational!"

"I'm glad to hear it," the waiter said as he turned toward me. "Can I get you anything else?"

"Oh, yes, please. I need another order of flatbread. And then I need as much as you can make, to go. Do you do to go on this side of the galaxy? Or is that rude? Anyway, I am starving. Can I get a doggy bag too? Do you do doggy bags? How many flatbreads can I buy at once?"

My stomach growled, pleading for more. I was lost in the fog, and my only release was to eat more slices. I had a need, an uncontrollable desire for those pizzas, for the alien food gripping my stomach and making it speak for me.

It was the only clear thought in my mind: more. Nothing else made any sense. I couldn't even see the restaurant anymore; my vision narrowed on my empty plate, but I didn't care.

Zander stared at me, not just anxious but full-on scared. He didn't even make eye contact with the waiter as he spoke. His voice was cold and clear, like a general giving a command.

"Please bring us the bill," he said, his voice carrying no emotion. "We'll have no more pizzas. But the food was wonderful, that's for sure."

"Would you like me to pack up your own food for you, sir?"

"No, we need to go," he said, handing the man the silver square he had used to pay for the taxi.

"But I need more flatbread," I whined, the words spilling out of my mouth before my mind had even processed them. My mind was no longer in charge. It would be offline for the rest of the night, by the looks of things.

Some part of me was still fighting for control. I felt my hands reaching for the glass of water, trying to bring it to my face, but I could barely hold it. My hands wouldn't respond; my fingers refused to twist around the barrel. Instead, my head moved closer to the plate, ready to lick it clean.

"Huh, this is the sixth time this week I've seen this," the waiter said, scratching his earlobe. "The flatbreads have become very popular of late."

The waiter took the card and processed it through the watch gizmo on his wrist.

Zander's face shot up to look at him, glaring. "What's happening to her?"

"Not to worry, sir. Everyone else was fine within a few minutes." The waiter seemed unfazed. "It's just a question of letting the brain calm down. Your friend will be fine. Our chef is very good."

"Is she in danger?"

"Oh, come on," the waiter scoffed, "We're a Da-Duhuian hotspot. We don't let bad things happen to our customers. We have some fabulous secret ingredients that might react weirdly with some subspecies, but they're harmless overall. We've had no complaints. Think of it as part of the experience."

"You should put a warning on your menu." Zander took his card back. He put it in the inner pocket of his new old coat, not breaking eye contact with me the whole time.

"We did, sir. What did you think all those cartoons were for?"

I licked the plate, screaming inside, filled with shame and embarrassment, but I couldn't stop. It was an animal drive, a primal drive, a craving I needed to fill.

"Sir, did you assault the cartoons? They will not be helpful if you assault them."

Zander helped me stand, but my hands grabbed for the tablecloth and held on tight. He reached to unclasp one fist, and I elbowed him in the stomach, forcing the wind out of his lungs.

I wanted to scream that I was sorry, but I wasn't in control. Zander said nothing as he grasped me around the waist and gave me a sharp tug, so fast I ripped the tablecloth from the table without anything spilling.

A few patrons *oohed* and *ahed*, clicking their tongues and clapping.

My fists dropped the tablecloth and turned their wrath on Zander, swinging wildly. My body reeled, not even trying to listen to what I was telling it to do. My feeble screams inside my head saying Stop, stop, stop!

I kept fighting him, trying to get his arms off me. The part of me that wanted pizzas saw him as a threat. As hard as I tried, though, I couldn't shake him off.

"Let me go!"

"No, you calm down first," he said in that same commanding voice, better suited for a battlefield than a bar.

"Not until I get my pizzas!" My foot collided with my chair, and it toppled over. The waiter rolled his eyes again, setting the chair back up.

"Come again!" the waiter said, shooting a wink at Zander, who flushed a deep red as he dragged me out of the restaurant.

Outside, the air was much cooler, and as we stepped into it, it was as if nature itself had slapped me.

"Breathe," Zander said.

This time, there was enough of me aware to do what he asked. My body calmed. Slowly, he let go of me, and I staggered away from him, trembling and ashamed.

"I'm done asking if you're all right, but … are you?"

I let out a loud groan, clutching my head.

"What the … what was that?" I leaned on a patio chair to steady myself. He patted me awkwardly on the back.

"Right, apparently some food hits you strongly," he said, and a smile crept onto his features.

"Ugh." I shook my head. This wasn't pretty. People were looking at me through the restaurant window; I think a cloud of gas was outright staring, but it had no eyes so I wasn't sure. "Don't laugh."

"I wouldn't dare," Zander said, punctuating the sentence with a short chuckle. I glared at him. "Feeling better?"

"Yeah, I think so." I wiped the palms of my hands against my eyes, hoping it would drag the drowsiness out of them. "Let's get away from this place. Please?"

"I know just where to go." He held out his hand.

· · · · · · · · ● · · · · · · · · ·

The universe is big. Freakishly big. It's the biggest thing we know, right?

I had been grass fed Star Trek and Doctor Who. I had grown up dying for adventure and wanting space. Needing space. Feeling a deep sense of emptiness when I realized I was earthbound for the rest of my life. I felt astrolust to my core.

So when Zander had said, "Hey, Sally, want to go on a quick trip to see the universe?" I had jumped at the chance. Of course I had. But I had expected a lot more running.

ALIENATION

And not so much shopping.

I had nothing against shopping, though I found it hard back home when money had been tight for the longest time. There was something magical about finding the perfect pair of shoes, feeling like Cinderella when you slipped your foot into it and it felt like it was made for you. Or when you put on a pair of jeans and suddenly, bam, you had legs.

I had definitely never intended to shop on another planet. And never had I expected it to be such a blast.

We wandered around the shops, and I ran into most of them, looking at their gadgets and admiring technology light-years ahead of my own. I tried on shoes with heels that adjusted to your feet, both around the foot itself and for height. You could adjust how tall you were with a series of confusing clicks, but it was impressive all the same.

Also, they had heels here?

It wasn't the main fashion, though. Most people wore loose sandals. Many were platformed with straps that were one continuous piece of material you had to wrap around your foot and leg in a certain way to keep the shoe from falling off. The feathered people, the Macreneens, had talon-like feet, so they covered their nails in individual, brightly colored socks.

"You know, you are allowed to treat yourself," Zander joked, patting his breast pocket where the card was kept. "There's no weight limit on this interstellar flight." I laughed, but he was completely serious. "Come on, I owe you."

"For what?" I asked, "You used your own money on Earth. I didn't lend you anything; I had nothing to lend."

"You looked out for me. You helped me in every way I can think of. When I leave … I want to make sure you're good, too."

My heart did a weird belly flop in my ribcage. Those were words I didn't want to hear.

"Right. Not what we're going to think about tonight," he said. "Come on, let's have a great evening, okay?"

"Oh, I'm fine," I said quickly. I wasn't lying. My stomach had felt weird after dinner; it was the perfect diversion. "It's just … my stomach is acting weird."

"Really?" Zander's face fell, his smile fading into a frown. I didn't like it. "Is it because of the pizza?"

"Maybe." I shrugged. "I'll be fine. You're right. We should just enjoy this."

"Great. Let's go!"

He grabbed my hand and dragged me forward. I laughed as I followed him, and we ran through the streets, deeper and deeper into the city, getting lost as we went.

"Pick a store, any store," Zander said. "Actually, close your eyes and pick at random."

I closed my eyes, giggling as I spun around then stopped, dizzy, in the middle of the street and of Zander's laughter. My head spinning, I staggered forward, somehow finding a door and pushing it open. It let out a little chime, a rainstick made of bells.

ALIENATION

As the dizziness left my head, I realized we were in a small dress shop, a room a little bigger than my apartment back home. Every wall was covered in fabrics with fancy prints, woven with strands of gold to highlight the designs. Deep violets and reds with a bright brocade looked down at me.

I ran my hand over the fabric. It was soft like silk but thicker, though this didn't make it any heavier. I looked up at Zander, who shrugged in response to the silent question.

"Hello, hello," came a sing-song voice from the back. A woman entered the room—a woman with eight eyes on her dark face. She wore a large, thick orange wrap around her head, which only accented her slender neck. This almost distracted from the extra pair of arms right below the first pair.

But as she came out and laid eyes on us, she froze. Well, when she laid eyes on Zander, I assumed. The two stared at each other in silence. Zander's face lit up with recognition, but the woman shook her head, jutting her chin in the direction of a small robot who sat on the counter beside her. The robot studied Zander as intently as she did, though being a robot, one could never be sure just how intent it intended to be. Zander's face dropped.

"Pleased to meet you," the woman said, ignoring the short repartee, as if that moment had happened in a frozen piece of time. "I am Tchilla, dressmaker to the stars. No matter how many arms, legs, appendages, or feathers you have, I can make you look fabulous. Are you looking for yourself or for a friend?"

"We're looking for Sally today," Zander said, unfazed. "I already have what I need. What do you recommend?"

"Ah, yes, a human?" she asked, nodding. I couldn't help but stare at those dark eyes of hers, eight great, black opals that reflected my body as she took me in, shifting through the colors of an oil slick. "Come here, human. I have just the thing."

She hustled me into a changing room and tossed me something thick and purple. It didn't look like a dress, and I couldn't find the neck.

Tchilla spoke of her home planet, a place I had never heard of, stringing poetry along with her memories of the purple skies of home and massive wild plants that roamed the great planes. All her wares were made of a sturdy silken fabric, a by-product of these gigantic plants, which took years to produce, apparently, but the end result would last forever.

I stepped out, and she laughed gently then pushed me back into the changing room. In seconds, her four hands had deftly fixed my mistake. She showed me how to drape the fabric, by wrapping the ends over my shoulders and then around my waist.

"I'm telling you, this dress can fit any number of arms," she said, "and it will make you look amazing, too."

And it really did.

"You see, my dear," Tchilla said sweetly, as she tucked the ends into the sleeves, "the perfect dress isn't the one you beat into submission. The perfect dress is the one that tells you just how much it wants to be worn by you. A partner, not a slave."

I looked in the mirror and was shocked to see a girl with an actual figure staring back. It made me look like I had curves, dammit. I turned around and around, taking it all in, in silent awe.

Zander purchased the dress for me. I couldn't believe I would be taking something so gorgeous and alien home. Not that I could tell anyone where I had gotten it.

"You come back if you need anything." Her gaze fell on Zander, and she nodded once. Like she knew him or something. There was much more going on here. But wasn't there always, when it came to Zander?

We wandered the streets a little more, this time focusing on the sights of the city rather than the shops. I felt my stomach rumble and hoped Zander hadn't heard it; I didn't want him to worry about me again, for nothing.

We talked, and, yet, we didn't talk. There was a distance between us that hadn't been there before—was it intentional? Not on my part. But all we exchanged was small talk, even if the small talk involved alien wares.

Each window held new wonders, each turn of the street new people, new alien species. We lingered in front of a jeweler's for a while, and I admired stones and minerals of textures unseen on Earth. It was there that I saw the price of gold.

"Zander." My eyes widened and my jaw hit the floor. "You paid one hundred Alliance things for dinner, right?"

"Credits," he replied. "Alliance credits. Yeah, I did. Why?"

"Tell me if I'm wrong, but does that sign say that gold is … five credits a gram?"

"Not a gram, a unit," Zander explained. "That would be a little over a gram. It's difficult to convert." He saw the look on my face and gave me a wink. "Let's go inside, shall we?"

The interior was even more impressive than the storefront. The walls were covered in transparent cases displaying jewels I had never seen the likes of before and some I recognized, including a ruby pendant the size of a goose egg. A small cabinet, not even locked, contained small gold jewels, incredibly intricate and incredibly cheap.

Zander shrugged at those. "It rains diamonds on some planets."

Silver, on the other hand, was worth a small fortune. The store owner looked at my simple silver hoops in longing, saying simply, "You have one caring boyfriend, miss." To which I froze, shocked and confused, as Zander's face turned a violent shade of red.

Anyone watching would have seen me leaving the store with a whole set of gold earrings, bracelets, necklaces, and gifts for friends back on Earth, and all for the miserable sum of a meal at a "high-end" snack food place.

I stopped to watch a street performer, a creature as long as a school bus with at least a dozen legs on each side. He blew bubbles out of the protrusions on his head, changing their colors and shape to make them dance together. It was mesmerizing, entirely enticing.

"You have to see this," Zander whispered, pulling me out of the trance.

"I'm watching," I replied. "It's incredible."

"There's more."

I followed him around the corner to a plaza the size of a small country, and my heart leapt in my chest.

It was a fountain. Or a mountain. Or maybe both. I couldn't see the top from where I was standing; it just kept going. All marble, beautiful gray stone carved into a tiered forest. It was surrounded by a moat of water with dancing jets, leading to an island with stone trees growing on it. The branches and leaves turned to dirt and roots for the tier above, all the way up as far as the eye could see.

I was speechless.

"You want to see it from the top?" Zander asked, hopping from foot to foot like a five-year-old wanting ice cream.

"Can we?"

"We're right next to Da-Duhui Tower." He pointed at a spacescraper that stood taller than the rest. "If we take the elevator to the top, we can see the whole thing from up there, not to mention the whole city."

My stomach made another little rumble, and he frowned.

"I'm fine," I said, smiling. "It's a human thing."

"I don't remember that from …" He shook his head. "Never mind. You up for a quick trip to the top of the tallest building in this solar system?"

"Heck, yes." I put on a good show, pretending my fear wouldn't get in our way. "And don't worry; I'm absolutely fine. It's not like I didn't have enough to eat."

He chuckled but said nothing. Wise move.

"And is the height going to be an issue?"

He remembered. Nice of him to ask, this time, before asking me to run across narrow ledges. Not that I was proud of my irrational fear, though it might actually be rational in my case.

"I hope not."

"I'll be here."

There was virtually no line at the elevators, so we walked right up to the building and rode the glass shuttle to the top. The higher we got, the more I saw of the fountain. Each tree was delicately carved to give the impression that you could walk through the stone thicket, like the forest had grown there and was still growing.

At the very top, however, was a tree stripped of all leaves, and there sat a large, bronze, well … bird thing. I would say it resembled an eagle the most, but it had more legs than any bird I had ever seen. It was caught between take-off and landing, as if it were ready to take flight at any moment.

"What is that?" I hitched my neck at the six-legged eagle.

"The griffon of Kalmara, the symbol of the Alliance from way back when."

"I bet there's a whole story to tell, right?"

"Always," Zander replied. "That's the thing about stories: they can't bear not being told."

ALIENATION

I was in so much awe that panic refused to kick in. Soon we were above the fountain, the city sprawling out at our feet. This tower really was tall; we were above the city, the smog, the hover cars.

The buildings spread out around us, split by the varicose veins of the city, glowing yellow and pumping life through the arteries. I could see, now, the rooftops of the tallest buildings, where spotlights glowed and plants flourished.

The elevator played a little jingle then stopped, throwing its doors open to an observation deck. A gust of wind blew, and for a second I thought I would blow right over the edge, before logic interjected and reminded me I was entirely safe.

Might have to tell my knees that, though. They were shaking like a cold Chihuahua after a bath.

I went over to the rail, as carefully as I could, looking down at the cityscape from this dizzying height. My breath stuck in my throat for a second—no, a minute; a full minute or even longer—as I saw Da-Duhui with my own eyes, overwhelming my every sense.

Maybe I could do this height thing.

Maybe.

"Impressed yet?" Zander asked, leaning on the rail beside me.

I shuddered, and not from the cold, and tightened my hands around the rail.

"It's… amazing." I stared down at the bright city lights, far below me and yet still vibrant. "I just imagined it to be a little more…"

"Foreign?" he suggested. "Alien?"

"Exactly. Like … they have pizzas here. So many of the people are bipedal, humanoid, or even human. They have cars and TVs and elevators."

"It's not all the same now, is it?"

"Okay, fine, it's pretty different," I said as I walked along the observation deck, a clammy hand on the rail to steady myself. In every direction until the curvature of the planet, there was a sea of buildings and neon lights. "This place is pretty alien. And yet I can't wrap my head around this being an alien planet, you know? It's like something I could have imagined in a fever dream or while high or something. They're still the same people. Living. Laughing. Eating, shopping. I expected—"

"What?"

"Hell if I know." I laughed, though it was an awkward laugh. "It's alien. But it's normal. It's … tame."

"Well, it's a lot to take in."

"That's for sure."

I watched the people for a while, in silence. From up here, they looked like ants, just small, black specks. No distinction between human or non-human, simply people.

"So, um," Zander started, taking his turn at being awkward, "what happened in the past two years?"

No avoiding it now. I took a deep breath.

"Not much," I said. "Honestly, though? It's been pretty tough."

"Oh?"

"We blew up a power plant. Most of the workforce got out, but I almost died, and they were sure you were buried under the rubble. I grieved for you, Zander."

"I promised I would be back."

"My anxiety wouldn't let me believe that." I tried looking anywhere but in his eyes. "Don't blame yourself, okay? You didn't know."

"I'm—"

"After the plant blew up, there was an inquiry. For some reason, Grisham named Matt and me as benefactors in his will, but after all that happened, all the safety questions being raised, they needed someone to blame, and the new head of the company would do."

"Oh?" he asked. "Who was that?"

"Me. For some reason, I was named the head of the company in Grisham's will. Probably some weird liability thing he had going on. I suspect that was the only reason he hired me. He needed a patsy in case something went down. I got dragged to court, but I had a great lawyer and we ended up turning the tables on them. I got a huge settlement. But, anyway, enough about my boring life. Marcy and Dany are getting married!"

I had to change the subject before I burst. It was hard enough talking about the worst eighteen months of my life, with the trial and the worst bout of depression I had ever suffered. I took deep breaths and smiled. He didn't need to know how broken I was after the plant. All he needed to see was that I was fine now.

"What?" Zander gasped. "The lovebirds are tying the knot?"

"Yup!"

"Oh my stars, that's amazing!" he said excitedly. "Marcy getting married? I should probably buy them a present or something, right? What are Earth customs on the subject? Do I need to prepare an interpretive dance?"

"Yes! Of course, but, um, that may be a little tough," I said, forcing out the words. "You see, they all think you're dead."

"Oh," he said, hurt, but there was no sign of surprise on his face. "I can see why. Oh, that is troublesome. I won't be able to come back to Earth, will I?"

"Well, if you wanted to"–I grinned–"we could say you survived in a secret World War Two bunker under the chasm, living off the canned food hidden there. Every day, you would dig yourself out a little more, and then, after two years, you finally made your way out."

He laughed, the echoes lost in the roar of the wind. "Or, you could tell them I'm an immortal, regenerative alien who survived by teleportation, but because of the relative nature of the universe I only came back two years later."

"Yeah." I shrugged. "Even then, I think my story's a little more credible."

"But mine's the only one that's true."

I stared into the rising smog of the city. It was easy to tell myself this was just another city on Earth. From up here, it could have been anywhere.

ALIENATION

"You and Matt broke up, though?" Zander interrupted my train of thought.

The question caught me by surprise, though I should have been prepared for it. I rubbed my sweaty palm on the back of my neck, forcing the bristles to lie flat.

"Yeah." The hardest part here was to keep my face straight. "We both got out okay, but the trial, you know. So, he moved out west to help out his aunt. I haven't spoken to him since. It was an ugly breakup."

"Did it have something to do with the whole aliens-blowing-up-his-office thing?"

"You got it."

"Ah, well, that's what I would say is my bad." He didn't seem too bothered by the news. "At least no one was hurt."

"Yup."

A blinding flash of white light, like a bolt of lightning in the dark, slammed down in front of me. I threw both hands onto the railing, scared that I would get zapped and that I was being attacked by an unseen electrical evil.

Zander, of course, was laughing and not scared at all. Stars flickered in my eyes as I tried to wipe the light from them.

"Are you pleased with the result?" The mechanical voice came from behind my field of vision. A man flickered in and out of existence, but that was probably because my eyes hadn't recovered.

"Um, with what?" I asked, blinking the flash out of my eyes. As my vision returned, I could swear I saw a robot in front of me, an actual robot. His arm extended as he held out a computerized tablet for us to look at.

He couldn't really be a robot, could he? I mean … he looked like one. His face was silver, with sharper angles than I had seen before, and his arms looked like ropes of metal wound around each other. Yet there was something unsettling about his face—namely, that it looked so much like an actual face. If I reached up and touched his skin, I expected it to feel springy and warm.

The robot became more insistent. He pushed the tablet at my hands again. I took it and looked down at the screen, and my heart skipped as I saw the pixels. It was a photo, an absolutely gorgeous photo. A candid picture of Zander and me as we leaned over the rails of Da-Duhui Tower, caught in deep conversation. The lights from the city below shone like beacons of different colors.

"If you like or want edits, it only costs fiiiiive credits," said a familiar voice. And there, standing next to the robot, was the terrifyingly clingy Mr. Gilmag. He spat out a pre-programmed jingle, "But for a credit more, you get four!"

"We'll take it," Zander said, pulling some spare change from his pocket and slipping the coins through the slot on the robot's front.

The robot froze, processing the order. His eyes went green and flickered, which was remarkably unsettling coming from such a human-looking face. The tablet pushed out a printed piece of glossy paper in seconds, the colors more vibrant than they had been on the screen.

Meanwhile, Mr. Gilmag locked his holographic eyes on me and spouted a few facts about the tower. "Da-Duhui Tower is the largest structure on the entire planet, standing at a striking five kilometers high," he said, and for a second I was thrilled my translator could give me metric units in space, though how accurate they were I didn't know. The next second, I scowled at that annoyingly cloying voice. "It was built during the twenty-second dynasty as a center of trade and commerce, while also serving as the largest radio broadcast tower on the entire planet. It can reach—"

"Thank you for the picture," Zander said and bowed to the robot. "We would like some privacy now."

"But I haven't told you about the subcontractors yet!"

"Thank you, but program off."

"Remember to check out our historic Da-Dahuian Unity Museum!" Mr. Gilmag disappeared. The robot, however, remained.

"Now I take my leave of absence." He gave us a short bow. "I'll be off until you need me again."

He rolled away, creeping backward so as not to break eye contact with us. He shrunk into the shadows until we couldn't see him anymore, though I was sure I felt his lifeless eyes on me.

"That last bit didn't rhyme," I pointed out.

"Don't be so nit-picky." Zander laughed. "It probably rhymes in a few thousand dialects, just not yours."

"True." I looked down at the photo in my hands. It was beautiful, and, yet, I felt an incredible knot in my chest while looking at it. Even as Zander laughed, I could tell the gaiety in his eyes was gone now, and I sensed what was coming.

"Zander … is this a date?" I was surprised those words came out. Of all the things I wanted to ask, that probably wasn't even near the top of my list.

Or maybe it was, and I just didn't want to admit it.

"Why?" He paused, cocking his head sideways. "Do you … do you want it to be?"

I stared at the photo. At the two of us, happy. But I knew full well that this was a one-time offer, a one-time thing. A late thank you for giving him a roof over his head and helping him out on my planet.

"I don't think that would be a good idea, Sally," he said slowly. "It's just … I'm immortal. I've been alive longer than most things in this universe, and in that time, I've lost—a lot."

"It's not me, it's you. Is that what you're saying?"

"I don't know what I'm saying," he said. "Only that this shouldn't be a date. I shouldn't … date."

"So, you never date? Anyone?" I looked up at his beautiful eyes, the silvery green muddled by the orange light from all around. "That must be incredibly lonely."

"Yes and no," he said. "I have Blayde. Whether I want her around or not, I'll always have Blayde. That's what family is for."

"But—no relationships. Not even friends?"

ALIENATION

"I have lost more friends in my lifetime than there are stars in the sky. I make friends too easily. It's a habit I'm trying to break. I just … I don't want to lose you."

I had been expecting it, waiting for it, for two years. I knew how the end would be. I felt it in my stomach, the knot that formed, twisting.

He didn't want to lose me, so he'd say goodbye forever. Logical.

I wanted to talk—really talk. But while this was the same Zander, I was a different Sally. And I knew what was coming.

"I'll never see you again, after tonight," I managed, my voice coming out in a whisper. Yet Zander still heard me. His face was empty and devoid of emotion, giving me the short nod I'd expected.

We weren't together, but it sure felt like a breakup. I couldn't take in the magic of this alien world while there was this alien feeling in my chest, the feeling of losing something, someone, I never really had.

"I'll take you back to Earth, but then I have to go. Like you said, everyone there thinks I'm dead. Coming back will disrupt their lives, and they don't deserve that. You don't need that. And besides, Blayde needs me out here. To keep—"

"Doing what you do?" I asked. Again, he nodded. "But why? Why not stay, for a little while? You said you liked it. Why do you have to keep moving, keep leaving?"

"It's all I know. It's all I've ever known. I can't remember doing anything else. I just … have to keep moving."

"There's something you're not telling me," I sputtered. "Look, I know you have secrets. You're good at hiding them, but not the fact you actually have them. Come on, if this is the last time we're ever going to talk, tell me … just tell me … tell me what you're running from."

"I'm not running from anything—"

"I don't believe you."

"Let me finish," he snapped. "I'm not running from anything. I'm looking for something. I'm trying to find my home, all right?"

"Home?" I asked, confused. "But why?"

Suddenly, the knot in my stomach burst. My belly wrenched in the wrong direction, twisting apart in a way that shouldn't have been physically possible. I fell to my knees, uttering a single, heavy gasp of pain. My body trembled, shuddering, the air catching in my throat.

"Shit. Sally!" Zander's hand was on my burning cheek, assessing the situation. "What's wrong? What's happening? Can you speak?"

I couldn't. I felt as if opening my mouth would allow my stomach to escape. Instead, I slapped my belly.

I almost threw up when I looked down. Slapping my belly had caused things to move there, a wriggling hive under my taut skin visible even through my shirt. Things were crawling inside me. My belly was swelling and writhing like it was a bag of termites and cockroaches.

My heart pounded. I wanted to scream, but I couldn't open my mouth. There was no air in my lungs, and my

ALIENATION

head spun until things turned dark and I fell backward, the dark, velvet sky filled my entire field of vision.

Zander's head was suddenly in front of the darkness, his eyes wild. An arm slid under my neck.

"Hospital," he said, lifting me into his arms. He dashed to the rail and jumped off the building.

SIX

EXACTLY WHAT I DIDN'T WANT TO HAVE HAPPEN, HAPPENS

SOMETIMES, YOU CALL 9-1-1 IF AN EMERGENCY occurs. In others, your best friend throws you off a spacescraper.

I probably would have screamed, but I was way past that. We were falling so quickly, I couldn't imagine ever going at that speed. Even with Zander's arms wound tightly around me, trying their best to comfort me, I felt as if I were a boulder and they were string. My head reeled and I jammed my tightly-shut eyes against his neck.

The wind strangled the air around my ears. It burned my skin with the icy coldness of a million particles being shoved aside by massive, plummeting humans. The drop in my gut was enough to tell me how dangerously fast we were falling, but the wind was an unnecessary emphasis.

Just when I thought we couldn't fall any further, when I thought we would smash into the pavement, it stopped. Zander was firmly planted on the ground, like he had walked off a boat rather than the tallest building this side of the galaxy.

But he did not stand still for long. As soon as he was on terra firma, he ran. I didn't think anyone could run that fast, but the wind was back in my ears as if we had never stopped falling. He was a bullet. I was the gun.

I couldn't see where we were going; my eyes pressed tightly against the cloth of his shirt as I tried to breathe through my nose. I didn't want to see anymore. The last image on my retinas was the horror of my writhing stomach. Zander held me tighter, and I almost imagined I could hear the blood moving through his veins.

But I couldn't hear any pulse other than my own blood rushing in my ears.

"Your heartbeat …" I struggled to say, shaking.

"I don't have one," he replied sharply. "Stay calm. I'm here."

My stomach was alive. It pulsed and swirled as it writhed under my shirt, little needles drilling their way out from inside my stomach. I felt numb, the signal coming from my nerves completely saturating my brain. I pushed my hand against my belly, trying to push the swelling down, but it was getting bigger by the second.

I wasn't helping.

I was safe, cradled in warm arms. But then Zander was pushing me away from him. I wanted to cling onto my hold, but he laid me on a sticky seat. Cold leather clung to my boiling skin. A breeze wafted over me, and

I forced my eyes open to see the same velvety sky I had been looking at when I'd closed them.

I was in a car. More precisely, a convertible.

The breeze wasn't enough to cool the heat of my skin, though. I realized the seat wasn't sticky: I was. I could barely move my hands, but Zander strapped me in as words flew out of his mouth faster than spilling M&Ms.

"She needs to go to the hospital, right now," he said, trying to keep his calm. It wasn't working. His voice was harsh, but it was commanding and powerful too.

"Who does?" I managed out of parched lips. Zander stroked my hair—or maybe he was pulling the sticky strands away from my face so I could breathe.

"No way," another voice sputtered. "That's my car! That's my car."

He repeated the last word as if he couldn't find another to convey how much this car was his. He sounded mad. He sounded distant.

"I have"—there was a pause, during which Zander reached into his pocket and pulled out every bill and coin he had on him; I watched the scene between fluttering eyelids—"fifty thousand. That's fifty grand worth of Allied credits—all with your name on it. Do we have a deal?"

"A deal?" There was a hesitation in the man's voice, but the sum must have been impressive because he sounded pleasantly surprised. "Of course you've got a deal. Just let me get my stuff out."

ALIENATION

The driver's door slammed, and suddenly Zander was on my right, his hands flying over the complicated driving console. Lights flickered on and off, and the engine revved, coming alive under his deft hands.

Apparently, people drove on the left in this solar system. Odd thing to focus on as I was dying.

"Everything's going to be fine, Sally," he said with as much reassurance as he could muster, but the tremor in his voice told me it wasn't enough to reassure himself. "You're going to be fine. I've got you."

"It's Alien!" I screamed as another twist of pain rushed up my spine. It felt as if my stomach was ripping in half. I grabbed my seat, trying to calm the agony, trying not to scream.

The car shot forward, slamming me against the sticky chair. We plunged off the platform parking lot into the nothingness of the highway, my eyes squeezing shut against the terror of the chasm.

"Don't be xenophobic, now," Zander muttered, his focus elsewhere.

"No, no!" I smashed my fists repeatedly into the soft flesh of my writhing belly. "It's the alien from *Alien!* Holy shit, it's a chest burster!"

I sobbed, pushing my hands against my crawling stomach. Whatever was in there was moving fast, sensing my panic and the car's acceleration. I pushed harder, trying to crush the thing—things, I didn't know. I just wanted to snap in half so the thing would break with me. Everything blared and mashed together.

"Sally, you have to stay calm." Zander swung the car sideways then down, dropping us a good hundred feet.

Tears welled in my eyes; from the pain or from the fear, I couldn't tell. They stung like they were liquid fire. Hair whipped my face, each strand going hundreds of miles an hour, ripping at my skin and sticking to my sweat. Even the inside of my head burned. My thoughts spun in circles, faster and faster, faster and faster.

"How can I stay calm? I can't … I can't breathe!"

The car dove. Like dropping a stone into a lake, we went down, and we went down fast. I clutched the seat with both hands, one of my nails snapping on it. I closed my eyes and held them shut. I wasn't going to open them for anything.

"Then breathe," Zander ordered, in that voice of a general commanding his troops. "Inhale and exhale."

"I can't!"

"Do it for Marcy," he snapped. "Do it for Marcy and Dany and Matt. Breathe."

"Matt's dead!"

"What?!"

My head swung sharply to the right as a huge, heavy vehicle collided with us.

Zander wasn't the only one speeding on this stretch of highway, but at least he was a good driver, though that was an understatement. As our car leveled out into one of the hovering lanes, joining the masses, someone sprung from left field and rammed into us. Our car turned into a plunging and spinning car, tumbling out of control, spiraling off and away from the road.

"Warning, warning," the car blared, lights flashing. *"Out of perimeter bounds. Please readjust course."*

And then, quite suddenly, there was nothing under me anymore. The seatbelt tore open. I felt my skin peel from the seat, and then nothing at all. I forced my eyes open and saw cars whizzing past me—above me.

I was falling.

Screaming.

My stomach lurched as I tumbled. I grabbed wildly at every passing thing, trying to hold onto something, anything to stop my fall. Unfortunately, nothing I grabbed was attached to our car, so we tumbled together, me and the old shopping bag, a random hat, anything the man who had sold us his car had forgotten to claim.

I got a last look at Zander as he clung to the steering wheel of the pitched car, his hand extended to grab mine. I saw him scream my name as gravity overtook me, pulling me down—

Crash.

My back hit a car. My stomach faltered, but now it was my back in pain, bruising, burning as I rolled off the hood of the vehicle, falling again, face forward in a nosedive. My fingers tried to clutch onto something, anything, but they were too slow to respond, and soon I was falling again—falling into the depths of the city.

Crash.

The car I slammed into next was driving quickly, and I gripped it. I was in luck. It was an antenna flag. The thing was dark blue and orange, and it burned my hands. We were flying, and I was being dragged forward, clutching the flag, my body flapping backward in the wind like an antenna ornament.

The driver turned around and glared. It was a big, burly looking thing, all hairy and with a slew of eyes that spiraled on a special head, leaving a round hole for a mouth in the middle. At least I thought it was a mouth. From all the teeth it flashed at me, I was pretty sure that not only was it a mouth, but an angry, scowling mouth.

It swung its controller sharply to the side. The car swerved. The flag snapped and sent me careening out of control. I was falling again.

Crash.

Crash, Crash, Crash.

All the way down.

The only upside? The rest of my body felt as bad as my stomach, so things evened out to a general agony across the board. I was going to be bruised in the morning.

If I survived until then.

And then the cars were gone. The world around me grew darker, like I was plunging into ink. For a moment, without anything around me to define my fall, it was as if I were floating, albeit on a gusty day. I saw nothing.

It smelled awful, though.

ALIENATION

At least I wasn't going to see the ground when I slammed into it.

Only, when I hit it at terminal velocity, I went straight through it, ripping the fabric as I fell—an awning. So old I didn't bounce but tore straight through it. Or maybe I was just falling too fast.

An awning, in pitch blackness. I didn't have time to think about how weird that was. Already, I was hitting another, only this time I bounced and rolled downward. My hands were too slow to grab it, so I fell to the next awning.

And the next one.

Finally, I saw a dim, gray glow below me. Somewhere between bounces, there in the darkness—light. I hit the ground, hard, landing on my back. My head smacked against the pavement as my lungs expelled all the air I had ever breathed in one go.

I don't know if I passed out; the world was black, either way. But as my eyes fluttered open, I knew there was no logical reason for me to still be alive.

But here I was, panting on the hard ground, moving my joints and assessing that nothing, not a single thing, was broken. Everything hurt—oh wow, it hurt—but everything was working.

I couldn't believe I could still move. I shouldn't have been able to. A fall from that height, I should have been dead. And, yet, here I was, with the palms of my hands numb and stinging. My kneecaps felt shattered, but I could still bend them—though that brought out another cry of pain.

I should have died.

I pushed myself up, whimpering and brushing the dirt off my clothes. I was alive. I could stand, even, but I was also in a dingy, smelly alleyway. Even looking up, I couldn't see the cars or even the city—only blackness, in every direction.

I was screwed.

More like Screwed. Capital S.

I gagged, feeling my stomach twist. The pain of it threw me back to the ground, back to my knees. I fell into a pool of stagnant water, but I barely noticed it soaking into my jeans. I braced myself on my hands as the contents of my stomach rose and spilled from my mouth. Thousands of beings crawled upwards and out, hitting the pavement and hightailing it out of there the second they were on solid ground, getting away from me as fast as they could.

I was extremely glad for the poor lighting. I had no urge to see the things that had grown in my stomach. The large, maggoty things escaped into the shadows, gray and fat and covered in slime.

The sight of them, the thought of where they had been, twisted my insides again. I threw up in pure revulsion. The idea that those creatures had been crawling through me sent my stomach back into knots.

Next time, no matter what I thought of the woman, I'd take Blayde's advice. I really should not have had that pizza.

I let myself breathe for a minute, but I knew I had to get up and going. I didn't know where to, though. There didn't seem to be much else down here, and I wasn't looking forward to wandering around and getting lost.

Zander would be searching for me right now. I shouldn't go away, but I couldn't sit around and do nothing. I was in pain. Every muscle screamed, and my entire body was probably one big, purple bruise. Just getting on my feet hurt like crap. Part of me felt better now those things were out of me. A rush of endorphins hurried in to fix me.

"Okay—assessment time," I said aloud, which proved that at least my mouth was working.

The rest of my body seemed in order. All my joints were stiff, but they bent where they needed to. Nothing felt broken, though it hurt worse than anything I'd experienced before.

Mind? My anxiety was strangely under control. Thank god for therapy and Prozac—neither of which I had with me right now. Crap. Just thinking about my anxiety was triggering my anxiety, so I forced myself through the breathing techniques, attempting to break the spiral before it began.

"Don't. Even. Think. About it."

Instead, I focused on standing again. I felt my wet knees and shrugged—a bad idea; my shoulder blades were not happy—and wiped my muddy palms over my jeans. Then, gingerly, I forced myself to walk, to put one foot in front of the other and head toward the source of light.

I guess miracles did exist. The light was coming from what looked remarkably like a telephone booth.

S.E. ANDERSON

It wasn't a TARDIS, but it would do.

It was probably the warmest gray glow I had ever seen, like a beacon beckoning me to come closer. I didn't need to be asked twice. I scurried in, closing the door behind me. It even smelled nice, radiating an air of freshly cleaned sheets. The little room was a haven of warmth in this weird darkness.

One wall held what looked like a very large mirror. Apparently it was a video chat booth as well. While I didn't like where I had landed, I had to admit the aliens had some cool tech. The little black disk on the top of the screen must have been the camera, watching me from its perch above.

What was the emergency number here? Not nine-one-one from back home, certainly—that number was of no use in my protection on an alien world—but there must have been a movement sensor because the computer powered up on its own, and the screen flashed blue. The first thing that flashed was a big, pulse button marked "Emergency Services." Perfect.

I tapped it, and a fresh face appeared on the screen. She looked human. Maybe they paired dispatchers accordingly. There was even a serenity about her, like she would lead me through a yoga meditation. Her cheekbones were high, and her skin polished like she were an opal.

"Emergency services, how may I help you?" she asked, giving me a motherly look. I tried to let her reassure me, but the smile ended on her side of the screen.

105

ALIENATION

"Hello, I'm Sally Webber," I said awkwardly, my knees trembling. "I just fell to the bottom of the city. I need help."

"Are you injured?"

"I threw up some parasites, and I'm not sure what shape I'm in. I don't understand why I'm in one piece—"

"Ma'am, I'll send a dispatch right now. Where are you?"

"I have no idea. Can you trace the call?"

"Easily. What did you say you name was?"

"Sally Webber."

"Can you stand still for a minute?"

I obliged and waited, not quite sure what was going on.

"I'm sorry. We don't have your name or face registered. Are you from an Alliance planet?"

"No, I'm from Earth."

"Never heard of it." Her patience visibly flickered. "Anyone we can contact for you?"

"My friends don't have phones," I said, realizing just how bad my situation was. "They could be anywhere."

"Don't worry, ma'am. We'll have someone bring you back in a few minutes."

"Thank you."

"Please present your hand for scanning."

"Scanning?"

"Yes," she said, annoyed. "We need your Identichip so we can process you."

"That's a bit problematic. You see, I don't have one. Our planet doesn't require them."

"Any other identification I could use? An ID card?"

"Sure." I reached to my side, and my heart dropped. My wallet was in my duffel bag, with Blayde. "I lost it in the fall," I answered sheepishly.

"Look, ma'am, we don't have your name, your face, or any ID. You're from a planet we've never heard of, and you seem fine to us. You know what I think?"

"No …?"

"You're a filthy Downdweller trying to hitch a trip to the surface," she snapped. "Sure, you may have better clothes, but you're still one of them. I've seen your tricks before. Now leave the emergency line for someone who actually needs it!" She disconnected the line.

"Hello? Hello?" I said frantically, repeatedly tapping the touchscreen, but it was no use; the screen was off for good, disabled by the woman on the phone.

The lights followed.

The entire street returned to darkness. Without a way to see, I used my hands to find my way out of the booth. I found the curb and sat on it. I guessed real cars had once driven on these streets because there were sidewalks here and gutters too, though they didn't seem to work very well.

I held my head in my hands and leaned forward, still nauseated from the fall and the things that had been in my stomach.

What was I supposed to do now? I was alone and lost in the middle of nowhere, in the darkness where not even the emergency services wanted to go, fearing those so-called Downdwellers.

ALIENATION

I was on the verge of tears. There was no way of letting Zander know where I was, no way for him to know I was down here, in the dark of this forgotten floor of the city. A modern-day equivalent of sweeping things under the rug.

I looked at my hands, or the lack of them. The darkness was perfect; I couldn't see them, or anything else. I wasn't even sure I existed anymore.

A warm, light breeze blew on my face smelling strongly of rotting fish, of bad morning breath, and of milk long past its sell-by date. It froze, the air pulling back, then threw itself against my face once more. My nose wrinkled, incapable of picking apart the scents. As it pulled back, I realized with a start that this was not wind—no, the air down here was much too stagnant for any kind of current.

Wait—bad breath?

SEVEN
THAT'S DARK, DUDE

THE THING BEFORE ME GROWLED, A LOW rumbling from a creature of monstrous proportions that shook the ground. My heart raced and my hands trembled as the breath of the unseen foe billowed on my face, taking in my scent as I tried to block out his.

Could it see me? Could it see how scared I was? How small and weak I was? How much could it tell about me, here, in the darkened world below the city? Did I stand a chance if I took off running? Could I even run? My mind cried for me to get away, but my legs refused to listen, keeping me firmly planted in front of the creature.

If I hadn't been scared of the dark before, I was now. For years to come, I would wake in cold sweats and imagine it was right in front of me, or at the end of my bed, or waiting for me in my dark hallway or kitchen.

ALIENATION

Panic welled in my chest. Panic of the attack that would surely follow.

The monster let out a long, earth shattering roar, showering me with basketball-sized balls of spittle. My knees turned to jelly as the stench of death saturated my every pore. It would eat me, I knew it. There was no avoiding it. No getting away. This was the end—

But I wasn't going down silently.

I felt panic rise from my gut to my throat, to my eyeballs and ears, the jagged sparks running through my blood.

I took a step back, bracing myself upon my trembling bones, forcing them to stay still. Wiping the spit off my face with a steady hand, I threw back my head, and with one strong, deep bellow, channeled all the oxygen I had into one roar. One war cry so loud it traveled through my entire being. It grew in my chest and exploded outwards, my voice resonating through the tiny streets and echoing back until I was no longer alone, until I was an army.

The creature roared back, but I roared louder. I would not let it take me. I would not end like this. I didn't survive the fall just to die in some dark alleyway. No, sir; no way.

I screamed until my throat felt red and raw then screamed some more. Soon my lungs were burning and my head spinning, but my knees would not buckle. Then, I was roaring at nothing. The creature had stopped, crawling back into the darkest dark from whence it came. The breath on my face was gone, the smell fading. The air was stagnant and muddy once again, the street around me silent as I dropped my voice.

The echo of the roar rang through my ears, and I inhaled in pure relief, feeling the shock and simple joy of knowing I was alive.

Quickly, the relief turned to hyperventilation. I found the curb with my trembling hands and sat to catch my breath. I needed my meds, but they were in my duffel bag, in the hands of a woman who probably wouldn't care that I was missing. A few small pills and all of this would be much more manageable, though I wasn't sure they were powerful enough to deal with the stress of being lost in an alien city.

I waded through the panic attack, letting my tears flow until my eyeballs were sore and my head was empty and heavy. My hands trembled as I clutched them around my body, giving myself a tight hug.

I knew Zander was going to find me. I was going to be okay. I just had to wait here, right here. He would follow me down here. Any minute now, he would find me. I just had to wait.

I reached into my pocket and pulled out my phone. I hadn't even realized it was there. While I had thrown my ID into my duffel bag before we jumped, I had forgotten to take the small mp3 player out of my pocket. It had cracked during the fall, the screen a spider web of glass, but it turned on, its light illuminating the tiny patch of darkness before me. A small, insignificant dot, but it was light.

ALIENATION

At least I had some music to listen to, so long as the battery lasted, that was. I didn't bring the charger with me, and even if I had, I probably wouldn't find a compatible outlet for another couple of light-years at least.

I pointed the screen at the buildings before me. No doors on their surface, I noted, only stone and more stone. One patch looked like it had once been an archway or a garage or something, but it was cemented in now, and poorly at that. If there ever were any doors, they sure weren't there now.

A quick glance at the building across the street showed nothing; the light wouldn't go that far.

"Holy cow," a voice said. "Do you see that?"

I flew to my feet, turning my head from side to side, but there was no one there. Not that I could see anyone, even if there were. The darkness was so thick, so complete, that even with the glow of my phone I couldn't make anything out.

"Hello?" I called into the dark.

There was movement around me—nothing I could see, but I could hear it, feel it. The sound of countless feet—small feet—pounding the street around me. I spun again, waving my phone around, trying to see something, anything.

Yeah, like that was going to help.

"Show yourselves," I ordered.

A light flicked on, then another. And then a whole lot.

Suddenly, the street was aglow. A wide circle of lanterns surrounded me, full of flickering blue flame that radiated bright against the glass. . Light, now that was a good thing, but there was no telling if its carrier was friend or foe. The people behind them held their lanterns at eye-level, so it was impossible for me to see their faces.

But they were short, that much I could tell. Up to my hip, maybe, if I was generous. Their clothes were strange, like someone had sewn rags together then tailored them. While rough, even scruffy, they fit them rather well, some better than others.

"The emergencies coming for you?" asked a voice, the same one that had just sworn. I turned, searching for it, and the creature lowered their lantern so I could see their face—a strange face, even in the blue and white glow of the alleyway.

Their skull was almond-shaped, literally. It was pointed at one end, around where their mouth was, while the other end was on the back of their head. Their hair sprouted from the apex in the back, creating a long ponytail they wore like a scarf, carelessly wound around part of their bare scalp. Their round, cat eyes looked me over, a reddish tint deep inside, like the creatures who live their lives in caves, never seeing the sun.

They looked like a child, but maybe that's how they all looked. But, hey, I had seen Galaxy Quest. Never assume *anything* when it came to aliens. Cute and small could just as well mean quick and deadly.

The universe is weird—I should have grabbed a guidebook—and I missed my towel. My knees were soaking from that puddle of water. I might have been better dressed than Arthur Dent, but he was better equipped.

I shook my head to answer their question then realized this could mean nothing to them, so I said "No" instead. They deflated.

"They don't know me," I said, pointing at the sky as if that would make more sense to them. "I'm not chipped or from an Alliance planet. Actually, they haven't even heard of my planet."

"Well, it's not like they care much about the Alliance." The stranger shrugged. "I am Kun, and these are my fellows in arms. We're the Street Sweepers."

"Sweeping away crime and bringing a clean dose of justice to the streets," piped up an equally small voice from somewhere to the side.

I glanced at the strangers and realized I had no sense of their gender. Was Kun male, female, neither? No clue, and no way of knowing. Did their race split the chromosomes, the way humans did?

They lowered the lanterns from their faces. Every one of them had the same pointed skull, reminding me of a fish I had once seen in the Baltimore Aquarium. Kun was the tallest.

"I'm, um, I'm Sally," I replied, stammering through dry lips. I wiped the tears from my face with my wrist. Hey, could you blame me for being in shock? "Sally Webber."

The stranger bowed, and I bowed back, hoping I was following their customs. I didn't want to cause a fuss on top of everything else. Not when I had quite literally just crashed into their neighborhood.

"You stood up to the Beast," one of them said, giddy. "That was frashing awesome!"

"Language, Cori," Kun snapped. "Sorry about him. We're all just, you know, impressed. It takes guts to stare down the Beast."

"What was that thing?"

I looked back up the street, but there were only a few strangers with lanterns. It was as if the Beast-thing were never here.

"You know when your parents tell you not to flush a dead pet down the sewers?" Kun shook his head. "That's what."

"Oh." I guessed I wasn't going to get more of an answer than that. "Can you tell me how to get back up there? I have some friends looking for me."

There was a hush, like they were holding their collective breaths. There was almost no air left in the circle to breathe.

"Crap, I'm sorry," Kun said.

"Language," someone interjected, and Kun glared at him.

"Look, Sally," he said softly. "They're deleting any files they have on you as we speak. It's over. You can't ever go back up there. They won't let you. You're a Downdweller the second your feet touch the ground. There's no going back from that."

"Wait, what?" But the circle was already dispersing. Kun waved me toward him as he walked away, but I had to stay to wait for Zander, didn't I? Except that I needed shelter more. Sticking around ran the risk of getting me killed.

So did following strangers, but it seemed like a chance worth taking.

"What do you mean there's no going back?" I followed Kun, trying to keep up. Falling from the sky tends to leave you a little sore and not all that enthusiastic about running.

No one said a word. It was incredibly odd. They seemed to appreciate the silence, though. There was no rumble of cars from above, or maybe the sound was so constant it had already faded into the background of my subconscious.

"There's gotta be a way back," I said, trying to get Kun to say something reassuring. I was fishing, sure, but I was also terrified.

"Sorry, but no," Kun answered, fixing his lantern onto a perch over his shoulder so he could stuff his hands in his pockets. He acted like he went through this a lot, almost like a bored college tour guide. There was no pity in his voice, none of the reassurance I craved.

Then again, I had just faced the Beast. I needed no pity, except I still had no idea what the Beast was, though, only that it smelled bad.

"Once you fall from that pampered pedestal, you can never get back up," one of the other people said, trotting along beside me and giving me a creepy, toothy grin. His teeth were sharp, like a shark's.

"Don't be like that, Rüt," said someone else.

I counted a dozen of them, including Kun. He was the only one with a scarf over his head; the others wore beads or a hat or nothing at all. Some had ponytails, others had braids. Some a knotted hairdo I had never seen before, like a rope to tie up a horse.

"But you have cars, don't you? Or a bus system?" I asked, but they said nothing. "Oh, come on … stairs?"

"Um, no." Kun gave a sharp laugh. "We don't have commodities like that. We're cut off from the Overcity, except for some running water, and even that's restricted."

"Wait, what? You're off the grid? Why?"

"It's complicated," Kun replied. Rüt trotted to keep pace with us, obviously eager to be a part of this conversation, though I couldn't see why.

"They royally frashed us over," a small voice said from behind, chirping like a bird.

"Sorry?" Kun's eyes, already large, seemed to bulge out of his head. He snapped his head around like an owl and glared at the small being. "Cori. You're not supposed to use words like that. They're bad for our image. You haven't earned that privilege yet. You know what I can do."

Kun was obviously a leader to be feared. I had to get on his good side. Rüt seemed to be his right-hand man, or small alien person, as it was, so I'd be remiss if I didn't get accepted by him too. The rest of his team, the Street Sweepers, were a close bunch. Finding my place within their community would be a struggle.

ALIENATION

Not that I planned on staying long.

"Ugh." Kun sighed and shook his head. "I don't have time for this. You can take the rear flank. We'll talk later."

Cori's eyes swelled from his head, like those rubber toys you squeezed too hard as a child.

"The rear?" he squeaked. "But…"

Kun pointed his fist—three fingers, I noted—toward the back of the line. Cori went without objection, though he huffed air heavily from his nose.

"Look," Kun said. "They only keep those emergency booths running so they know who to delete from their systems. They never actually rescue anyone. Trust me, there are a lot of your kind down here."

"My kind?"

"Humans and so on." He shrugged. "Upfolk. City people. Your lot."

"But I have friends," I sputtered, trying to decide what to pick up on first and coming up short. "They know I fell. They'll come after me."

"They can try." He popped his eyelids up, an odd but unmistakable ocular shrug. "But the cars are hooked on a magnetized grid, and it doesn't extend down here. They can't drive under it. Don't know how it works, don't ask me, but we had a Higher Up fall a few years back and he went on for hours about it. That's why most people survive the fall. If you have a lot of metal on you, the magnetic grid pulls you up, if only slightly. Maybe enough to stop you from breaking your neck on the pavement." He continued his polite rant, waving his hands around to emphasize whatever point he was trying to make. To me, though, it sounded like the ramblings of a child.

"So they abandon their own people?" I shuddered. Da-Duhui's glow was wearing off on me. "How long have you lived here?"

"All my life," Kun said, shrugging his eyelids again. "I was born here. Raised here. I'm a Downdweller, born and bred."

"Downdweller? What is that, anyway? The woman on the phone really didn't like them."

"Figures," he grunted. "In any case, you're looking at one. That's what they call those of us who live in the Undercity. Technically, you're one of us, now that you're stuck. You're a Downdweller, Sally Webber."

A shiver traveled up my spine, all the way to the top of my head, and spread through my bones.

We continued in silence. Kun's team led me along small pathways, through the foundations of the buildings above, knowing their way around in the dark better than I knew my own apartment. Strange sounds filled the darkness. Large things moved and slithered in the distance, but the Street Sweepers seemed not to notice. I sure did. It was like the foundations of the entire city were moaning in agony.

Kun pointed a thick finger down another small alley, and I followed. I was Dorothy arriving in Oz, only the munchkins were aliens, the witch a beast I had shooed off with a panic attack, and I didn't have Toto with me. I glanced at my phone. That would do fine; it could be my Toto. Now to meet the good witch and track down the wizard.

Hopefully, they didn't have anyone for me to melt using water. That would be awfully gross. Not my cup of tea at all.

Kun led me to a small door in the wall, holding his lantern boldly before it so that I could see. The entrance was blocked with wooden boards, and someone had written the words "unsafe" in chalk, making it clear this was not a building to trifle with. I wondered how many of these old homes were accessible down here. This had been the first doorway I had passed that wasn't cemented shut.

But before I could say a word, the Street Sweepers pulled the wooden slats away. They came off easily, as if they were never nailed on to begin with. Kun reached forward to open the door.

"Welcome," he said, with a flourish, "to our secret hideaway."

Well, the place sure looked cozy, but it smelled awful. The stench hit me the second he opened the door, a gust of mold and mildew rushing at my face like I'd been set upon by a wizard. Dank age and urine were not a nice mix.

The hideaway looked like a child's clubhouse: backless benches in various states of disrepair, a threadbare rug on the floor, pillows piled in the corner into what could easily have been a fort. Drawings on the wall, which, while lacking any artistic talent, sure brightened up the place.

"Are you coming?" Kun asked as he dashed inside, grinning as he threw himself on the padded armchair. He waved me in after him.

"You don't have to get excited about it," Rüt said, giving me a look that could easily have come from Droopy the dog, "but you could try to be polite. It's not like we had to bring you."

"Oh!" I said, feeling the blood rush to my face. "I'm sorry. It's just … wow, this place took my breath away."

"Better," said Kun. "Now come on in. Let me show you where your stuff is."

"My stuff?" I asked, but he ignored me.

I followed him through the house, which was much bigger than I had expected it was even tall enough for me to walk through comfortably. Everything was lit with the same soft blue light, the little flames flickering inside jars set on the floor every few steps.

The rooms were wide and under-furnished, though there were mattresses in every corner. There were blankets and rags, sometimes indistinguishable from each other, piled all over the place. It looked like a squatter's hovel, or maybe a drug den.

Not that I had seen either, except on TV. And this wasn't Earth, anyway.

I forced myself to smile out of politeness, but hiding my disgust was going to be difficult.

ALIENATION

They had called it their hideaway. Maybe it was a place to hide from the Beast. Their lives must be difficult down here, in the dark and constantly having to evade a monster who smelled like the sewers. They were just barely surviving.

Rüt brought me to a room that was completely empty except for an old pump in the center. The floor was tiled in white on one side and brown-green on the other. One step on the brown tiles made me realize it wasn't paint, but mold.

Alien mold. I gagged. I should have taken shots before this trip. I'd probably die of space flu after all this.

"The larder is through there." Rüt opened a door I hadn't seen. It was dark and had stairs leading down into a darker space. "We're going to need a nice dinner. And be snappy about it."

"Excuse me?" I stammered.

Was he really asking what I thought he was? I glared at the stranger. I was taller than him, by a lot. I bet if he had a clone stand on his shoulders, I'd still be taller. I could take him down easy. Who did he think he was anyway, bossing me around like this?

"You heard me. We need a meal," he snapped. "And the food has to last for a week. So be smart about it. You might want to plan ahead. We eat twice a day, and we get pretty hungry."

"You seriously expect me to make you a meal? We just met. If you think—"

"We saved you," Rüt said. "Without us, you would be wandering the streets until you got lost and starved to death. With us? You'll always have food. All you have to do is make enough to share."

"Hey, I faced the Beast on my own, remember? Doesn't that count for something?"

"Maybe." He offered up a shrug with his eyes. "But that was just one Beast. They travel in herds, you know."

Well, that was terrifying as shit. The shiver came back and took me for a spin.

He picked up on this and nodded slowly. "Look," he said, "we all have jobs to do in order to survive. You don't know your way around the streets, you're human, and you don't have the Light like we do. Your kind wasn't meant for the Undercity. So let's help each other out, okay? You cook. You clean up. Make this place nice. And in exchange, we'll let you stay with us. All right?"

I nodded, slowly. Not that I was okay with this deal, but I was exhausted, bruised, hungry, and not in the mood to argue. He was right—I didn't know my way around. They were the only help I would get.

And I was happy to cook. It wasn't a big deal.

At least for now.

"Good." Rüt grinned. "Now get us some grub. You can use the roof-shrooms to see down the stairs. Thank you."

He dashed out of the room before I had time to ask what he meant. At least he was polite enough to say thanks.

EIGHT

I HEAR WEDDING BELLS: MAKE THEM STOP!

THE ONE THING NO ONE TELLS YOU ABOUT falling a few miles down a highway is that you feel pretty sore after it.

Probably because it was a no-brainer.

With the adrenaline wearing off, I felt the soreness I'd wanted to avoid. I desperately wanted to sit down, but that would irritate my bruised rear, a literal pain in the ass.

I stood on wobbly legs by a small door leading to the larder, staring into the cave black darkness down the stairs. What had he meant by roof-shrooms? I looked up at the dripping stairway ceiling, and sure enough, there were little mushrooms there, gray and seemingly lifeless.

It was odd how you could travel light-years and still see something recognizable. I reached up to touch the hood of the delicate little guy, hoping to the heavens it wouldn't kill me. The second my skin touched his, he lit up.

And so did all his friends.

A ripple of teal light flew down the staircase. The bioluminescent fungi made the room look like it was midday in the Sahara.

Though maybe a blue-green Sahara. Or that planet from Avatar. Panorama? No, Pandora.

I thought of my phone and my definite need for the familiar. Luckily, my music selection was fair on its own, so I put in my earbuds and hit shuffle. If I was going to be Snow White, I needed a musical entourage. And so, with the dulcet tones of Taylor Swift in my ears, I got to work.

I marched down the stairs in pure awe. The light was magical, like something out of a fairytale, all bright and glimmering. But the roof-shrooms gave off no heat, and soon my teeth were chattering. It was time to stop looking up and instead look at the job ahead: preparing food for over a dozen small aliens whom I knew nothing about.

Not what I had planned for today, that's for sure.

I grabbed what I could and ran upstairs, too cold to stay down there much longer. I had what appeared to be an onion, maybe, and a block of either meat of cheese. There was also some potato-looking lumps and maybe some grubs.

Grubs?

I dropped everything. The grubs didn't care, they were latched onto the alien potatoes and paid no attention to me. I brushed them off with the edge of my toe, biting my lip in disgust and leaving a brown smudge on the tuber's skin. Of course, the fake-potato was now covered in mold from the ground. I wasn't sure which was worse.

Gross. I wondered if I was supposed to eat them then shuddered at the thought. Please, no.

I put my hand on my stomach, carefully. Not even an hour ago, it had been writhing with creatures, and even though they were gone, it still hadn't settled. I never wanted to think of pizza again, and I didn't want to touch a bite of food in this terrifying world.

My belly gurgled with hunger.

No. I turned my entire focus to the job at hand. I would suck it up, work through it, then find a way out of here. I was Dorothy from Kansas. I was Snow-freaking-White, and I would beat my witches. I needed to get back to the city, and this was the only way to do it. I grabbed a bucket, pumped the water in the middle of the room, and got to cleaning the taters.

They had everything in the larder. There were cooking utensils, old pots and pans, and things I had never seen before and could only guess at their use. I grabbed what looked familiar—cutting, frying, seasoning—and made do, hoping to high heaven I wasn't poisoning myself or anyone else. Soon, the smell of frying onions filled the kitchen. I was proud of my weird alien creation.

It looked like potato rösti, so good I probably would have Instagrammed it, had I been back home. Heck, I pulled out my phone and snapped a picture, just for good measure. There.

Kun must have smelled the food because his face was suddenly in front of mine. I crouched over my makeshift stove, a pan over one of their upturned lights. He rubbed his belly like a hungry child.

"This smells good. What is it?"

"It's … Earth roast," I said. "A specialty of my … um … grandfather's. Yes. Grandfather's Earth roast."

"How much longer?"

"I'd say it's ready."

Kun let out a shrill sound, like an awful whistle, and suddenly the Street Sweepers were running around, grabbing plates and utensils and cups and drinks in a whirlwind. My hands flew to my ears, trying to keep out the noise. In less than a minute, they had taken everything into the living room, where they sat on the floor despite having actual chairs to sit on, eager for dinner.

I followed Kun out holding the frying pan, walking around the small group and scooping out ladlefuls of my creation. They had their own order of seniority, with Kun at the top and Rüt close behind. I hadn't learned any of the other names yet, and no one cared to introduce me.

When I had dished out a plate to everyone, Kun gestured for me to sit next to him, giving Rüt a not so delicate shove to make room for me, which made the latter pout. I did as I was told, sitting cross-legged next to their leader, emptying the last of the saucepan on his plate. There would be no seconds, for anyone.

"You won't eat?"

"I… I can't," I said. "Nothing's been staying down on this planet."

That was as gentle as I could put it. There was no way I was eating anything here, not after those… things. I shuddered at the memory. Kun's glare, though, made it clear that it was not the right thing to say.

"What if she's trying to poison us?" suggested Rüt, scowling. A slice of potato slid out of his open mouth and onto the floor before him.

"She's not going to poison us." Kun laughed, but the expression never reached his eyes. "Right, Sally?"

"I wouldn't dare."

Rüt pushed his plate forward. "Well, I'm not going to take a bite until she does. And I suspect none of us will."

He was right. The rest of the aliens pushed their plates forward, all staring at me. I gazed down at my plate. The food looked good, that was for sure, and it smelled amazing. Even so, my stomach was doing flips at the thought of eating it.

"Fine," I said, and picked up the metal skewer in front of me. I stabbed a Da-Duhuian potato, closed my eyes, and brought it to my mouth.

It tasted like bananas had cross-bred with a cucumber. But it didn't burn. It didn't hurt. And I wasn't crazy and addicted, yearning for more. I swallowed it, opening my eyes and holding out the skewer like a proud sword, victorious in defeating the not-actually-poisonous food.

"Hum, this is pretty good!" Kun said, and instantly, his crew devoured their meals. They ate with metal spatulas, utensils like flat spoons, the kind of thing used to scrape paint off the walls, rather than skewers. I watched as the aliens finished their plates before I had put my utensil down.

They burped in unison. Then laughed.

"Sally Webber has made us a glorious meal," Kun announced, giving me a fond look. I edged away. Something about his voice creeped me out. "Her presence here has made this place feel more like a home. And for that reason, I wish to announce that I am marrying her!"

I spat out my food like someone had slapped me on the back. It didn't all go out. Some I inhaled down the wrong pipe and started to both laugh and choke. Rather than coming to my help, Kun laughed.

I caught my breath, wiping tears from the edges of my eyes. I felt winded, not only from the laughing fit but from the shock of hearing those words from a perfect stranger.

"Kun … I'm not going to marry you," I said, softly.

"Why not?"

"Well, for starters, I don't even know you, and I don't want to get married. To anyone. And it would have been nice if you had asked me first."

"Well, you're going to say yes, so I didn't think that mattered." He shrugged.

"What makes you think that?"

"Because you have to."

"But what if I don't want to?"

"That's not fair!" he said, getting up in a scurry and glaring at me. He crossed his arms over his chest.

"Life's not fair."

"You're mean!" And with that, Kun took off down the hallway, covering his eyes with his hands and sobbing. I watched him go, awestruck.

I turned to look at the rest of the Street Sweepers, but their eyes were already on me. Glaring, actually, as if I had just stabbed someone. There were no thanks for the food, only pure anger.

They got up and moved away from me, casually, like they had all simultaneously planned to do something else. I rose to my feet, stepping over their dirty plates and spatulas as I made my way to the door.

"Where do you think you're going?" Rüt asked, suddenly in front of me.

"I'm not welcome here," I replied, wondering why I was so nervous. My hands shook, and I stuffed them into my pockets. "I'm leaving."

"On your own?"

"Yes," I said, trying to move past him. The small alien stood his ground. I'll blame that on his low center of gravity, not on my weak arms. "Look. If you're not going to help me find my way back up to the city, I'm going to do it myself. Without you and the Street Cleaners."

"Sweepers. But it's *impossible*. You'll die! And what do you mean, you're not welcome here? We opened our doors to you. You're getting married tomorrow! Isn't that hospitable enough for you?"

"I don't want to get married," I snapped.

"But Kun wants to."

"I'm not Kun, and I don't want to. He'll have to wrap his obloid head around that fact. Capiche?"

I shoved my way forward, but Rüt was joined by another Downdweller. I frowned.

"Let me out, Rüt."

"No. This is for your own good."

"I'm the only one who gets to decide that. So let. Me. Out."

"No."

They glared at me. And not just them. The Street Sweepers formed a barrier between me and the door. They advanced on me, blocked my escape.

I knew I could take them: I was taller, after all, and probably stronger. But they had strength in numbers, and I didn't have enough arms to swat them all at once. Instead, I put my hands up.

"Fine. I'll stay. But I'm not getting married."

"We'll talk about that after you clean up," Rüt said. "For now, I need to console your fiancé."

I shuddered at the thought. No way was I marrying that infantile stranger. No way was I marrying anyone in this unbearable city.

And for the first time since I got to their weird planet, it hit me: I wanted to go home, more than anything else in the universe.

ALIENATION

Talk about culture shock.

I clenched my fists and stormed to the living room where I picked up the dishes and brought them to the kitchen. I cleaned them, violently throwing them into the bucket under the pump, trying to keep my mind off my imprisonment.

I would leave when they were asleep. They wouldn't be able to stop me then.

All the while, the Downdwellers kept popping their heads into the kitchen to talk to me. Sometimes it was to ask about the world above, but mostly it was to congratulate me on my spontaneous engagement. I groaned internally as they rambled on about my future spouse's accomplishments.

"He's very kind," one said.

"He's very handsome," said another.

"One time, he ate fifteen nuts at once!"

"You'll be marrying a leader," they all agreed.

I didn't care either way. I had only just met him, and there was no foundation for a relationship. Not to mention I was not of his world and that I had to leave, yesterday.

Did I mention that I never got a say in this? Because I would have liked a say in my own engagement.

It must have been getting late because they stopped coming to see me. The noise in the house died down until all I could hear was my own breathing.

I poked my head out of the kitchen—nothing. Slipping out of my shoes, I grabbed them in one hand, taking care to step as lightly as I could on the cold stone floor. I reached the first room with the mattresses, and, yes, there they were: three little Downdwellers snoozing in a pile. I got out of there quickly, balancing on the tips of my toes.

The other rooms were the same—the Downdwellers' sleeping forms rising and falling gently in the near-dark. They had left their little lights on the floors beside them, floating flames trapped in jars like a small swarm of fireflies. It was just enough to light my way out of there.

I reached the front door and panicked. I had never seen a locking system like this. Latches and knobs and hooks and string were all over the door, with no rhyme or reason. I wondered why half the things looked like they didn't serve a purpose.

I had to be quiet.

Of course, as luck would have it, the second I nudged the first latch, a loud ringing exploded into the room. Instantly, they were upon me, racing at me, suddenly awake and very, very angry.

I pulled the latch again, but it wouldn't give. I tried another, but there were hands around my waist, my legs, my arms, dragging me down and away from the door.

I cried out in pain as one twisted my arm backward.

"Quiet!" Rüt snarled, raising his hand. A small plume of blue light appeared in his palm, dancing delicately in the air above him. The light from the lamps; the Downdwellers were the ones creating them.

I watched wide-eyed as the thing grew, sucking energy from the room and making the air crackle and hiss. It

ALIENATION

grew larger and larger in his palm until it was bigger than my head, and then he raised it, ready to strike…

"That's my future spouse, you brute!" Kun yelled, leaping into the air and kicking Rüt's face. The fire fell to the ground and set the rug ablaze, but together the Street Sweepers stomped it out, while the two angry aliens stared each other down.

"You kicked me!" Rüt cried, holding his palm to his face.

"You tried to incinerate Sally Webber!" Kun retorted. "You're not allowed to do that. I'm telling on you."

"Oh, yeah?" Rüt snapped. "Well if you tell, then I'm telling too!"

They glared at each other. Stalemate. I took my window of opportunity and leaped at the door, trying to rip the latch, but still I grabbed the wrong one.

I missed my shot. The Street Sweepers were upon me again, holding me tighter than ever. Four of them grabbed me, two to an arm, and it was enough to render me immobile. One curled around my leg, weighing me down. They brought me before their leader.

"Sally Webber," Kun said sadly, his fight with his friend forgotten. "Why are you trying to go?"

"Um, look, Kun," I said, as politely as I could, "It's been great and all, but the truth is, I need to get back to my friends. To my family. It's not you, it's me."

"But you can't," Kun insisted. "Why don't you believe us? We're your family now. You're going to be my wife!"

"I need to at least try to go home."

Kun let out a heavy sigh. He dropped his head, closing his large eyes and breathing deeply. When he looked back up, he looked resigned.

"Very well then," he said, a pout on his mouth as he crossed his arms across his chest. "If you're not going to stay here willingly, we'll have to help you. Get the ropes."

"The what, now?"

The five Downdwellers dragged me into the living room, pulling so hard I thought they would yank my arms out of their sockets. They forced me into a seat by the wall with the old pipes and tied me to them quicker than I could say "Don't you dare!"

Their knots were haphazard but tight, nothing thought out. They wouldn't know how to undo them, even if they tried. In the end, I couldn't move, and I think they had cut off the circulation in my left arm.

"Let me go!" I snapped, trying to find something more dramatic to yell and failing miserably. I struggled at my bonds, but that only seemed to make them tighter.

"We're going to get married—tomorrow," Kun asserted. "And then you'll be my sweetie, and you can't go anywhere! Forever! And you'll cook for me and we'll have lots of kids."

"Oh for the love of… " I swore under my breath. "I don't want to marry you. We're not even the same species. There's no compatibility. No kids, Kun."

"You'll fall in love with me," he said, puffing up his cheeks and chest, standing tall and proud. "And then we'll kiss under a full moon and—"

ALIENATION

"Wait," I stammered. "Is that ... hold on, what now?"

"Sleep tight, sweetie of mine." Kun smiled like this was completely natural. "I love you!"

"But... "

And then they were gone.

NINE

MEET THE INLAWS

IT FELT LIKE HOURS HAD PASSED AS I SAT THERE IN the darkness, plotting my escape. I worked the ropes, but they were incredibly tight. Already, my left arm was going numb and limp. I panicked first about toxic blood, if that was even a thing, then amputation, and my situation in general began to hit me.

First of all, I was trapped. In the underbelly of a city with no way out. On another planet.

Secondly, no one knew where I was or how to get to me. Everyone I knew and loved thought I was on Earth, and yet here I was, in the basement of an Undercity almost across the galaxy.

Well, still in the same galactic arm, but it's the same difference, right?

And last but not least, Zander would find me.

ALIENATION

I jerked awake. How had I fallen asleep? How long had I even been asleep? Two minutes, an hour?

The knot in my stomach tightened as I took in my dark surroundings. Panic began to take hold as fear flowed through me like a current, and I struggled to reel it in.

I told myself that I had control, but that was a lie. I was just as trapped now as I had been when I'd fallen asleep. That, and my left arm was completely numb now.

It slowly hit me that something was different. There was light now, though it had been moved around since dinner. There was a plate of food—bread, possibly—next to my now completely useless arm. Though the thought was nice, there was no way for me to eat anything. No way for me to move.

And then, there was a knock on the door.

Nobody moved to answer it.

No one was here.

"Zander?" I struggled to sit more upright, but it hurt to move.

"Kun!" a voice shouted, deeper than any of the Street Sweepers'. "Get your ass out here, young man!"

My heart fell—not Zander. Whoever it was, they were angry, though.

Still, no one showed. The Street Sweepers were gone; no one was in the house but me. I hoped to high heaven that the voice outside the door was on my side.

"Help!" I shouted. "Help me. They tied me up!"

The door burst open in a blaze of purple flame. A Downdweller stepped inside, his face almond-shaped and his features fierce. His eyes sparkled with determination and fury. As they landed on me, they bulged from their sockets. The stranger was at my side in an instant.

The alien was at least a foot taller than the Street Sweepers. His face was longer and narrower, more elegant and almost handsome. The ponytail that hung out of the point of his skull was wrapped in a lovely silken scarf around his scalp. He looked altogether more refined and more put together than any of the Downdwellers so far, even as he stormed in with flames in his palms.

And that's when it hit me.

Kun and Rüt and the rest of the Street Sweepers. They weren't just childish, they were children. And this man, this Downdweller barreling toward me, he had to be a parent.

Their secret hideaway, this house, was their clubhouse, where they would hang out and play.

And I was the unknowing tourist who had fallen into one of their games.

"Did they hurt you?" the stranger asked, kicking the food aside and reaching down, working his hands at the knots. I shook my head.

He burst a rope open with a well-controlled flame, and suddenly the blood was flowing through my arm again, sending jolts of painful tingles down the length of it as the nerves turned back on. I cried out as the ropes loosened.

He took my hand and turned it over, looking for signs of harm. "How long have you been here?"

"About a day, I think." I staggered forward as I tried to get up. The stranger gave me a sturdy hand to help me stand. "I fell … and they … they …"

"Don't worry." He gave me a sweet, reassuring smile. "My name is Tamashi Owasurete Shimat. Call me Tam. And your name?"

"Sally Webber." I forced a smile. "Sally. Thank you, Tam."

Now standing, I felt the full pain of my last day: the soreness in my joints and muscles from being cramped in a seated position for so long, the bruising along my entire ribcage, my slowly revitalizing arm. I tried to step forward and howled in pain. Tam reached for my sore arm, which only made me hiss.

"I'm sorry for how my child has behaved," he said, half apologetic, half furious. "Rest assured that when I find him, he will face a stern punishment. And speaking of… "

Kun had returned to see the door of his beloved hideaway shattered to pieces and singed to a crisp. He stepped into the house and froze. All color—the small amount there was to begin with—drained from his face.

"Kunoch," Tam said sternly.

"Kota?" Kun replied, trembling. The other kids poked their heads in the door, gasped, and took off in the other direction. Only Kun stayed, paralyzed with fear.

"Wait until your koty hears about this!" Tam's face was purple and getting darker by the second, his fury lighting a fire behind those large black eyes. "Home. Now. March!"

Tam walked Kun through the dark streets of the Undercity with his hand clutched on the collar of the child's shirt, shouting the entire way. I followed close behind, rubbing my wrists where the ropes had dug into them. My arm hurt like hell. Shit, everything hurt like hell, and if Tam wasn't yelling, I probably would have been letting loose a few slurs of my own. Kun said nothing. How could he? His parent wasn't giving him a single opportunity to even attempt to crawl out of this mess.

The streets were dark and stuffy, like the last time I had been outside. Tam seemed to have no problem navigating them, though. His fire crackled in his hand, angry and sparking, unlike the gentle flame I had seen back at the house. The light was my only way to see as I followed them, trying not to think about what lurked in the dark.

We turned a corner, and my jaw dropped. Suddenly, there was light. Civilization.

Tam let the fireball dwindle as we stepped onto the clean pavement. A vast market was illuminated by the flames of the Downdwellers, the street vibrant and alive with people. It looked glorious under the purple and blue lights, each stall selling a bounty of food and trinkets so completely out of my world they took my breath away.

But Tam wasn't stopping. He stormed through the street, the crowd parting to let him and Kun through. Even though his legs were half the length of mine, I struggled to keep up, accidentally bumping into people as I forced my way through, trying not to get distracted by the stalls.

I had never seen anything like them. The people behind the stalls shouted and roared at each other, bartering and chiding, making trades and advertising wares. Mounds of oddly shaped fruits and vegetables laid on one table, mountains of spices on another. One sold small metal bowls in intricate patterns, some of them holding flames, their light bouncing and reflecting off the polished sides of the bowl and illuminating his stall.

The Downdwellers were packed thickly in the street, going about their daily lives with no regard to the bustling city above. They were nothing like the crowd of the Upper City, their hair and clothes varied and they were packed closer together. Some glanced at me as I walked, and they looked away just as quickly.

But there weren't just Downdwellers here: There were humanoids, too. There were even humans, albeit a few in the masses, though easy to spot with their height difference. But they didn't look much like me, not anymore. They looked … worn.

I shuddered. Is that what would become of me, if I couldn't make it back to the surface?

No. I couldn't think like that. I was getting back up there, even if it meant giving up everything else. There was no other option. I was going home, whatever it takes.

Zander would find me.

We rounded the corner from the bazaar, walking down residential streets with beautifully lit fronts. Each home was well-kept, even if it wasn't the pinnacle of sophistication. Flowers hung over their doorways, beautiful bioluminescent blues and purples, like the mushrooms of the cellar.

Tam stopped in the middle of the street, turning to steer Kun in front of a house and shoving him up the steps. It had a light of its own, emanating a bright, warm orange glow, fronted by a beaten-down, rusty door. In one swift move, Tam retrieved a key from his pocket, jammed it into the lock, and threw the door open, shoving Kun inside.

Fires of different colors burned in jars on the shelves, as if floating there by magic. As neat as they were, they only dimly illuminated the room ahead. The house had what resembled a sofa and a table, but nothing covered the walls except long, dark stains. It smelled like sweat and salt, like the rest of the Undercity, even though the house looked as clean as it could get—not a cobweb or any dust, proof of a caring owner. Unlike the kids' hideaway, this home felt warm and smelt faintly of flowers.

ALIENATION

And it was cozily furnished, too. As little furniture as there was, it was properly coordinated. I stared at the couch, wanting to collapse on it then and there from exhaustion. My sleep in the clubhouse hadn't been restful, and every part of me still hurt. I needed rest. I was practically falling over as it was.

"Marth!" Tam called, and Kun stiffened under his grip. "Get out here. Now!"

A Downdweller in a trim suit stepped into the room, his clothes tight and elegant. Rather than a ponytail, his hair grew in a crown around his skull, leading to a point and back down either side, brown and flecked with gray. He reminded me of a goblin, though a tall and fishy looking goblin. He crossed his arms over his chest, and I wondered if Griphook had relatives on Da-Duhui.

"You found him!" Marth exclaimed, fierce and stern all at once. "Where did he run off to this time?"

"The clubhouse, of course," Tam replied. "But he had a houseguest …"

"Oh, skies above." Marth's jaw dropped as he saw me. But his shock was replaced by determination, the look a parent puts on when they were about to lecture their kid. A look I knew well enough from my own family.

"Hi, I'm Sally Webber," I said, forcing a smile. "I fell?"

"Yes, Yes, that much is clear," he muttered. "Kun. What did we say we did when we find someone from the Overcity?"

"We bring them to you or Kota," Kun replied, abashed.

"And what don't we do?"

"We don't—"

"We don't play freaking house with them!" Tam snapped.

"Tamashi!" Marth exclaimed. "Language! Now, Kun. You realize what you did was astoundingly wrong? How long has she been down here?"

"A day?" he squeaked. "Not even!"

"Oh, thank the skies," Marth murmured under his breath. "Did you hurt her? Did he hurt you?" His head snapped up, his eyes meeting mine.

"No, I'm fine," I said, a shiver passing through me. His eyes were intensely dark, like miniature black holes.

"He and his friends tied her up," Tam said angrily.

"Kun!" Marth's jaw dropped again. "Go to your room! You're grounded. I'll speak with you in a minute, but first I have to repair the damage you did."

"But, Koty," Kun whined, "I was going to marry her!"

"Marry her?" Tam scoffed. "Kun, this is ridiculous. You can't rope an Upper into your games like this. Their lives are not your playthings. Go to your room now."

"But, Kota!"

"Now," Marth and Tam said as one. Kun ran off down a hallway, covering his eyes with his hands.

"Miss Webber, we are so sorry for the actions of our offspring," Marth said, striding forward then freezing in place. "I'm going to get you something to drink. Tam, can you make her comfortable?"

"I'll get some blankets."

It was weird, how quickly they acted. Marth left without introducing himself, a whirlwind flying out the door he had come in without making a sound. And Tam had left too, dashing off somewhere else entirely while I tried to follow Marth.

When Tam came back, his arms were laden with thick, fluffy blankets. He ushered me to the couch and handed them over one by one, wrapping me gently in a bundle until I could barely move. I was a burrito of warmth. It was only then that I realized how much I needed the heat. Tears trickled down my face as it hit me how royally screwed I was.

I was free from one prison, but I was still stuck down here.

"These are really soft," I said, slowly.

"Beast pelts," Tam replied.

"I thought the Beast was more slithery, like a snake."

"Snake?" Tam clinched his eyes in a shrug. "What the … no, never mind. What did the children tell you about the Beasts?"

"They didn't say anything. I saw one. Well, not exactly saw. It was dark. It smelled rank. It was more like… confronted."

Tam's expression was one of shock, his eyes wider than I could have imagined them going. "You what?"

"I screamed at it until it went away. That's when Kun and his friends found me."

"Hot glass of Jee, coming though," Marth said, grinning as he handed me the mug. "Here. It's warm, so it should help."

I had trouble getting my hands from under the blankets, but Marth was patient and waited. I took the goblet with both hands, smiling as I thanked him. He beamed.

I took a long sip, letting the heat of it flow through me. It tasted of warm cinnamon and thick molasses, and it coated my guts like an internal blanket. Already, I felt calmer. I sank deeper into the furs.

"Again, we apologize for Kun's actions," Marth said, reaching for Tam's hand and giving it a tight squeeze. "He's never done this before. We don't get a lot of new people down here. He's not used to it."

"Not to excuse his actions in any way," said Tam. "Trust me, he's not going to leave his room for months. We want to make this right. Whatever you need, tell us."

"Just get me out of here," I said, stubbornly. "I need to get back to the city. My friends need me. I mean, I need them. I need to get home."

"Poor child," Marth said, shaking his head like a bobble. "There's no way back up. Once you're here, you're here."

"Hold on, what?" I sputtered, almost spilling drink over the thick hides. "I assumed after you came along … I thought the kids were messing with me?"

"No, no, they were telling you the truth." Marth sighed. "We're cut off down here."

ALIENATION

"We need to find her somewhere else to stay," Tam said, in hushed tones, as if I wasn't here. "We don't have room in this house."

"But she needs a home," Marth replied, shooting Tam a harsh look, "and we can provide one, for a little bit, until another unit is cleared out. I mean, Plutarch is at the end. She can have his place when the time comes."

"Thank you," I smiled warmly, willfully forcing myself not to shudder. I had no intention of staying in the Undercity for long. I was going home. "Don't worry, I'll be gone before long. My friends will find me."

"Poor child," Marth muttered, nodding solemnly as if he had heard it all before. "I don't know how much Kun told you—or how much of it was true—but there is no way back up to the city. We're fully cut off down here. We have been for thousands of years."

"Oh." All of this was incredibly sudden and weird, half of it not even making sense. I don't think my situation had become clear in my mind yet. But it was beginning to.

"And they don't help you?" I urged, glancing back and forth between the two of them. They looked impassive.

"Politics, I guess," Tam said. "It's complicated, as most things are. You look exhausted. Are you hungry? Are you hurt from your fall?"

"No, no, I should be all right." I cringed at the thought of putting anything in my stomach. Even that one bite of potato from the night before wasn't sitting well. Or maybe I was just too hungry.

"You must be tired," Tam continued.

"Very."

"Then come. Your room is this way." Tam led me across the room to the hallway, picking up a small metal plate and a glass bulb on the way. He waved a few fingers over the bulb and coaxed a flame into existence, without any kind of matches, before closing it off with the metal plate and handing it to me.

"You can," I muttered, awed, as I held the floating fire. It looked delicate and blue, like a jellyfish.

"A gift us Theosians have mastered in the dark," he said, extending a hand and letting small sparks flicker above his palm like little fireflies.

"Theosians?"

"Downdwellers who haven't fallen." He chuckled. "Anyway, sleep well, Sally. Don't feel obligated to get up right away. Sleep as long as you want. We're all here for you."

Tam turned and left without another word. I took to my room, which, despite its inhabitants being rather short, was close to my size, like Kun's hideaway. The room itself was small but well-groomed, like the rest of the home, and I barely noticed the smell.

There was a small basin in the corner, and a quick glance at it told me there was water. I was desperate to wash off the past day, to get the horror of it off my skin. There wasn't enough water for a cat bath, but at least my hands and face would feel clean.

I dipped my hands into the lukewarm liquid and brought it to my face with a splash. Sweat and grime washed off in a cool and refreshing touch. My skin felt slimy, oily even under my fingers. I dug them in deep, practically clawing the dirt from my face.

Tears leaked through my closed eyelids, tears of stress and fear. Scrub, scratch, splash. I repeated the sequence, trying not to think, as if the mechanical motion would be enough to cleanse my soul.

I had fallen. I was weak.

I had faced a Beast. I was unhinged.

I had played Snow White to a band of children. I was an idiot.

How had I not seen this was all a game to them? How had I been so quick to play along, to put my survival in their hands?

I scrubbed the memory from my mind. What would have happened if Tam hadn't gone looking for his son? Would I be married to Kun, slaving away as his wife and servant and waiting for my alien prince to rescue me.

I scoffed. Zander was no prince. He had dropped me. The image of him as an infallible white knight riding through the universe on starlight and saving it from destruction was fading fast.

In the end, he was just a man. He wasn't perfect, and neither was I.

Not that I ever claimed to be.

But he was all I had. I put my hands on the basin, gripping the edge as I forced myself to breathe. Focusing on the difference in temperature from the air I inhaled versus the air I exhaled. In. Out. In. Out. I was calm. I was in control. I would not give into my panic.

Where was he anyway? Where was the great Zander, the one I had heard so much about in hushed, terrified tones? If he was anything like the man I thought he was, he should have found me hours ago, rescued me from the dark.

Zander needed to hurry his ass up and get over here to do some rescuing.

I sat down on the bed—a mattress suspended from the ceiling by thick ropes—which creaked and groaned under my weight. My mind raced, running away, going anywhere but here.

Zander would find me. I put my head back on the pillow. "He will find me," I said, hoping that repeating it a few million times out loud would make it true.

But as sleep crept over me, my resolve in this elemental truth faded.

He had promised to keep me safe, and I wasn't feeling very safe right now.

TEN

UNDER THE CITY, UNDER THE CITY

I WAS AT HOME, SITTING ON MY COUCH clutching a cup of warm tea. The smell and the heat of the drink was soothing.

I ran a hand awkwardly over my scalp. I felt soft hair growing under my fingertips, slowly coming back after being singed off. The baldness was unsettling. Every time I passed a mirror, I thought the person staring back was someone else. I could not, would not, get used to it.

Marcy sat across from me, Dany having left to bring us a takeaway. Pizza, I think it was. She wore a black dress, which really wasn't her color. It wasn't joyful; it was sad.

Today was a sad day, after all. I ran my hands through the fabric of my own black dress, something I had bought at Target—or had ordered it online. I couldn't remember. I didn't want to spend a lot of money on a dress to mourn someone who wasn't dead.

"How are you holding up?" Marcy asked, cocking her head to the side. I looked up at her, poking out my tongue. A peppermint melted there.

"Sorry," she said.

I said something, not sure what. A few words like that's okay, or maybe just thank you. Nothing special. I ran my hand through my hair and missed. There was no hair to play with.

"That was the weirdest memorial I've ever been to," she said, and I could tell she was trying to read me. I didn't like that. We had always trusted each other, but today, she was judging me. "I can't … I just can't believe our friends are gone."

I nodded, my eyes dry. I said nothing about who Grisham really was; I had never told her Zander's secret. But I knew if I tried to talk about Matt, his sacrifice, that I would cry tears I didn't know I had left.

"You killed them," she said, her eyes snapping up and capturing mine in a vice grip. "You killed them all."

"What? No." This was wrong. Marcy would never say that, but it was her voice, and they were her lips the words tumbled through, and they sounded real and harsh and cruel.

"You killed Matt," she said, rising to her feet. She was growing now, growing larger than life, taking up the entire apartment. It was getting dark, the light being sucked up by this non-Marcy.

"You're unnatural," she snapped. "You stole his life for yours. You killed him. You did. No one else."

ALIENATION

"Marcy, stop," I begged.

"How are you still alive?" Her teeth were long now, and sharp at that. "How did you survive? You should be dead. You should be dead and Matt alive."

"No, I—"

And then she lunged at me.

· · · · · · · · · ● · · · · · · · · · ·

Waking up in a strange bed is always unsettling. There's that moment where you still believe you are at home, wrapped up in a bundle of your own sheets, in your own room. The second you see that you're not, however, the brain panics. And that was me, right now.

The last time I had slept—really slept, in a bed and not tied to a pipe—I had been in my apartment. I had been in my own bed with my sheets and my warm pillows. When I had woken up, light had shone through my window and my roommate/ex was making us tea.

About five minutes before we had a fight and I kicked them out. Or they ran away. But that's a story for another time.

In any case, waking up in a strange bed was unsettling, but waking up in said bed in cold sweats made matters even worse.

This room had no light. Not natural light, anyway. The small light of floating fire gleamed on the shelf. It looked the same as when I had gone to sleep.

I got out of bed and stumbled as I put my clothes back on. My body still smarted from everything that had happened the day before, like I were an old piece of wood that was stiff and creaking. The jeans were dry-ish now, having had time away from the mess that was me, and I wished I had something clean to wear. Gosh, I would give anything to feel clean right now.

I'd had that dream before. Call it a recurring nightmare. Almost always bringing me back to the moment right after the memorial service for the Grisham Corp plant disaster. Three deaths, one injury.

Zander, the alien. Grisham, the villain. Matt, the hero. Although, to the people of Franklin, it was just the accountant, the boss, and the protégé.

I was the injury.

No one else had been hurt. The evacuation had been perfect. Grisham had certainly planned the most efficient plant there was, even when it came down to fire preparedness. Too bad he hadn't been alive to see it in action.

I shuddered at the memory. Two years had gone by since, and not all that much had happened. Life was different, but it moved on. I was still without a job, but money was no longer so tight. I was still rooming with an alien, but they weren't like Zander. Except for the bit where they were extraterrestrial.

I wasn't sure they would be there when I got back.

I reached up to brush a finger through my hair. It should never have grown back. Not this fast, not this thick. It shouldn't have grown back at all, not after the burns that had covered my head.

More had happened to me in the last day than in my last two years combined, but now, I wasn't so sure that was a good thing. My astrolust was quenched. Now I was just, well, scared.

Scared I wasn't going to make it home. Scared I would be stuck here forever. Scared I would be stuck in a culture I did not know, to never see the sun again. I shivered, the fullest body shiver I had ever experienced.

Today, I would find a way back home. I would find Zander and leave this planet. And I would not ask for a second trip anywhere else, ever again.

The smell of hot Jee wafted through the house, bringing memories of autumn back on Earth, all warm and spiced. That alone was enough to force me up and out of bed. I tied my laces on my trusted Chucks, straightened my t-shirt, and left the small room, closing the door behind me. The scent was heavy enough to give me a clear path to follow through the house.

Everything looked identical to how it had been when I had gone to bed. I passed a study filled with books, huge shelves lining the walls; and a kitchen, much better stocked than the Street Sweepers' playhouse and cleaner. I shuddered at the memory.

Marth was in the dining room, sitting at the end of a long table with chairs enough for twelve. The entire surface was empty, save for two glass chalices and a little kettle. As I entered, he filled the empty chalice from the weird looking kettle—it just looked weird, okay?—and pushed it to the seat beside him. I took that as an invitation to join.

"Did you sleep well?" he asked, smiling warmly. I watched the steam rise from my cup and breathed in the heavenly scent of Jee.

I nodded then remembered this wasn't Earth, and certainly not the United States, and voiced my agreement instead.

"Yes, very," I said. "Thank you for letting me use your spare room. You are too kind."

"It's a pleasure," Marth replied but caught himself. "I mean, we're glad to be of help. I am so sorry about your situation."

"It's okay. No, I mean, thank you," I said. It was definitely not okay, and I had to stop saying that as a response to everything. It just wasn't right.

"And sorry again about our offspring."

I kept my tongue locked between my teeth and drank my Jee quietly, staring ahead at the bare wall. The light on the table caught my eye and I turned to it, watching the little fireball float and flicker under the glass.

"How long did I sleep?" I asked. I no longer felt sleepy, but I sure as hell still felt tired.

"Not very long," Marth replied. "A few hours. I guess your body is still on Alliance time. You'll get used to it here."

I nodded sheepishly, never having worried about jet lag on other planets before. Was it still jet lag when there were no jets were involved? Planet lag? Space lag? Either way, I didn't understand which way was up and which day it was anymore. Was it even daytime?

I distracted myself from these thoughts by staring at the globe of light. It was so pretty, the way it floated and flickered like it had a life of its own. Marth watched me, saying nothing and drinking his Jee.

"Can everyone produce fire?" I asked and looked away from the small sun.

Marth chuckled. "Where are you from, Sally Webber?"

"Earth."

"Is that part of the Alliance?" Marth sipped his own drink then continued. "Our history isn't all that up to date. Any new additions to the Alliance in the past century or two might not have made the news around here yet."

"Oh," I replied. "No, but the Alliance knows about us. We haven't made first contact. I'm here with a friend. Or at least … I was."

Marth bobbed his head. Was that a nod?

"I wondered if us Theosians are still part of Alliance history," he said, "or if they cut us out of that, too. But you won't know many elemental races if you haven't made contact yet."

"That's for sure." I laughed and sipped my Jee. This stuff was amazing for a weary soul. "I only know of humans. And humans can't do what you do. I don't even know what an elemental race is."

"Elementals have a certain degree of control over their environment," Marth explained. "Like us. We can excite particles to give off light, either hot or cold. But humans can do a lot of things we cannot even fathom. Honestly, some of the things I hear humans can do truly scares me."

"Like what?" I asked.

"Take how fast you adapt, for instance. You get sick and then move on. Not every person who falls down here survives, you know. But humans? Humans seem to take to this just fine. Anything avian doesn't last longer than a month. Take away sunlight, and they wither away."

I didn't like the sound of that, so I focused on my Jee. But it was too late; the chalice was empty. I had already downed it. Marth quickly filled my cup, smiling as he did so.

"But what about the fire?" I asked, indicating the glowing orb on the table. He did the bobble head thing again and extended his hand forward. Filaments of light lifted from his palm and stuck together, growing into a small hovering ball, gently turning, like a miniature star, a tiny blue giant. I watched in awe.

"Take it," he said, pushing his palm forward.

"What?" I shifted back. "I can't. My skin will burn."

"It won't," Marth smiled, and his smile was warmer than the little sun. Literally. As I reached out, I felt no heat from the tiny ball of light. It was cold, but so alive.

I held my two hands together like a cup, and Marth reeled back.

ALIENATION

"That," he said, incensed, "is incredibly offensive!"

"What?" Not even a day in this stranger's house, and I was doing cultural faux pas. I put my hands on my lap, and he burst out laughing.

"I'm kidding!" Marth reached for my hand, gently, and lifted it to the same level as the light. "You don't need to be afraid of us, Sally. This is your home now, so think of us as family. Here, take this."

And I took the light. The tendrils reached for my hand, and I felt nothing, nada, zilch, as if the light were all in my head. I pulled my hand away, and the ball stayed with me, hovering an inch above my palm.

"Yes, us Theosians can create plasma," he said, "and flame. But mostly light. Anything that burns takes practice, so you won't see children with a dangerous heat. But while we live in darkness, we have light in our veins."

I was listening, but just barely. The light was so … fascinating. It swayed, and when I ran my finger through it, disturbing whips of light came right back in place once my finger had passed. I giggled.

"They needed us, once." Marth sighed, leaning back in his chair.

"Who did?"

"The Alliance." He shrugged, his eyelids squeezing and dropping. "They needed us to stoke the great fires of the first ships. Our people fought together side by side. But then … well, you know."

"I don't know. I just got here."

"No, you know." Marth's eyes met mine and held them there, captivatingly dark. "You're down here with us now. They did the same thing to you that they did to us. Welcome. Anyway, keep the light. You're going to need it. Light isn't always so easy to come by down here."

ELEVEN
THE WORLD BENEATH THE WORLD

MARTH MADE ME TAKE A WALK.

He opened the front door and practically pushed me out, giving me a stick and a lantern for me to stuff the little light ball into. It would be good for me, he said, so I took his word for it and went for a walk.

The market was shut, but there were still people in the street. Orbs of light shimmered as I walked by, and I kept away from them, trying to not draw attention to myself. Either no one cared about the human who had just fallen, or they were being polite. I was thankful either way.

I didn't know where I was going and soon realized that I had left the habitable sector entirely. There were no more warm street orbs, only my own lantern. I wondered why some parts of the Undercity were settled and others not. If the city above stretched across the entire planet, were there settlements down here with other Downdwellers? More Theosians? Did they talk with each other? If I was to live here, I had to know these things.

Not that I was planning on staying. I clenched my fists around the lantern pole as I walked. I was getting out of here. I would find Zander and go home.

I stopped by a wall and stared. Yes, this would do nicely. I was getting out of this place if I had to fight for my freedom by tooth and nail. Probably nail, because it looked like I'd need to climb my way out.

I slipped my fingers between the cracks of the old bricks. I pulled. My arms burned like they were on fire. I found a foothold and then another.

And I began to climb.

I had hooked my light onto a pole and propped it through my bra so the lantern hung near my face. I probably looked like a human anglerfish, though much more attractive, if I do say so myself.

"What are you doing?"

The voice sounded like that of a small boy's: calm, composed, unsurprised by anything, like everyone I had met in this odd place. Turning my head, I spotted him in his own little pool of light ten feet below me, his eyes wide as they gazed back at me.

He was half the size of Kun, his clothes more ragged and not as fitted as what the others wore—a loose, red sweater and fourth, maybe fifth-hand cargo pants. He stood in the street, unmoving, his hands stuffed deep into his pockets. He looked like one of the Street Sweepers, though one whose name I had never learned.

"I'm going home." I cringed as I stretched my hand to the brick above me, feeling around for it and taking a deep breath before gathering the courage to move to the next ledge, a fanciful divider between the floors of the buildings. I hadn't yet thought about what would happen when I reached the awnings, but I'd figure that out when I got there.

"My Kota says no one ever goes home."

"Well, your Kota's about to be proved wrong," I replied. I forced my knee to budge, but it was being stubborn and refused to fold.

"You're not the first to try," the kid continued. "Mooli tries every week—well, he did until about a month ago. Now he just sleeps a lot."

"I'm not Mooli." I pulled myself up, finding firmer footholds. I was a few meters up now, but there was no end in sight to this climb, what with me not having a good source of light. Would the orb Marth had given me run out? And when that happened, where would I be?

I looked down to get my bearings. Vertigo hit me like a punch in the gut. I had barely made it up one floor, and already I was high enough to make me nauseated. I turned my gaze back to my hands.

"You could fall," the child said, not trying to hide the worry in his voice. "Koty says to never get too high that falling will hurt. Xia broke her leg last week."

"I'm not Xia, either," I replied, annoyed. I grabbed a filled-in windowsill above me, taking a deep breath before tackling the wall once more.

It was more difficult at this point. The sloppy bricks were replaced by cemented-in windows, dropping the number of footholds tenfold. I kept my focus, though. Stopping now would mean never getting home. And I was going to get home by any means possible.

"Then who are you?" he asked, suddenly sounding excited.

"I'm Sally," I replied, glad that I had taken rock climbing as an extracurricular in high school but regretting how out of shape I was. My arms burned as they clung to the vertical surface. I didn't know if I could hold on for much longer, but I needed to get high enough to signal for help.

"Sally who?"

"Sally Webber." I grunted as I slid my foot on the ledge my hands had been on earlier. There were dents in the wall, as if someone had tried hacking at it with a pickaxe, deep enough for me to use them as hand holds.

"Aren't you going to ask who I am?" he whined, his voice getting quieter as I climbed away from him. I took a deep breath, trying to calm my pumping heart. I wasn't going to look back. I would not make that mistake again.

"Who are you?" I asked absentmindedly, swinging my hand to another hold, hoisting my body higher into the unknown. The next ledge was wider and separated the stories of the building. So close, but just out of reach.

ALIENATION

"I'm Jomar."

"And how old are you, Jomar?" I paused to take a breath and wipe the sweat from my brow.

"Seventy-six," Jomar replied, pure joy in his voice.

"Seventy-six?" I didn't want to look back, but my curiosity was piqued. I peeled my eyes off the wall to look at his face. It was not the face of an almost-octogenarian.

Woah. Too much. I closed my eyes and breathed a deep, cleansing breath.

"And a half," he added.

I turned back toward the wall, lifting my hand to slide it into the handhold above. A sharp pain shot through my fingers, freezing my body, and then I was falling, spinning, landing flat on my back on the ground below. My lantern shattered in the dark beside me. The pole dug into my spine as the small light died in the street.

"You all right?" Jomar let some flames dance on his fingertips, holding them painfully close to my face. The brightness made me cringe, and I squeezed my eyes shut.

"I think so," I replied, shocked. This was the second time I had survived a fall in the past twenty-four hours. I really was lucky.

I pushed myself to my feet, ripping the pole from my bra and tossing it into the distance. My muscles hurt, but other than that, I was fine. Well, except for the foot-long dart stuck in my finger. Jomar's eyes widened.

"Wow," he gasped. "A Stinger's quill? You found a Stinger's quill?"

"I what now?" I remembered having read, years ago, to keep calm after being stung, to stop the panicked heart from pumping venom into the blood stream. Was there venom? I couldn't tell, but my hand was on fire.

"Can I have it?" Jomar begged. "Please, please, please?"

"After you tell me some more about it. First off, is it venomous?"

He bobbled his head. "The Stinger doesn't want to kill you." He plucked the quill from my pulsating finger. The pressure abated, and my finger tingled. "It just wants you to keep out. That's his hole. He doesn't want you moving in."

"Does he, now?" I chuckled. The child, for indeed he was a child, seventy-six and a half years or not, was so joyful I couldn't help but smile, no matter how much everything hurt.

"They live anywhere dark."

"I bet the real estate's great for them down here."

"Real estate?" he asked.

"The Stinger has a lot of places to live down here. Listen, Jomar, has anybody made it back up there before? Anyone at all?"

He did the bobble head thing again.

"Grandpa says that his grandpa's grandpa could come and go as he wanted," Jomar replied. "But I haven't seen anyone leave."

"Ever?"

"Never ever."

ALIENATION

I fell back down on the street, letting my back lie on the cold asphalt. There was no light above me, no orange glow to light up the velvet darkness, no stars beyond, twinkling on their pedestal. It was as if someone had flooded the streets with ink, yet I could move and breathe freely through it. But seeing ... that was something entirely different.

"You sure there wasn't anything on that quill?" I asked, feeling drowsy. The boy nodded.

"I'd better get back then. Try again in the morning, whatnot."

"What will happen?"

"What do you mean?"

"If you get out."

"*When* I get out."

"What happens to the rest of us?" he asked.

I froze. A wave of guilt flooded me. I hadn't even thought of them, even after their hospitality. I hadn't once thought about what I would say once I got back up. Zander would know what to do. I would ask him once I got back, and we would solve this problem together.

Jomar left with his new quill but without an answer. I waited for his footsteps to fade before getting back up, taking a deep breath and looking up at that wall.

Two stories. Tomorrow, I would climb it again. And I would not be so careless as to get stung by anything.

Whatever this city threw my way, I would fight it. I just wanted to get back to Earth.

I went back to my new home, using my phone to light my way. I put it on airplane mode. If they had the Internet here, it sure as heck wouldn't connect, let alone while I was in the Undercity. I needed the battery to last as long as possible, as much as I kept telling myself this situation was temporary.

I hadn't wandered far from the Shimat house, knowing I wouldn't find my way back easily if I had. I meandered through the empty market again. People paid no attention to me, and for that, I was grateful. Honestly, I didn't want to talk to anyone, not after what I had just gone through. I never wanted to be held hostage again.

Or, you know, fall a few miles, either. Not a fun way to spend what was supposed to be your only day off-planet.

I wondered if anyone was worried about me. Marcy, probably. I was supposed to take her to her dress fitting right about now. Hopefully one day I'd be able to tell her what I had been through.

I found Tam's street easily. As I walked to the front door, I realized how paper-thin the walls were. Hushed voices rose from inside, even though it sounded like they were trying to be quiet. And they were angry.

"—Never get another shot at this. Any of this," said someone I didn't recognize. They sounded jumpy, agitated, even through their whispers.

"But we need to be careful. We're still missing an element of this puzzle."

ALIENATION

"Actually," answered a third voice—Tam's, I was sure of it, "I might have a way to resolve our little problem."

"Really? How?" the first voice replied.

"I know someone," Tam said. "She just fell, and I think she'll be eager to help us, once she learns it's her only way out of the Undercity."

My heart stopped. If I had half a mind, I would have thrown the door open and begged to have a shot at whatever they were planning. But my mind was still trying to compute a way out of this place, considering whether Beetlejuice would get me out of this if I called his name three times. I just stood there, frozen.

"We can't force her to do anything," the voice continued.

"Upfolk'll do anything to get back to the city," Tam said.

"If we succeed, she'll get back on top. But if we fail—"

"She'll still be on top. We give her a trip upstairs, and she does a little job to help us. It's not too much to ask." Tam seemed confident, In charge of the group, from what I could tell.

"She needs to know what she'll be facing. It will be dangerous. Very dangerous."

"Of course," said Tam. "She's out right now, but I can send Marth to find her."

Danger? Ouch. A chance to get out of here? Yes, please. My list of ideas had run dry, so this might be my only shot. I stuffed my courage into my feet and pushed open the door.

TWELVE

MISSION: IMPOSSIBLY WEIRD

"YOU DON'T NEED TO GET MARTH," I SAID, striding through the doorway. I felt embarrassed the second I did. Maybe I should have dimmed down the drama. Theatrical entrances weren't really my thing, and I hated making a scene. Six pairs of black eyes were on me, three mouths agape. Talk about awkward.

The three Theosians sat cross-legged on the floor. I tried to look confident, but I was anxious and my hands shook on the doorknob. This did not dissuade Tam, however. His face lit up.

"This is Sally," he said, standing up and reaching for me like we were old friends. "She's from the Overcity. Well, as a tourist, right? Sally, meet Shu and Ratta. They're friends of mine."

I bowed. They bowed back. I was proud I had gotten the hang of that greeting, but it was still very surreal.

ALIENATION

"Come sit with us." Shu, whose hair was bright yellow and wrapped in a bun, tapped the floor next to him. The trio ignored the sofas around them, like their conference was too important to be comfortable. Why did people in this city need chairs if they never used them?

I sat with them, crossing my legs like I was back in kindergarten. My ass was still smarting from all my falling lately. They stared at me, as if waiting for me to speak, making everything a lot more awkward than it already was.

"So, um," I said, trying to break the silence, "you have a way of getting me back to the surface? Well, if you do, tell me. I need to get back up there. I need to get home."

"Would you do anything for it?" Tam asked.

"Anything," I asserted, not even needing to lie. "Though, on second thought, maybe not murder. Yeah. Not murder. I can't do that. But anything else—"

"Leave the child alone, Tam," Marth snapped, blowing into the room like a breeze and placing his hands on my shoulders. He was short enough that he didn't have to bend over. I was like a child sitting at his feet.

"Marth, we've talked about this," Tam replied. "We're going to get our planet back. Believe me, I'll do anything to return our people to the sunlight."

"Leave her out of your stupid games," Marth snapped. "The planet we knew and loved isn't even here anymore. It stopped existing the moment they left us down here. This is our home now. The Overcity will never be ours. Accept it."

"You're the one who's always saying our resources are running dry," said Tam. "If they keep abandoning their people with us, casting them off to the dark, maybe it's time to bring some of our own up to meet them."

"Tam, you're an imbecile," Marth replied, "but it's not up to me. It's up to Sally. If you dare force her into one of your schemes, I will be out of here before you have time to say another word. Do you hear me?"

"Yes, dear," Tam answered, seemingly unaffected by all this.

The hands left my shoulders. Marth muttered under his breath as he made his way out of the room, leaving it quiet once more.

Tam was unfazed, not even watching his partner leave. Instead, he stared at me a little too closely, eyes intent and gleaming. He looked me up and down and smiled. "You don't know us. Our people." It wasn't an accusation but a statement of fact.

"No," I replied.

"But do you know *about* us?" Ratta said awkwardly, shooting a glance at Tam. He seemed more troubled by Marth's outburst than Tam was. "About Theosian culture? What did they teach you in school?"

"I, well, I didn't go to school in the Alliance. I'm from Earth."

ALIENATION

"Never heard of it," Ratta muttered. "Which quadrant is it in?"

"I don't know. I don't know anything about the Alliance. This is my first day … off-world? Is that the right word?"

They exchanged glances, staring at each other in turn. I studied the rug. There was a stain in front of me in the shape of Florida. I wondered if I would ever see that state again. If I would see my parents again.

"So you don't know anything about our history or politics?" Shu said.

"Not our politics," Ratta pointed out. "Their politics. Their history."

"Fine." Shu blinked slowly. "Do you know anything about Alliance history or politics?"

"Um, no."

"All right. This is going to get long, then," Shu said.

"Just give her the short version," Tam suggested. "We don't have much time."

"Well, let's start at the beginning," Shu said, calmly, turning to face me with a warm smile. "Eight thousand years ago, this arm of the galaxy was attacked by an enemy we remember only as The Darkness."

"It wasn't literal darkness," said Ratta, "but this enemy committed genocide, killing many civilizations. Wiped out their history, culture, everything. This was at the very beginning of space flight, so news traveled slowly, if at all. So, basically, darkness. One day we just stopped hearing from them, and we didn't know why."

"Thanks, Ratta, way to keep things short," said Shu. "In any case, those who had at least some technology banded together to fight them. This planet was one of the first to join the Alliance. Our ancestors signed the Pyrinian Treaty with the other nine planets in order to end the war."

"Ugh, treaties, seriously?" Ratta interjected. "Go ahead. Bore her to tears."

"Shorter version, then." Shu nodded. "After the worst war in history, ten planets signed an agreement and created the Planetary Alliance. The planets were equals, every race on the same level. The treaty was to ensure none would forget that fact as they began to work together in a new era of camaraderie. As a gesture of our commitment, our ancestors invited the round heads—namely humans, though all races were welcome—to come and live on our planet. Combine forces, for a better future."

"Over the next few years, centuries even," Ratta blurted out, unable to let Shu tell the story on his own, "through a series of complicated socio-economic events, the separation between us and the round heads became larger. Eventually, without any of our ancestors realizing it, we were on the bottom heap, and we couldn't get on top again."

"They cut off our electricity," said Tam. "We were left in the dark without a light to let us climb back up. They don't want anything to do with us anymore. They don't even send dispatches for those who fall down, but we can change that now. We've got the codes to their robots."

"Wait—what now?" I did a double-take. Of all the things he could have said, that was probably the one I least expected. My eyes widened so much I felt them drying. They could have rivaled any Theosian's.

"We can shut them off." Tam grinned so broadly that the corners of his lips touched his ears. "They can't live without the robots doing their dirty work. We'll use that as our way in, reintegrate with society by taking on the jobs they don't want."

"We need a spy." Shu sat up straight, his lips drawing into a thin line. "We need a round head to go to the central computer and enter the code that disables the robots."

"That's it," added Tam, for good measure.

"The other round heads have adapted to life down here," Ratta continued. "Their eyes are too wide from their prolonged exposure to the terrible lighting. Their hair is thin due to the lack of basic minerals and sunlight. They look old, overworked, too sick to look normal in the fancy Overcity."

"Even in a world with hundreds of different intelligent species, they would stick out." Shu waved his hands around his face, though what he was trying to convey I wasn't sure.

"The ICP, their central computer, is kept in the mayor's office," Tam piped up, sounding like Jerry from Totally Spies. "It holds the master control over the robots in case of a…"

S. E. ANDERSON

"Well, a robotic uprising," Ratta interjected.

"Yes, that." Tam shot a glare at his friend. "They have to be powered down manually."

"Lucky for us, we have a window of opportunity." Ratta seemed positively excited, his fingers twitching in the air. "Tonight, the mayor and his family are hosting a fancy ball to celebrate his birthday and to encourage possible voters. That's when you get in. Our source, the one who gave us the codes, has prepared everything."

Holy shit, this was a heist. Webber, Sally Webber: interstellar woman of mystery.

None of this made any sense anymore, not that I was sure it ever had. I stared at Tam, Shu, Ratta, and at Marth, who peered in silently from the kitchen. Were they all insane? Or was this how things were handled on other worlds?

"But I'm not invited," I muttered, the only words I could get out in this onslaught of weirdness.

"Not a problem. We have acquired invitations. Again, thanks to our source."

"We're not alone in this," Tam said. "We have help from the surface. Our contacts have been helping us plan this for months, but we lost touch with our agent on the inside, so we need you."

"Your agent?"

"The last one of you we sent upstairs," said Tam. "They didn't survive being reintroduced to sunlight."

"Wait, hold on." My head was reeling. I had too many questions. "Why not ask someone who's already up

177

there? Why does your contact need someone from the Undercity?"

"They insisted," squeaked Ratta.

"Your contact did?"

"No chip in the hand, you see," explained Shu. "Anyone who falls is wiped from the system. If by any chance you get caught in the palace, they wouldn't be able to identify you. It's using the Alliance's own misdeeds against them."

I blinked. They weren't planning an uprising or a coup but a silent takeover. It was sly, cleverly cunning, and completely idiotic.

But try telling Tam that.

I saw why Marth thought his plan was crazy—because it was. If all they had was to take over some robots and reclaim the menial jobs, there wasn't going to be much, if any, change.

Fact was, they could control fire. I had only seen them manipulate it gently, to create light, to calm themselves. But it was still fire, and fire burned. They could easily turn this on the people above and take over far more quickly than whatever their plan was now.

I could tell them this plan was pure insanity, destined to fail. Even if I somehow dismantled the robots with a master code, it wasn't like people wouldn't repair them. It wasn't like the Downdwellers were anyone's first choice for a replacement.

But if I said anything, I wouldn't be going up.

So, I made one of the truly selfish decisions of my life. I nodded, and kept my mouth shut.

I did say I would do anything to go back home.

"Good," Tam smiled. "All right. I'll tell our contact things are back on, but we have to get going, and soon. There's only a small window for this."

"Just tell me what to do," I said.

They didn't waste any time. They rose and dispersed. Shu and Ratta left to gather the others, while Tam made his way to the back of the house.

"You coming?" he asked, turning back to me.

"Um, yeah."

I got up and dashed after him as he walked off. Marth stood in the doorway to the kitchen, glaring at me.

"You realize this plan is idiotic, right?" he asked, arms akimbo. "And certainly doomed to fail?"

I guess the look on my face was enough of an answer. Marth's eyes pulled together, a scowl drawing his lips up. Without a word, he turned away, not even leaving the room, just showing me his back. I guess that was an insult in his culture because I felt waves of coldness emanating from his small frame. I hurried after Tam, trying to ignore the guilt gnawing the back of my neck and digging at the pit of my stomach.

Oh, hello, anxiety. Been a while since I've seen you here. Where's my Prozac when I need it?

"Causeway, Causeway. Come in, Causeway." Tam spoke clearly and eloquently. I stepped into the small room after him. This had to be a home office, but it was

ALIENATION

small and cramped, the walls stuffed with brown scrolls. I had to squeeze in just to fit.

"Go for Causeway," a voice replied, filling the small room. "Come in, Tam."

"We have the package. Ready for transport. Over."

"You do?" The voice sounded surprised. "Splendid! We will send a convoy to transport the package for delivery. Congratulations, Tam."

"Thank you, Mr. Causeway, sir."

I was the package. Well, I didn't expect royal treatment, but the name felt wrong. Still, I could handle that if it meant getting out of this place.

The two of them arranged a place to meet; they didn't need me there. I stepped out into the hallway, taking in the small house I had lived in for a day. It was small, but it was a home. And I was dishonoring this family and their hospitality by going ahead with this foolishness.

Or I was paying them back in full. This is what Tam wanted. This is what I would do.

Kun glared at me from his room and shut the door. If I was doing something good for these people, why did I feel like shit?

And so, they decided a fanfare was the best way to see me off. Everyone in town—every Downdweller, Theosian, or other—gathered to send me off.

We stood in the middle of a wide avenue, so large that even the light from the many Theosians didn't reach the walls. Everyone was there: Tam, Ratta, Shu, even Marth, who looked glum next to his partner. Kun and the other children stood off to the perimeter, climbing over each other so they could see over the shoulders of their parents.

They lit the way with their little palm fires. Some had set them in little lanterns, so they didn't have to focus on keeping them burning. Others twisted the flames through their fingers like a pet snake or magic coin, barely paying attention to what they were doing.

Others played music.

So Tam wasn't the only one who knew about the plan. As more people crowded around me, I realized that maybe I was in too deep. Not only did everyone know about the plan, they believed in it.

They believed in me. A stranger.

I wondered who their contact was. Who was this Mr. Causeway? Some high-ranking government official who wanted to put things right? Someone rich and powerful who would put all their resources at the Downdwellers' disposal? Whoever it was, they were my ticket out of here, and for that I was thankful.

It really was a fanfare, though. Some of the Downdwellers played together: poppy music, heroic and uplifting all at once. Their instruments were like nothing we had on Earth. Each person handled a different tube or box of some kind, producing sounds I would never have associated with their looks, somewhere between cords and horns.

I watched them out of the corner of my eye, trying not to stare too long at any one thing. Not polite, after

ALIENATION

all. If that even was the standard on this planet. I scanned the crowd, taking in the music, the fire, the tears, and my heart sank. I was probably the only one here, except maybe Marth, who didn't believe in Tam's scheme.

Ouch.

Hello, guilt.

Welcome back, anxiety. I didn't miss you.

My eyes fell on somewhat familiar faces, the first round faces I had seen since falling. Human faces. And the Theosians were right: They were barely recognizable. Their skin sagged and wrinkled like cheap fabric, and a shiver went through me.

This is why I was doing this, why I was lying. There was no way I was going to fade away down here.

I wanted to live.

But so did everyone else here.

"It's time," Tam said. All at once, we looked to the sky. At first there was nothing, and I wondered if Tam was making things up, but the rest of the Downdwellers were staring exactly where he was pointing. They could see whatever it was, but I saw nothing except darkness.

And then a rope ladder fell right on my head.

It rolled down my face, knocking me back a step. Tam grabbed it and steadied it as the audience looked on.

"So," I said, one hand on my head to caress the throbbing. "I just … climb?"

"That tends to be the point of ladders," Tam said, punctuating his sentence with a smart grin.

I nodded. "Best of luck, Tam. I hope we meet again, under better circumstances."

"I do too." He bowed, and I dipped my head in response. "Here, take this." He handed me one of the homemade lanterns, only this one was smaller than my thumb, with a bright jellyfish of blue fire swimming happily in the bulb. "We're counting on you, Sally. Our lives are in your hands."

I shuddered, and my hands shook as I took his gift. Definitely not steady enough to hold anybody's lives there. Even the little ball of light rattled. I slipped the tiny lantern onto the cord of the necklace around my neck. It wasn't hot against my skin, or cold. It simply was.

But my hands still shook. I clutched the ladder, making them look steady. Perfect, or at least much better.

"Goodbye, Tam."

"Goodbye, Sally," he replied. "Our futures depend on you!"

I climbed, my mind racing, trying to find a dramatic response to what he said. By the time I came up with something halfway decent, I had already climbed a good distance, and enough time had passed that it would be weird if I said anything now.

So, I said nothing, and kept climbing.

It was a long ladder. Soon, the lights from the Theosians were mere pinpricks. Above me, there was still darkness.

ALIENATION

I guessed it was better that way—I wouldn't see how high up I was.

Gosh, heights made me sick to my stomach.

I climbed past more awnings that glowed pale in the light of my necklace. Not the same ones that had broken my fall, I don't think, but they were still riddled with holes and tears from years of neglect. Some had shop names on the front, the letters peeling after all these years. I focused on them as I continued to climb up and up, and I put the drop beneath me out of my mind.

"I'm coming, Zander," I said to the sky.

I reached up and hit metal instead of another rung. It came out of nowhere. I ripped my hand back, losing my grip. And in that moment of shock, my feet slipped. I clung onto the rung with one trembling hand.

You're in deep shit, Webber, Sally Webber, interstellar woman of mystery and klutz on a ladder.

THIRTEEN

I CLIMB THE ANTI-SOCIAL LADDER

I WAS DANGLING FOR A SPLIT-SECOND BEFORE A hand grabbed my wrist.

"Hold on tight. I've got ya," came a warm voice. The skin was silky smooth, like the paw of a cat, and the grip firm, instantly reassuring. I swung my feet forward to grab the ladder, relying on the hand to stop me from plunging back to the Downdwellers, failing before my mission had even began.

"Thanks," I grumbled, out of breath, as I climbed up to the metal. It must have been a car or a ship or something like that because there was an actual solid floor. A very inviting one at that.

The arm dragged me up, and I collapsed on the metal, my arms screaming. I hadn't started any kind of workout regime—never expecting Zander to take me into any kind of space danger—so I was, unfortunately, out of shape and I felt it now.

Note to self: if you ever want to explore the universe, you need to exercise sometimes.

"You okay?" The person who had saved me crouched at my side. We were in a van, like the old VWs from the sixties back home, at least in terms of space. Someone else shut the door, sliding it off the roof like it was a storefront.

"Yeah, never better," I groaned.

The lights were out, but I could tell there were three people in the van with me: the silk-handed person, the one closing the door, and the one at the wheel. I guessed these were the militants fighting for Downdweller rights, the big shots with the money and contacts.

"Punch it, Mal!" the door person shouted to the driver, then threw themselves in the passenger seat. The driver didn't need to be told twice. The second the door shut, they forced the car forward, rising like an elevator on steroids.

"Five, four, three, two, one…" the driver named Mal counted, "and we're back on the drive-grid. Resuming power to the mags now."

They hit the switch, and the van was bathed in light. Finally, my saviors came into view, and my heart joined the Olympic gymnastics team.

The one who had grabbed my arm was humanoid but certainly not human. Her entire body was covered in a short, thick film of white, velvety hair. Her features were arranged more closely to the center of her face, and she had wide, open ears, like she was a rabbit-human hybrid. And yet, as outlandish as that was for me, she looked amazingly classy. She sported a tight, dark blue robe, embroidered around the waist and elbows.

The person at the door had skin like a gummy worm: semi-transparent yet bending light like Jell-O. They looked fragile, like poking them would cause permanent damage. They were bipedal but had an extra pair of arms hanging out of the backpack they wore. Their eyes were wide and childlike.

Finally, the driver turned around, and I realized with a start that this person could have been on Earth, and I wouldn't have paid any attention to him. He had light brown skin and high cheekbones, but cute, round features. His face was covered by big, black marks, like he had let a five-year-old draw on his face with Sharpies.

"Yo," he said. "You sure you're okay?"

"Me?" I scoffed, pushing myself up. "I'm good. Thanks for the rescue." I grinned.

The humanoid rabbit stroked my shoulder with a reassuring velvet touch. They were gentle and kind, but I felt like I was the pet bunny rabbit.

"Oh, poor doll!" the rabbit said. "You're free of them now. You're back in civilization. Don't worry. You're safe. Did they treat your poorly down there?"

"No, they were really nice, actually," I replied, and her eyes widened.

"Wow, you learn something new every day!" she stammered. "Anyways, I'm Qeetzal. Call me Qee! Our getaway driver is Maloka, and our extra pair of hands here is T'Poxggen."

"Just call me Pox," the latter laughed. "My parents were kusil when they were young. Makes sense now, right?"

"Um … sure," I said.

"Your skin, it's so pink! I've never seen anything so light on humans. Did that happen when you fell?"

"No?"

I wasn't all that pink. My abuela had given me a light olive tone, which I guessed wasn't all that prominent on this planet. They obviously had never seen a Theosian if they thought I was pale.

It was unnerving.

"So, who are you?" Qee asked, her voice rising in pitch, "How long have you had to live … down there?" They shuddered.

"I'm Sally," I said, as they helped me onto one of the bean bag chairs, "I fell down there … yesterday. I think. I've kinda lost track of time."

"Wow." Qee nodded to Pox. "Incredible."

Like it was the most unbelievable thing in the world to lose track of time when there wasn't a dawn or a dusk. I leaned back and closed my eyes. Finally free.

So why was I feeling bad about leaving? Why was I feeling guilty for people I didn't know? Shit, just how much of a conscience did I have? I didn't like this side of me.

I really wanted to sleep.

"Do people who fall down there become the Downdwellers' pets?" asked Pox, sitting down across from me. "Like in the stories?"

"What? No! They're nice people. They gave me a place to stay and everything."

"Oh," replied Pox, their frown visible right through their head. "What was it like?"

"Leave her alone," said Mal. "Can't you see she's been through a lot? Let her rest. She's got enough to worry about and a huge job tonight."

"Thank you," I said, and I drifted on the bean bag chair. I watched the rabbit woman and the Jell-o person as they stared back at me, and I wondered how either of them pooped. Then I realized how ridiculous a thought that was and shoved it away. But still, I kinda wished Jell-o person had some visible organs for me to freak out about, the way they were freaking out about my 'ordeal' with the Downdwellers.

"You're not from here, are you?" asked Qee, eyeing me cautiously. I shook my head.

"I'm from Earth."

"Never heard of it!" Mal shouted from the front seat. "It's not Alliance, right? I don't think it's on the list. I should know; I know them all."

He boasted like my prom date, Mr. Scott "I can name all the countries and their capitals but also their GDP and HDI" Fleming. Now that was a night to forget.

"No, we haven't made first contact yet."

ALIENATION

At that, Pox and Qee's eyes bulged. They stared at me, at each other, then back at me again, almost like in an old Loony Toons cartoon. But the staring got too intense, even for me.

"What?" I asked.

"Holy drang!" Pox let out a small blubbery sound. "Are you a child hire?"

"A what now?"

"A child—no matter. It's not like you would know anything about them." They laughed, their voice sounding like gelatin being swung back and forth. "But, like, how do you cope?"

"With what?"

"Like not being civilized," said Pox.

"Come on, Pox," Qee scoffed. "You can't ask someone that!"

"Sorry, sorry," they replied. "I'm just curious. I mean, do you all live in trees or something? Oh my gosh, do you have trees? Do they smell as bad as everyone says they do?"

Gradually, it got lighter outside, which meant that slowly but surely we were rising. The façades of the buildings became more elegant and detailed, and the awnings that had broken my fall became cleaner as we ascended. I stared out the window over Pox's shoulder as they tapped away on what looked like a phone in the shape of a pyramid.

Some buildings dropped away, shorter than the rest. The streets widened as they became avenues and highways, wider than airport runways. Every once in a while, a large ledge indicated a shopping center, going from thinner strips littered with stalls to wider ones with modern shops on the sides.

Soon, something hit my eyes that I hadn't expected to see for a long, long time: sunlight.

The glare was incredibly strong, and Mal pulling down the visor did nothing to help. No one seemed bothered by this, and I realized my eyes had actually adjusted to the darkness below.

The van rose without having to go vertical, which was a huge relief; however, it meant ascension took a while. I would have asked about it, but I didn't want to talk to these people. Any question about their technology would probably have prompted questions about my own. So, we kept rising, at an annoyingly slow pace, with me fascinated by the brilliance before us.

"Second tier," Mal said, reading the indicator on the car's dash, some kind of GPS system in three dimensions. Pox nodded slowly.

"I could kill for a pizza," Qee muttered.

"You say that about most foods," Pox replied.

"Yeah, but I'm hungry." The rabbit shrugged. "When we get up there, I'm having a meal. Sally? Sal? Can I call you Sal? Want something to eat?"

"Yes, please." I nodded. "Oh. Um, last time I ate some food up here, I got some … larval parasite things, though. I should be careful."

ALIENATION

"Oh, don't worry. You can only have them once," Qee said eagerly. "I had them when I was a kid. Ate right through my abdomen."

"She's, like, part cyborg now." Pox giggled.

"Part robot," Qee said, frustrated. "Part robot. I'm a cyborg because I'm part robot."

"Whatever," said Pox. "I have a robotic foot, but you don't see me bragging about it."

Mal sighed. "Everyone's got parts these days."

"But not you."

"Nope, one hundred percent human," he said proudly. "Da-Duhuian, born and raised."

"So am I, dingbat," snapped Qee.

"Yeah, but your robotic innards aren't," the driver teased. "All right, we'll park here and get something to eat then it's down to Mister Boss Man to drop off Sally. Good?"

"Whoopee!" shouted Qee. "Finally! Food!"

Mal drove up to another of the openings in the wall of the city, deftly maneuvering the van through the small entrance, like a bee flying into its hive. Once inside, the place opened, leaving ample room for parking. He found a spot and set us down with a sigh of relief from the hovering suspension.

Pox opened the door and we piled out, and for a second I thought I could maybe be one of them, a young adult taking on the big city. Going for a bite to eat with my closest friends. But I wasn't; I couldn't be. I was from Earth, and these aliens had grown up here, while I have been light-years away.

That and I wasn't too sold on having them as friends yet. But hey, new planet, new me. Let's see about making connections.

"I don't have any money," I said, cautiously.

"Don't sweat it," said Mal. "We'll expense this to the boss. Come on, I'm starving!"

The world up here was not as glamorous as the level I had been on with Zander. Sunlight trickled down through layers of grating, but it was so dim the streetlights were on, even in the middle of the day. The streets were a little gross. Actually, a whole lot of gross. The Downdweller streets—the ones they lived on— were cleaner than this. I hadn't seen any litter there; whereas here, it was all over the place.

"Are you coming?" urged Pox. "We want to get there before the lunch rush."

"Yeah," I said, noncommittal, and trotted to join them. Together, we walked the soiled streets, following Mal as he led us to, well, I had no idea where we were going.

"Oh my drang, zoommies!" Qee squawked, rushing to a street vendor. The stall held a large selection of boxes, all open at the top, letting out the sound of small shuffling and little chirps. She reached into one without hesitation, pulling out a small, squirming figure barely bigger than her hands.

"Isn't he precious?" she asked, holding the thing out to me and Pox. The creature was cute, I could give her that. It was shaped like a puppy but covered in feathers, its mouth a weird assortment of stunted tentacles, like the face of a mole. The fleshy appendages moved around in hypnotic circles as the small creature whimpered in Qee's hands. Its eyes were closed, if it even had any.

"You can pet it," she said, eyeing my expression. "They don't bite. They don't do much of anything."

I reached out, nervously, to stoke the tiny zoomie along its back. It let out gentle cooing noises, obviously liking the attention. It felt soft, like Qee's hands or the down of a pillow. Not what I expected from a small touch of the strange-looking bird-mole.

"I can't believe your folk eat these," Mal muttered, butting his way into the small circle we had formed.

"Shut up." Pox scowled. "You all eat poultry, and you know the chicken is our holiest creature, right?"

"It's also delicious," Mal said, flashing her an obnoxious smile.

"Screw you." Pox ripped the tiny zoomie from Qee's hand and swallowed it whole before any of us could stop them. Even the tiny critter didn't have time to react and went down silently. But we could see it squirm as it went down their gullet, the transparent skin giving us a full window of the zoomie as it began to be digested.

I recoiled. Pox didn't seem bothered by this, making a scene of licking their fingers as we stared. They paid the store clerk, who couldn't have looked any less interested.

"You know I'm a vegan, right?" Qee said, obviously uncomfortable.

"Sorry, darling," Pox replied. "I know you think they're cute."

"So freaking gross." Mal shook his head. "I'm still hungry, though. Come on, everyone."

I followed, now reluctantly, as Mal led us around the corner to a fast-food place he was excited about. We walked right in, found a table, and took our seats. The menu popped up digitally where a placemat would go.

"Pick anything you want," Mal said.

"Thanks," I said, scrolling through the options and not understanding a lick of them. Pizza. Pizza. Pizza. Probably for the first time in my life, I was glad for a menu with pictures. Nothing looked familiar, except maybe the pizzas that actually were pizzas, and I knew well enough to avoid *them*.

In the end, I settled on something that looked like noodles. The second our orders were placed, a resounding ding flew through the restaurant, forcing open a small door in the wall that I hadn't even noticed. Out rolled an old and battered robot, scruffy and graffitied in places, one eye lit and the other dull. It rolled up on caterpillar treads and slid the food in front of each of us before returning to his stall.

Those were not noodles.

Every single thing we ordered had come in the form of foam. Mine was a bright red, while Qee had some green sludge, and the other two plates carried

ALIENATION

something pure and white. They each grabbed straws and sucked as I watched in awe.

"Tuck in," Qee suggested, taking a break from her foam. Her soft pink nose twitched in every direction, though I wasn't sure if it was meant to be doing that.

I grabbed courage in both my hands and jammed my straw into the foam, taking a long sip. I immediately regretted it. The foam was heavily spiced. The entire thing was overwhelming and confusing. I coughed the way I had when I'd tried my first cigarette, and I felt the same nausea in the pit of my stomach. Bile threatened to rise.

The group laughed.

"You like it?" Qee asked politely.

"It's … an acquired taste," I said, and she laughed again.

The second sip was not as strong, seeing as how I knew what to expect this time. By the fourth or fifth, I appreciated it a little more, though there was no way it tasted like noodles.

It tasted like pizza.

Crap. They say everything tastes like chicken, but they're wrong. Everything tastes like pizza in the big wide universe. There was no escaping it.

And it wasn't even good pizza.

I wasn't done before the others ordered more. By the time my plate was clean, they had made it through at least three helpings, and it didn't look like they would stop anytime soon.

S.E.ANDERSON

"Um, shouldn't we be going to see your boss?" I asked, wishing there was a glass of water available.

"He can wait." Mal waved me off.

"Are you sure?" I continued. "Because I have a deal to uphold, and I really haven't gotten the details on the whole of it."

"We're going, we're going!" Pox said, taking a break from their fourth serving. You could see pretty much the entire esophagus through their skin now, all white like snow. I wondered if the zoomie was digested yet, but I wasn't sure I wanted to know. I was very glad for their outfit, as weird as it was, since it covered the most gruesome part of the gut.

"And you're sure he's going to pay for this?" Qee asked Mal, nose bristling.

"Of course," Mal replied. "It's nothing to him. Where's that bot when you need it?"

The sad-looking robot came back, and Mal shoved some paper money at him. The thing reacted after a lag, picking up the cash with its flat fingers.

"Thank you for dining at Grotto's today," it said, gathering the payment and verifying it was correct. "We hope you come back soon. A well-filled belly is a happy belly."

The three of them mouthed the words along with the robot before it spun its torso and went back to the stall, the panel sliding shut over it before they could respond. Not that I think they would want to. I didn't think they were too fond of that robot.

ALIENATION

"All right," Mal said, standing, "best not keep that boss man waiting. Let's get a move on."

I followed him out of the eatery, the women straight on my heels. A man in a maroon jumpsuit picked up litter with a cold look on his face, glaring at each of us in turn. Three robotic street sweepers were working with him, but of course they paid us no mind.

"But what do they want me to do?" I asked Mal, trying to ignore the street cleaner's glare. "The Downdwellers only got the main gist of the plan. They didn't tell me much."

"Their minds aren't ready for that kind of complexity." Mal snickered, stuffing his hands deep into his pockets. "Don't worry. It's very simple. Anyone could do it. Maakuna planned it himself."

His hands flew to his mouth, his eyes widening as if he had spilled a deep, dark secret. But the word, the name, meant nothing to me. The second he realized that, he not only relaxed, he got cocky again.

"Well, well, well," he said, "you really aren't from around here, are you?"

I shook my head. Did shaking your head mean the same thing here as it did back home?

Behind us, the girls were hushed, whispering with their heads close together. Whatever event transpired with the zoomie was forgotten. They looked at Mal repeatedly, smiling as they did. Was there a crush I didn't know about? Then again, I knew nothing about any of their relationships.

"Maakuna is one of the most powerful names in this sector," Mal explained. "Maybe even the entire Alliance. You must really be out of the loop for his name to mean nothing."

"I'm telling you, never heard of him before."

Mal shrugged and opened the door to the van with a twist of the wrist, inviting everyone in. I took my seat in the back again, running the name through my mind over and over again. I was sure I had never heard of Maakuna before, no matter how much Mal wanted me to.

Qee closed the door, and we took off. Mal unthreaded the needle to get us to the main avenue. There, I was surprised he did not drive up. Instead, he banked us, slowly, across the road to a series of dismal homes.

"I can't believe you don't know who he is," Pox stammered. "He's the … he's a household name."

"Not in my household." Qee showed her teeth. "Veganism, and all. An evil spirit invoked inside a house becomes bound with that house. We were never allowed to say the name, even when we wanted to share some juicy gossip."

"You're actually a vegan?" I asked.

"All hail the great and mighty Vega," she replied, making the sign of a star in the air.

"Anyway, he's ready for you now," Mal said as he turned off his com. "And don't worry. He's very reasonable. Just do everything he says, and no one gets hurt."

FOURTEEN

THE ALIEN-FATHER AND TOTALLY LEGITIMATE SPACE BUSINESS

I KNEW THE SECOND WE DREW UP TO THE HOUSE that this was shady as hell. Or, at least, much, much shadier than I had expected.

Tam and his friends made their nameless helper out to be a philanthropic hero. Mal and the gang made him sound like an intense businessman. But from the looks of the house we were heading to, it seemed more likely that we were heading to a *legitimate* businessman.

As in I think I accidentally joined the mob.

Let's look at the signs, shall we?

One. The place looked grim, and ultimately kinda creepy. It stuck out from the rest of the buildings because its façade was just a little bit nicer and more polished than the others surrounding it. Still, it was dark and looming with brass ornaments around the windows and doors. Even the little sidewalk out front where the car could land seemed cleaner than the ones around it. All the buildings on this strip had their metal shutters rolled down and looked empty.

Signs number two and three would probably be the men standing outside the front door. Lurking? Nah. Guarding it, but putting on a big act of lurking. They looked practically identical: tall and lean, wearing crisp suits in one piece—which looked altogether weird, yet gave off the same effect as suits back home. Their bald heads were both covered entirely in intricate tattoos.

Tattoos that seemed to move with each breath.

Mal parked the van on the ledge, and we got out. I froze as my foot hit the pavement. I just couldn't stop staring at those tattoos, mesmerized by the weaving patterns. They looked fixed, like tribal tattoos. But out of the corner of my eye … there was no way I could be sure, but they were putting me on edge.

"Itzi," Mal proclaimed, as if to an old friend. He waltzed up close to the man on the right looking like he wanted a hug. Itzi glared at the boy, not returning the affection.

"Sonota," he said. "That's Itzi. Get it right, boy."

Mal gulped but stood his ground. He wasn't going to show weakness in front of this man, and it made me suddenly frightful of who they worked for.

Sign number four that you might have just joined the mob: if their guards were enough to put Mal on edge, then I wondered just how unsettling the man in charge was.

ALIENATION

Itzi waved and grinned at Mal, showing off a row of shark-like teeth. A shiver went through my body. These were the type of men that mothers would see and pull their children closer to their bodies as they walked down the street. And from what I could tell, from the cold chill of the air around them, those mothers probably had the right idea.

I looked back at Qee and Pox, surprised to see the color had drained from their faces, which was impressive, considering that Qee's fur was white and Pox was entirely transparent. They kept a healthy distance from the two men, practically still in the van.

"You're late, little man," said Itzi. The way he said it made it sound like this might be the last time Mal would ever be late to anything.

As in, you know, the alive capacity.

"You know the Downdwellers," Mal said, trying to shrug him off playfully but failing oh-so-badly. "They took forever to get her to us. No sense of time, you know."

The two men glared at Mal, identical stares on identical faces. Mal took a hurried step back.

"Relax, kid," Sonota said, putting a heavy hand on Mal's shoulder. "He's waiting for you, but you're lucky he is a patient man. Go on in."

Itzi was already at the door, opening the polished wood for Mal with a loud creaking noise. Mal trotted up nervously then turned to look back at me, giving me a wary look as if to say, *You coming?*

I hustled to catch up with him, sidestepping around Sonota, who sniggered as he watched me walk. I had no idea what he meant by that, but I sure didn't like it. Itzi grunted as he closed the door behind us.

We were in a tight hallway, more tall than wide, dimly lit and grimy. The wallpaper, or tapestry or whatever was covering the wall, was peeling and decaying. There were a few cobwebs in the corners—which glowed a bright shade of blue and formed patterns I had never seen before—but the spiders, or whatever had made them, were nowhere to be seen.

The place smelled of mold. No, it reeked of it. Like week-old bologna and cheese. I held my breath as we walked, but it did no good. The smell seeped into everything, and I knew it would never come out of my clothes.

But it looked—and smelled—incredibly familiar.

A woman stood, bored, at the top of the stairs, smoking what looked like a stick bug, while wearing a long-draped nightgown that revealed more than I wanted to see. Turns out the three-boob thing wasn't just something dreamed up by Earth boys.

She glared at us too, like we were the spiders making all the webs, and she wanted to squash us under the heel of her fluffy, green slipper. I tried to ignore her, looking instead at the few pictures on the walls, mostly of pressed flowers from planets I had never heard of.

Possibly the only flowers I had seen on Da-Duhui.

Itzi led us through a small maze of thin hallways, some so tight we had to turn sideways. Finally, though, we reached a sitting room, one large enough that it could easily take up an entire floor of someone's house. The smell here wasn't so bad, or, at least, different enough that I didn't want to gag anymore. Maybe I was just getting used to it.

While there were windows here, they were covered in heavy purple drapes, the kind of thing you would see at a Victorian funeral parlor. Everything else was lit with harsh electrical lighting, which buzzed and hummed like a fly on steroids.

"Sir, they've finally arrived," Itzi announced. I couldn't be sure if he was trying to be dismissive or sarcastic. Either way, I didn't think I was making the best first impression with Itzi.

He turned out of the room and slammed the door shut, leaving us alone in the dark with an ornate pink couch. Or at least, I think it was pink. It was dark.

"So, the Downdwellers really did find a *round head* for their cause," a deep voice resonated through the room. I realized then that the couch was not a couch. Or, more reasonably, the couch was part couch, part something else. "Come around. Let me look at you."

Mal gave me a quick shove and I trotted, knees trembling, in front of the sofa, trying to keep my head held high.

My heart fell. I knew this species. I had seen it before, just yesterday: an Oexasie. But the look in his eyes matched mine—recognition.

"You!" it said.

"You!" I echoed.

It was no longer nude. The Oexasie had squeezed into a tight, pink suit, like an overstuffed sausage spilling out of its casing. I stepped back, ready to run. The thing knew who I was. He knew I was with the thief who had raided his museum.

I understood now why the place had felt so familiar. I recognized it from when I had been running for my life down the hallways and stairs.

"Well, well, well," he said, his voice both deep and wheezing simultaneously. "I think she'll do just fine."

"I did good?" Mal asked, practically begging for approval.

"You did fantastic, young Mal." The creature beamed. "Congratulations. You deserve a reward. Itzi will see to you."

"Really?" Mal's face lit up. "Awesome. Is that it?"

"Yes, yes." The stranger waved a thick hand at him, limply. "I'm a man of my word, I'll give you that. We're finished here. I no longer need your services. You and your friends will be … taken care of."

Mal was practically glowing, but I clenched my fists, knowing what was coming. I half expected bullets to emanate from this very room. But Mal walked out freely, alive, and probably into a trap.

I would have run then, if I could. I wanted to storm out that door, screaming, because this was not what I signed up for. Then again, what had I expected, signing up for a coup?

ALIENATION

I tried not to make eye contact with the Oexasie, but it took up most of my field of vision and looking away wasn't going to help my situation.

"I'm impressed," said the Oexasie. "It takes guts to return to the scene of the crime, especially without your … infamous escort. How did the Theosians find you?"

"My escort dumped me," I replied, trying to keep my chin high. "Literally."

The Oexasie laughed, letting out a resonating sound that could have been him choking. His breath smelled almost as bad as the Beast in the Undercity. Maybe they were cousins.

"If I had known I could catch the great Zander by simply hanging up his coat, I would have set a trap ages ago," he said, his mouth distorted into what could have been a grin. "So, does this mean the siblings have returned?"

"I have no idea," I lied. "I was a convenience for them. They left me the second they were able to."

"Left you to fend for yourself in the Undercity. How pleasant. What makes a woman like you want to help the miserables downstairs? You don't look like a Downdweller."

"You don't look like someone who cares about them."

He slapped the arm of the chair, and the room flickered out of existence. For a split-second, I stood in something brilliantly white and over-lit, like an operating room. The man laughed and slapped the chair again. The room returned to its old, haggard look. An illusion.

"I doubt you care either," he scoffed. "Tell me, why are you here?"

S.E.ANDERSON

"What do you expect?" I said, trying to play along. "I was a Downdweller for a day, and I don't want to be one for much longer."

"I can understand that." He nodded. "I have heard of the way they live down there, in their own squalor and filth. They are nothing. You deserve more."

So, he hadn't been down there either. No one had. I guess what Tam had said was right: Once you went down, you never came back up. Ever.

Still, I felt oddly gross, and I wasn't sure why. Maybe I was just disgusted by the people who were my only ticket out of there. I shuddered-I was doing a lot of that lately.

"They deserve more," I said. "If I can help, even in a small way, I think I will. For justice."

"Oh?" he replied, his eyes growing wide. "You think it's justice, bringing their people into a world where they'll be mistreated? Where they will be on the same level as mindless automatons?"

"It's one step closer to equal rights," I told him, sternly, half believing my own words.

"Equal?" He laughed yet again, his mouth opening wide, breathing pungent air into my face. "I like your naivety, girl. Sit down." He pointed to the armchair across from him.

"No, thank you. I would prefer to remain standing."

He laughed. "I like you more and more. But please, sit down before I have someone shoot your head off. You know I can."

"Actually, I don't." I shrugged. "I have no idea who you are."

ALIENATION

He stopped laughing suddenly. He stared at me, as if trying to take me in in one gaze, staring like I had stepped out of a UFO and claimed his world as my own. His bizarre, lizard-like eyes blinked rapidly.

"Oh?" he said. "Don't you, now?"

"Not a clue."

My heart pounded. This was new. All this blathering to save my own hide was sinking me deeper into this pit of trouble. I wondered, mildly, when this defense mechanism became a part of my personality. Was it when Grisham had turned into a hellbeast? Probably. That stuff had messed me up.

Or maybe it was the moment I had realized that my chances of going home were getting slimmer by the second. Or that Zander wasn't coming to my rescue, so I had to throw everything I could at this fire and hope it would die down eventually.

"You're not from around here," the man said, doubtfully. I nodded. "So, where? Border planets? Outer rim?"

"Unclaimed territory. Outside of Alliance control."

He let out a low clicking noise I took to be the equivalent of an impressed whistle.

"Well, then, you're a long way from home." He sniggered. "Allow me to introduce myself. I'm Maakuna Ik'Imo'No, fifth of my name," he said, as if still expecting his name to instill some kind of terror. Not a chance. I couldn't care less. I didn't know it when Mal had said his name in the car, and I didn't know it now.

But I think I was going to.

"You're rather insolent, I take it," he said.

"And you seem pretty nefarious. I think that makes us even."

His face went cold. "Don't for a second believe you are on equal standing with me, girl. You are here because I wish it. And I might not want you around all that long."

"I'll be gone as soon as this is over," I insisted. "That's the point, after all. If you still have a mission for me to do, that is. It doesn't sound like the Downdwellers are in on your full plan."

"Listen, kid," he snapped. "You really think I care for those … creatures? I've got better things to do than dwell on petty civil rights."

He waved his hand and a woman walked in, her dress a plastic sheet that only barely covered her rear. She stuck an orange stub in his mouth, lit it, and rushed out of the room in a polite trot as Maakuna watched. He took a deep, relaxing puff, blowing the smoke in my direction. I tried not to breathe it in, but I couldn't help but notice it smelled like pond water.

"So why are you even dealing with them?" I asked.

"You're an interesting specimen," he said, taking another puff of his cigar-looking thing. "Up from nothing, come from nowhere, and yet you expect me to tell you everything."

"I expect you to let me know what I'm getting into," I said, realizing I was pushing it too far and yet incapable of stopping. "I need to know what I am doing if I'm expected to do it well."

He puffed the smoke in my face again, this time giving me no time to prepare. My body screamed for me to breathe, but I held my own, refusing to give him the pleasure of seeing me flinch.

"Suit yourself." He shrugged. "You're going through with tonight whether you like it or not, so what comes afterward is up to you. You perform poorly, and it's your own ass on the line."

"What comes afterward?"

"Ah, ah, ah!" He waggled a slug-like finger back and forth. "I keep no secrets from my family. On the other hand, I have no reason to tell you anything."

"Not that I would understand, right?"

He nodded. "Exactly. Nothing a small human girl like you would understand. Leave it to the slugs."

"Oh, yes, I understood that quite clearly," I said, going with it. I sat in the armchair like he had asked me to, leaning on my arm childishly. "Nothing a humanitarian like me would get, one who joins a team of losers to ease her guilt of her own upper-class privilege."

"Precisely," he said, taking a long puff of his cigar.

"Nothing a dummy like me would understand. A clumsy girl. I might even slip up tonight, I'm so incompetent."

He perked up at this. "If you mess this up, I'll have you killed."

"I wouldn't doubt it, sir. I know you're capable of that," I said. "But wouldn't that be done by someone else if they caught me? I'll denounce anyone to save my own skin."

"You have no idea how big this operation is."

"Oh, yes, I have no idea." I grinned now, tilting my head provocatively. "I'm just afraid I'll mess up tonight."

"You won't mess up." A command.

"Not if I know what's at stake. I mean, if I knew what would happen if I messed up … I know the codes won't shut the robots down, you practically said so yourself. What if it makes them blow up? I could turn your whole operation in rather than getting arrested for something I didn't know I was even doing."

He grunted. "You want the truth?"

I gave him a curt nod. "Maybe if the stakes were clear, I wouldn't slip up."

"Have it your way," he said monotonously. He puffed out another cloud of smoke, and I breathed it in, ignoring my burning throat. "You heard right, the codes won't shut down the robots. Quite the contrary: they weaponize them."

I let out a fake gasp. I wasn't all that surprised, if the mob was involved. "But, why?"

"After the robots are under our control"—Maakuna paused for effect—"the population will be under our control."

"What would you do with them?" I asked. "I mean, I hear many people talking about 'taking over,' but what would you do when you're in charge?"

ALIENATION

"Simple," he said, and I realized he didn't care about what he was telling me. He probably thought I wouldn't come out of this alive, one way or another. This time, I stopped myself from shuddering before the shiver came out. "The robots won't come out with guns or anything. No, that would be too messy. This is one of the biggest cities in the Planetary Alliance; people come here to shop and eat. We raise the shopping taxes, slowly, pushing the prices up ever so slightly. The government won't even notice. They don't track the bots. They're too well-programmed to ever mess up. The extra money gets funneled to us. It's that simple. The Downdwellers will think the plan failed and go back to living their miserable lives, and no one gets hurt."

This whole plan was becoming more insane by the minute. Was this how other people operated on these planets? Maybe it's true what they say: The universe is a big, chaotic place. Earth was no exception, sure, but I was used to that strangeness, mostly.

"So, even if I get caught"—I forced myself not to roll my eyes—"nothing will be wrong to start with?"

"That's right: No one will even know." He chortled.

"That's a relief." I gave a fake sigh. Internally, though, I didn't have a clue what was going on. His plan sounded just as ridiculous as the one he had fed the Theosians, maybe even more so.

"But if you do get caught," he continued, "make no mistake, the Alliance will hide you away where no one can find you, chip or no chip. And if you mess up in any way at all, even slightly, I'm sending you back to the Downdwellers for the rest of your miserable life. Understood?"

I nodded quickly, knowing full well his threats were legitimate. He probably had hands in the police, and I would end up in the Undercity in mere seconds; that was, however, if I didn't find Zander first. And I had to find Zander first.

"Why me?" I asked, my veins running thick with fear. "Why not some random woman. There are probably people who want—"

"None are desperate enough."

"And what makes you think I'm desperate?"

"Because," Maakuna waved his short arms feebly, "it's this or the Undercity. And I don't think you're ready to resign just yet. I'd say you're desperate enough, desperate enough for me to know you won't fail, whatever you say. You don't want to go back down there. And don't give me that look. You can claim to want to help the Downdwellers' cause because you believe in it, but make no mistake, you're like me. You're in it for yourself. Not to mention, you don't exist."

"Because they deleted me from their systems?"

"Exactly. When you fell," he explained, despite me having made it clear I knew this bit, "any record they had of you was wiped. And you weren't from the Alliance to begin with. You can go anywhere undetected. If you get caught, you can scream and cry all you want, but they're never going to connect you with me. Anyway, what was your name again?"

ALIENATION

"Sally," I replied. "Sally We—"

"Well, Sally." He handed me a note, with numbers scribbled on it. "You need to memorize this map."

"What?"

"The plan is simple," said Maakuna, slowly, as if I wouldn't understand. "You're going to the ball. You'll mingle with the crowd, and then you'll break into the palace. Be casual. Try not to attract the attention of the Travoshella. Then, you'll enter the commands into the ICP. And that's it. No harm done. You can leave and never see any of us again. Easy. But you have to blend in, and there's no way you'll do that with what you're wearing now. Get this layout memorized, and then it's straight to hair and makeup."

My knees wobbled, leaving me unable to speak, while trying to ignore the creature's sharp glare and desperately figure out how to change this situation to suit my own needs: finding Zander again.

But would he still be here?

FIFTEEN
THE WEIRDEST BATH OF MY LIFE

ITZI AND SONOTA CAME TO FIND ME SOON AFTER that. Maakuna was tired of me and waved me away. I would never see him again. For that, I was eternally grateful. I was sure if Zander's offer of wiping my memory still stood, I would use it on my memories of Maakuna; his ugly face would haunt my nightmares for years to come.

Sonota smirked, as he led me through the house, his partner picking up the rear. "The boss man likes you."

"It didn't seem that way," I said, trying to ignore the sailing patterns on his head. It was probably just as rude to stare on this planet, not that it stopped people from doing it.

The two of them grinned, as if they were in on a private joke. Whatever it was, I was glad I wasn't in on it. I didn't want to know what those two found funny.

ALIENATION

We left the living room, Sonota ahead of me and Itzi behind, following the twisting hallways out and about in a direction we hadn't gone before. I wondered just how large this house was before we ran back into the stairs we had passed earlier, the one with the woman who'd glared. This time, though, she and her triple bosom were nowhere to be found.

They led me up the stairs, one, two, three whole floors until we were in another identical hallway, only this one had blue trim rather than red. Small differences that made no difference. How many of these rooms were illusions, I did not know, but it explained how they could clean up so quickly after the mess Blayde had left. I followed the men down the corridor until we reached a door like any other, which they opened without knocking.

Inside, the room was warm and inviting. A fake fire burned and churned in a small chimney, giving off a red glow and basking the room in real heat. The woman in there was setting up a mannequin, tossing a gold-yellow gown over it and pinning it in place. She turned as she heard us enter.

"Ah, it's you," she said, nodding at my two escorts. "I suppose this is the girl?"

Her eyes fell on mine, and in the same instant we both understood. We had seen each other before. She had been above, at the Da-Duhui plaza. Tchilla.

She had sold me the dress that I had—where was it now? Either with Zander or lost in the fall. In any case, she was the woman who had fitted me, the one who could dress anyone, any life form.

Why was she doing work for the mob?

If she knew who I was, she said nothing to the men, but I could tell she recognized me and that she knew I recognized her. Her spider eyes sparkled and gleamed black as they met mine. Thankfully, she kept her mouth shut for the both of us.

"All right you two," Sonota said, giving me a sharp push into the room. "You don't have much time. I'd suggest you get to work, but that goes without saying."

Tchilla and I both nodded. That was all my guards needed, and they left. Itzi shut the door behind him. It would be a safe bet to assume it was now locked.

The woman and I stared at each other for a hot minute, taking in the familiarity of each other's faces combined with the weirdness of meeting here, of all places. Finally, she stepped forward to touch my face. A strange act from an almost stranger.

"I've sold you a dress before, haven't I?" she said, her voice almost a mutter as she slipped a lock of my hair behind my ear. She was a small woman, shorter than me, not exactly human, and, yet, not exactly … not. Her proportions seemed off, and it wasn't the extra pair of arms that made it look so. The turban was off now. Her hair was so gray it was almost blue, and her skin was so wrinkled it reminded me of Chinese paper.

"Yesterday," I replied, hushed and rushed. "Or two days ago. I don't know anymore. How do you remember

ALIENATION

me? You must have hundreds of customers. I was just a face in the crowd."

"The man you were with," she explained, speaking quickly, "he came to me, searching for you. He said you were lost. He wanted my help finding you. I had nothing to say."

My heart leaped. Zander was searching for me. He was still here, still looking. He wasn't giving up, and neither was I. I would get through this. I was going to go home.

"What happened to you?" she asked, indicating, well, everything, with a sweep of her four arms.

"I fell into the Undercity. That Maakuna guy promised the Downdwellers a way out in exchange for me crashing a party tonight. It's been weird."

"And you're all right?" she asked, smoothing my hair down yet again. "No one has hurt you?"

"I've got a few scrapes and bruises, but I'll manage." I heaved a sigh of relief. Speaking to her was like unloading huge weights off my back. She clasped my shoulders tightly.

"Your name, girl?" she urged.

"Sally," I said. "Sally Webber. From Earth."

"Tchilla," she replied. "Tchilla from Meegra. I'm going to get you out of here."

She ushered me to the curtain draped across part of the room, and I understood she wanted me to get changed. I slipped behind it and took everything off. The t-shirt and jeans had become stiff as cardboard

218

after the muck they had been through. I had to practically peel them off my skin.

When I emerged from behind the curtain wearing my undergarments proudly, Tchilla made an audible hiss. I looked down. The partitions had cut off the light from the room, so it was only now that I saw the damaged state my body was in. A huge bruise graced my chest and belly, radiating so many shades of blue and purple that it could have been Blayde's hair. My stomach was littered with small pock-marks, little red bruises from where the maggot things had tried to burst their way out, before I had forced them out through my throat. My legs and hands were scratched up, but they were the least of my worries.

Tchilla put the dress back down on the form. No, we were not going to try it on while I was in this state, her face said. As I stood in the middle of the room, quasi-naked and feeling like a train had hit me full force, she gathered help from outside. Within minutes, the woman from the staircase brought in a robot, who in turn carried a large metal basin—large enough to fit me—and they filled it with scalding water, which made steam rise and fill the room.

I wasn't even thinking at this point. Exhaustion took over the second I admitted just how tired I was. Tchilla helped me strip entirely, peeling the bra from my skin and taking off my earrings, setting them aside for later. She held the silver with reverence. Then she led me into the water, which burned and soothed all at once. Motes of dirt rose and swirled around my limp body.

My bra went into the fire.

"Hey!" I shouted, though I was too tired to protest. Tchilla said nothing. Instead, she sat down on a chair, pulled out her garment basket, and sewed me a new one without a second thought. Her four hands flew over the small fabric, holding it and cutting it and stitching it all in one go.

"Why are you here, Tchilla?" I asked, as the water reached my chin.

"The same reason anyone comes to Maakuna: I had no choice. Now relax and get clean."

I took her advice and let my hair sprawl into the water. Nothing felt as good as this. Every ache and pain in my body washed away; every joint and muscle relaxed. My skin felt slimy, but a basket of what looked like soaps and sponges would see to that.

I felt nonchalant about being nude around this stranger. She did not care, and neither did I. It was a relief to feel this comfortable around someone in this city, to have her work with me with no judgment.

"Did my friend leave you a way to reach him?" I asked, scrubbing the muck from between my toes.

"Yes and no," Tchilla said. "He left me a way to signal him. Whether he sees it will be up to the stars, but I will try. I will tell him you plan on being at the mayoral palace tonight. Hopefully, he will find you there."

"Oh, thank you," I replied, sinking deeper into the water. I imagined he would be worried sick by now, if he truly did care for me. But I was worried too. I was under the impression he would be on top of things a little more than he was. He promised to keep me safe, and he wasn't doing anything like that right now. Was he really the man he claimed to be?

"Did he tell you his name?" I asked Tchilla, and she looked up, making eye contact with me. In her hand was a beautiful, simple bra, a basket of gentle lace that dangled over her fingers. She had seven of those, I noticed, on each hand. Her arms were covered with tight metal bangles that stuck to her skin and never moved, even as she wove her many fingers through the motions of crafting.

"He didn't need to," she replied, her voice lowering to a whisper. "I would recognize him anywhere. I saw him as a child, you know."

"You what?" I slid out of the water, shocked by the sudden cold, but Tchilla returned to her work, her eyes twinkling.

"How? When?" I asked, dumbfounded. "What happened?"

"He did say you weren't from around here." She chuckled. "Anyone here would know not to speak of him. The official stance is that he is a criminal, after all. Or a myth. Maybe both, depending on which version you like best. But in mine, you get handsome princes and heroic rescues."

ALIENATION

"Zander?" I asked.

"Shush," Tchilla's face went cold. "Don't say that name so freely. But, yes, him. Him and his fireball sister. But it's a long story and not for tonight."

"Oh, please. I want to know."

She grabbed a handful of white powdery balls from a little bowl and crushed them in my hair before I could ask what she was doing. She massaged the powder into my scalp as she talked.

"I mentioned before that I was from Meegra, but I grew up on Pyrina," she said, her voice slipping into a tone reserved for storytelling and legends. "A planet much like this one, the home-world of the Alliance. It's beautiful: pink and orange skies any time of the day, a deep and dark ocean, and stars that still come out at night. I lived in a nice neighborhood, a place with tall trees lining the streets and fresh markets every day of the week."

"Why did you leave, if you liked it so much?"

"Reasons." Tchilla gave a sharp push with both thumbs on the nape of my neck. "Now, hush. You want the story, right? Well, it just so happens that when you live in a nice neighborhood in the capital planet of the largest alliance in the known universe, you might just get held hostage by terrorists. They came down one day, falling from the sky and taking the entire block as their own. They wanted money or something. It wasn't even all that special. We were told that if we stayed inside, we would not be harmed, but they cut off water, electricity, everything. We were adrift and alone.

"And then one day, we weren't.

"One morning, after about a week of being locked up on my floor with my parents, there was no one left on the streets to keep us trapped inside. No one knew if it was safe, but I didn't care. I was a child, you understand. I snuck out while they were debating the relative safety of trying the outside world.

"And it was safe. The streets were empty, but I stuck to the shadows. Hold on," she said, pushing on my head. I dunked instinctively, rinsing my hair in one swift move. When I brought it back up, she combed it, removing the water with an occasional pat of a towel.

"Zander got rid of them?" I asked.

"You've really got to work on your patience," Tchilla chided. "We're not there yet. But, anyway, I turned a corner, and someone grabbed me. Completely out of the red. He had his hand over my mouth before I could say anything. 'Stay quiet, and nothing will happen to you,' he said. 'Who did this? Who's in on it?'

"I had no idea what he was talking about. He was jittery, and sounded panicked and paranoid. I knew something had happened, but I didn't know what.

"And that's when your friend appeared. I was out of the stranger's grasp as quickly as I had gotten into it. Your friend had the terrorist on the ground, stunned, before I knew what was even happening. And he looked at me. That face, I could never forget it. I knew who he was. We had all heard stories, seen the wanted posters. This was centuries ago, you see. People back then knew he existed, though they had no idea what he was. I knew, though. He was a hero.

"And then he spoke. It was odd, unprepared. He blurted 'Um, stay in school?' before his sister turned the corner hair ablaze—I mean quite literally on fire—and the two of them disappeared."

"Wait, how long ago was this?" I asked, my words tumbling from numb lips.

"Oh, years and years ago." Tchilla tugged the knots out of my hair, a little harsher than I would have liked. "The official report was that our own troops liberated the street that morning, but I knew the truth. The heavy lifting had been done for them. The siblings weren't criminals; they were heroes. So, when I was old enough, I left and came here. I couldn't stay there anymore, knowing what had happened there."

Zander was centuries old, a fact I had somehow known all along, but it something that had never registered in my brain. I remembered the stories I had heard, from aliens who all knew his name but told a different tale. Was he the same Zander from them all? The criminal centuries ago, maybe the myth from millennia before?"

I shivered. Tchilla stopped combing for a beat, then resumed just as quickly.

I knew Zander was immortal. I had seen him die and come back to life as if that had been nothing. I knew that time was messed up for him. I had waited two years for him to return, only for him to tell me it hadn't been more than a week. But it had never resonated with me what that could actually mean.

Just how old was he?

"Come on, time to get out," said Tchilla. "We're not going to have enough time to get you ready, otherwise."

I stepped out of the basin, letting her towel me off. She passed the fluffy mass to me as she turned back to her basket, handing me my new undergarments, which were heavenly light. Finally the gown, which she traded for the towel so I could put it on.

With her extra fingers and hands, she stitched me in in just a few seconds, stitching and adjusting like none of it was any trouble. It was snug—snugger than I liked—around the belly and bust, but wide around the hips and legs, meaning I could walk fine in it, just not very quickly or I'd be out of breath in just a few steps.

Tchilla was a talented seamstress. I studied my reflection in the basin, surprised at just how flattering the gown was. In all the excitement, I hadn't realized that I was wearing a handmade, designer dress to some once-in-a-lifetime alien bash.

"Done," she said, as she helped me put my silver earrings back on. "I suppose Maakuna will have other convincing jewelry for you to wear tonight. Now, if things get hairy, I have stitched a little pocket in the gown, on your left hip, where I may or may not have slipped a few smoke pellets. They're very thick, so if you need to use them, toss them away from you and hold your breath. Then run like hell. Do you understand me?"

ALIENATION

I nodded slowly.

"Good," she replied. "Your audio device is in the other pocket, on your right hip. They're going to want me gone, now. I will try to relay your location to, well, him. Good luck, Sally."

It was as if she had heard them coming. The door to the room flew open and in came the same people who had brought in my bath. Now they were here to take it away, along with the dress form, the basket, and everything that had made this room a dressing room.

Sonota had joined them and dragged Tchilla away without a word. He touched her on the shoulder, leading her away. She did not fight it, nor did I. But I watched her leave, clutching my fists under the fabric of my skirts.

And then they were gone. I was left alone in the room, wearing a gown far too fancy for me, my feet bare beneath it, practically shaking as I tried to compartmentalize the thoughts in my brain.

Zander was looking for me.

Zander was old, way old.

And I was going on a mission for the mob that was highly, *highly* illegal and would probably get me killed.

But, hey, my dress was swishy. I turned back and forth, playing with the lag in the fabric. Anything to distract from the existential dread of it all. Adding anything more to the fact that I was on an alien planet with no way off it wasn't going to make me feel any better.

If anything, it would make everything a whole lot worse.

SIXTEEN

HEIST PLANNING 101

I HAD HALF EXPECTED THEM TO COME FOR ME right away, but instead, I sat in the room, waiting, as absolutely nothing at all happened.

Had they forgotten about me? I made my way to the door and tried the handle. No, it was definitely locked. I grunted in annoyance. I *really* didn't like this.

I turned back to the fake-real fire, staring into it. The underwire of my last bra was sitting there, gently melting in the ash. My last remnant of Earth.

Where had my clothes gone? I searched the room. Had Tchilla tossed them too? I felt a pang of sadness at the thought of losing my Chucks. I'd had them since high school. They had been there for me when John died, when I had run Zander over with my car, when I had been abducted, and now, through the streets of a murky alien city. They were only shoes, but it was like another link to Earth had just been snapped.

It physically hurt.

I jumped when I heard a knock at the door. Someone was finally here for me. But then I caught myself. They had *knocked*. This wasn't Itzi or Sonata. This was someone else.

Could it be Zander, so soon? My heart fluttered then fell. That was far too unlikely … and knowing him, he would probably abscond through the window. Tchilla, then, coming back to pick up something she forgot? Also, highly unlikely, seeing how empty this room was.

But the person did not wait for me to answer their knock. They pushed the door open, popping their head inside, and there was Mal, black Sharpie marks on his face and all.

"Sally?" he said, beaming.

"My god, Mal!" I replied, rushing to him. "You're alive!"

"Of course I'm alive," he scoffed. "Why under the stars wouldn't I be?"

"Because Maakuna … no matter. I thought he was different. I'm glad to see you're all right."

"Thanks," he said. "Same goes for you."

"And Pox? Qee?"

"I drove them home. They weren't feeling all that good. I'd blame it on our lunch, but, you know, not everyone has the stomach to do what's right."

"United for the Theosian cause," I muttered.

"The what, now?"

"The … Downdwellers. The original race that lived here, the ones relegated to the Undercity? You know, the ones you're trying to help?"

"Wait, they're another species?" Mal stepped back. "Shit! I thought they were just people who had got stuck down there!"

"Um, nope. And they can create fire. They're Elementals."

"Now you're just poking my nose."

"You're seriously telling me you didn't know? You have no idea who you're helping?"

"We're just trying to do a good deed," he said, making his way closer to the fire. Tchilla's stool was there, and he sat, patting the space next to him. It was far too small for me, so I stood. I wasn't very happy with him, anyway. I might have been glad he hadn't been executed, but I wasn't sure I liked him all that much.

"You look beautiful, Sally," he said, his eyes drawing wide as his voice lightened. I felt the heat rise to my face. I had not expected a compliment, and certainly not from him, this kid. Although, was he a child? The Sharpie made it hard to tell. He could have been my age, another young adult taking to the stars.

"Thank you," I said.

"You look tense."

"I'm fine," I lied, stepping close to the fire, holding the hem of my skirt to keep it from the flames. It kept my hands from fidgeting.

ALIENATION

"You say you're from a place called … Earth?" he said, making conversation. I nodded slowly. "Have you ever *been* with an alien before?"

"Excuse me?" I asked, startled. Of all the things he could have said right then, I had not expected that. I guess it would be best for me to stop expecting anything anymore. I dropped the skirt then grabbed it again, stepping away from the fire before it became any more of a hazard.

"I mean, have you slept with anyone who's not from your planet before?" he asked, raising his eyebrows. "Ever tasted the stars?"

"Um, no. And I don't want to, if you're offering."

"But I'm curious," he said, getting back up. "We're all human, but we're not. Not really, you know? Not the same kind of human, at least. Every one of us is slightly different: different parts, different pieces, different … sensations."

I felt vomit rising, and I gagged it back down. My hands tightened into fists on my skirt. "I said no, thank you."

"But aren't you the least bit curious?" he urged, stepping closer. I could smell him now, his breath like an overripe peach. "Don't you want to know a different species? I'd sure enjoy the challenge. I've tried thirty-two different kinds, and they've each been fun. I'm sure you would be, too. Care to be my thirty-third? Lucky double number!"

"But … you're a kid!" I sputtered, not knowing which part of that sentence disgusted me the most.

"I'm two hundred and three. Come on, I know you want me just as much as I want you. I saw you looking at me, back in the van."

"I'm not interested," I snapped, stepping back, feeling the wall press against me. Damn. Not where I wanted to be.

"But there's no risk." He sniggered. "No compatibility, you see?"

"Oh, I'm sure Kirk is just crawling with alien STDs," I pointed out. Mal looked confused.

"What did you say about Kirk?"

I shook my head.

He was starting to smell now, a weird, sweet scent, like someone had dropped a bottle of rose oil over him and set him out in the sun. Part of me was warming up to the idea, the hint of curiosity that had tugged at my brain from when puberty and science fiction had hit at once. Wondering what it might be like. If we all worked the same, if we could …

No. One day, maybe, but not with him. Not with this pushy, two-century old kid creeping me out and, I think, trying to win me over with … were those pheromones? And they were working, too. I wondered if his seduction tactics were legal on this planet.

"Sorry, I ramble like that when I'm mad. And right now, I'm pretty pissed. I said no, so please stop."

I ran my hands along the wall behind me, hoping for a way out, but I was stuck. He had me pinned, and he was stepping closer.

ALIENATION

"Come on, you're just tense." He reached a hand out to me, taking a strand of my hair in his mouth. And then, he began to chew.

"What the hell are you doing?" I snapped, ripping my hair away from him, leaving a substantial chunk between his teeth. Ow, that hurt. My scalp was on fire, but I bit down hard on my molars and stifled my cry.

"Not doing anything for ya?" He sniggered. "That's all right. Everyone's turned on by something different. Just let me find what works."

He reached out for me again, and something dark kicked in. With a yelp, I grabbed his arm, twisted it behind him, and tossed him away from me. He turned and came right at me, livid, and that's when my fist collided with his nose.

"How's that for new sensations?" I snapped, as he cried out, clutching the appendage. "Don't mess with Earth girls."

"What the Veesh?" Mal barked, clutching his bloody nose. "You hit me!"

"I was defending myself." I marched to the door and threw it open, glad the idiot had left it unlocked, and abandoned Mal to gather his senses. I wasn't going to pity him.

Out in the hallways, Sonota was waiting, his eyes wide, tattoos swirling rapidly on his head. Mal rushed past him without a word or even a look.

"What the hell just happened?" Sonota asked, cocking his head to the side.

"You don't need to know," I replied, unclasping my hands from my skirts. It was no time to relax, but I had to get my pounding heart to slow down or risk losing it completely. "I need a purse. And maybe a thumb drive with a certain pile of codes."

"Well, that was a thrill to see," Sonota said, leaning into the room and taking in the scene before closing the door. He shook his head, smiling, and let out a small chuckle, a sharp rasp at the back of his throat. "He's going to be mad, you know."

I rolled my eyes. "He can handle it. He's got to be used to rejection by now."

"Not Mal." Sonota pointed through the floor, taking me back out toward the staircase. "The boss man. He thought you'd be a nice treat for the boy. Now he'll have to pay him actual money."

"Oh, come on, are you kidding me?" I stopped, and Sonota's gaze turned cold. He issued me forward with a jerk of his head. "He can't be serious. I thought you said we were in a rush?"

"He thought you two could squeeze a minute into your schedule."

"A minute?"

"What? Is that too long for you?" he asked, casually curious. "Does it take that long for your kind?"

"Excuse me?" I snapped.

"You Earthlings are weird," he said, and pushed no further.

I shuddered. If Maakuna thought I could be traded and sold that way, then I truly was less than nothing to him. I would have to succeed tonight and slip out before he drew me back into his so-called family. I knew he had power, but I wasn't sure how much weight his word had. I personally didn't trust him as far as I could throw that giant, bulbous creature.

We went back to the landing where Itzi was waiting for us, casually chatting with the woman from the stairs. She took off by the time I reached them, slipping out of the hallway and into one of the dark rooms.

"Right, time to plan a heist." Itzi winked at me. "Did you have fun?"

"What?"

"She punched him in the nose." Sonota laughed. "So, really, I'm the one who ended up having a good time."

Itzi's face broke into a huge grin, and he laughed too. "Oh, oh, this is too good! Did you hit him nice and hard?"

"He was bleedin'," Sonota cheered.

"That's incredible." Itzi slapped me on the back, hard, like I was one of the guys. The skin screamed under his touch, but I forced a smile. "That kid had it coming. The way he scribbles those marks on his face, like he's evading the cameras? Why the heck would they be looking for a prissy, middle-band rebel like him?"

Right about then, Mal stepped down the stairs onto the landing. There was a terse moment of silence as the three men eyed each other, ignoring me completely. Finally, Itzi and Sonota broke into laughter again. Mal stormed out the front door, slamming it behind him.

"Good for you," Sonota said squeezing my shoulder a little too tight. "You probably made more of a man out of him today than he was expecting."

"Yeah," Itzi added. "Though a swift kick could have done the same. I was all for shooting him."

"The boss isn't going to be happy," Sonota pointed out.

"So what?" I said, crossing my arms over my chest. My back smarted as I forced my spine straight and tall. "Mal won't tell him anything about this. He's a coward. He won't admit to not getting an easy lay that was handed to him on a plate, will he?"

Both men laughed at this, slapping my back one after the other. I guess this earned their trust or something. Go, man talk!

The bruise screamed at me. I told it to shut up.

"Right, come on," Itzi said, finally, opening the double doors behind him. They opened onto a conference room with a large steel table covered in maps and odd trinkets. He instructed me to sit down.

"Now, your job is to get to the ICP and implant this code into its matrix," he said bluntly, handing me what looked like a thick fridge magnet. "Do you know how this works?"

"No?"

He sighed, looking at his partner, who shrugged. With exaggerated gestures, he took the magnet back, held it up in front of my eyes, then stuck it to a small donut shaped box that sat on the table. And, just like a magnet, it stuck.

ALIENATION

"There, now you're in the system," Itzi said. "Is that too hard for you, or should I do the tutorial again?"

I scowled at him and ripped the magnet off the donut. "I've got it."

"Good," Sonota said, a smile creeping up his pale features. "We're putting the chip into this pocket mirror. Being as you're a girl, no one will suspect anything with you carrying it around."

"Right, because vanity is a feminine trait on every planet."

"Veesh, relax, Earth-wad," Sonota snapped, taking the magnet from my hand and putting it into a mirror. "Smile a little. It's just a stereotype."

I found myself losing my patience more and more with these two. Maybe Tchilla was right. Maybe I needed to be more patient, but I just wanted to get out of this place as quickly as I could.

"Now, you're going to enter here." Sonota pointed to a spot on the map. As he touched what I thought was paper, it suddenly came to life. The lights of the room dimmed as the glowing 3-D layout of the palace rose in the air before me. I held my breath. Sonota pointed to a gate outside the building, in front of an empty lawn. "You're going to have to socialize tonight," he continued, "and you know nothing of the royal ways. We were hoping the person we got would be more familiar with Da-Duhuian etiquette, but you'll have to do. Just … remind everyone you're new, and they should extend foreign leniency. Got that?"

"Tell everyone I just got here from Earth. Got it."

"Good." He smiled one of those false grins with his sharp shark teeth. "Avoid the Travoshella at all costs. You are not worthy of their presence. The signal will be a waiter with a green mask, on the north lawn. He's one of ours and will let you in."

"At that point," Itzi said, taking over the relay, "head around the back side of the palace. Do not let yourself be seen. You got that? Do. Not. Be. Seen. Hide in the shadows. You get caught back there, you'll have to lie through your eyeballs to get out. Actually, from that point on, that should be the general rule of thumb."

"Seems logical," I said, taking a page from Spock's book. Just sit there, nod, speak with poise. If anyone knew how to behave it would be the crew of the *Enterprise*. Too bad I didn't have any federation training.

"The kitchen entrance is hidden here," Sonota continued, pointing to the map with a lean fourth finger, "and that's your way in. Our man will leave the door open for you. It's a change in course, so most in the kitchen will be distracted. Now, you need to make it past the staff, but then the palace should be clear. Use the servant passages to get around. Take a little time to memorize them before we go. You're going to have to find your way to the ICP's main room, which is here."

In the middle of the map was a room with only one entrance and exit, and you had to climb through floors and floors of the most important building on the planet to get to it. He reached his hand into the hologram to show me this one. It was at the exact center of the palace, as if the place were a safe, not a building.

"No guards?" I asked.

"Only electrical," Sonota explained, "and we'll have them covered."

"That's why you have to wait for the waiter, dumbass," Itzi added.

"Also, hand them over," his partner said.

"What?"

"The smoke bombs." He held out a hand, raising his eyebrows slowly. "I scanned you. If I can spot them, then so will the gate guards. So, hand them over, or you're not going anywhere tonight."

"Except maybe back in a room with Mal-child. Heyo!"

I fumbled for the secret pocket at my hip and pulled out the small black pellets. I could run, I thought to myself. I could throw them right now and dash out of the room. I could grab a car and drive my way out of here. But before I could try anything, Sonota snatched them from me and put them down, hard, on the table. He handed me a replacement for them—a small, red purse.

"Don't you lose this," he added, as an afterthought. "The drive is inside the collapsible mirror, and the invite is on this cuff." Before I saw it coming, he snapped a metal bracelet around my arm. It pinched, hard.

I looked down at the copper ring. How was this meant to be an invite? It was more like a shackle. It didn't appear as if it would come off easily.

"And this is a loaner," Itzi said, tossing me a heavy crystal necklace. I caught it from the air and slipped it on, without even looking at what it was. It was damn heavy, that was for sure. I hung it above the Theosian's light-in-a-bottle. "The boss man wants it back. Once you've finished the mission and placed the chip in the computer, meet us outside in the parking lot. You'll return the necklace, and we, in return, will drive you anyplace you need to be. You can even keep the dress."

I nodded slowly, biting down hard on my molars. They were taking a bit of a beating tonight.

"Okay," I agreed.

I pushed myself up and studied the map. The palace looked large, with more rooms than I could count. It would be easier to memorize a single route than the entire layout. I would have to take a right here, a left there, go up a few floors and back down one to get around a pesky bedroom. I hated the fact that I was putting my life into the hands of two men I trusted less and less.

"Hurry up, then let's get going," Sonota said. He sighed. "We want to be fashionably late, but no later."

SEVENTEEN

WEBBER, SALLY WEBBER; INTERSTELLAR WOMAN OF MYSTERY

THERE WAS NO POINT IN DELAYING THE INEVITABLE.
We stepped outside into the darkness. Being this far down in the buildings, the sun set earlier, I guessed. Then again, I had lost track of time entirely, not that I ever had a concept of it on this planet.

There was a stretch limo parked along the street—a long hovercar as classy as a '50s Chevrolet, a deep chrome color reflecting the lights that bounced off it. Sonota ushered me inside, neither gently nor gruffly, a sort of neutral indifference in his pose that told me he didn't care about anything this evening, except maybe carrying out his boss's wishes.

The windows were tinted, so dark I couldn't see a thing outside. For that, I was incredibly thankful; I didn't want to see the plunging depths anymore. I had pushed myself enough with those already.

We began to rise, drifting upward this time rather than taking the vertical angle. I guessed some people could afford better cars, and Maakuna seemed like he could afford the best.

I hit the light on the ceiling, basking the car in a soft red glow. The compartment was closed, Itzi and Sonota having the partition raised to block me. That was fine. It gave me time to breathe.

I held up the cuff on my arm—an invitation to a ball, the most prestigious event of the year, the mayor's birthday. A party, and you know how I feel about parties. The copper shone in the red light, and I wondered how I would feel about this if I had been born and raised in Da-Duhui. I suspect I would have been over the moon, not that they had a moon, but right now, my stomach was tied in knots, and all I could think about was getting home.

Did I mention I don't like parties?

Though, admittedly, part of me was excited, at least a tiny bit. I had never been to a reception this fancy, and going to one on an alien planet, no less? It was somewhat sensational. Not to mention that I was well dressed, wearing an expensive gown and gorgeous jewelry, and expensive—

Crap. I wasn't wearing any shoes.

Should I say something? I scooted up the seat to the partition. Was it worth bringing it up? It was too late now, after all. And if no one had noticed yet, maybe they wouldn't notice at all.

ALIENATION

We stopped rising, and the car eased to a stop. Not a very long ride. When Itzi opened my door, I saw why: the mayor's palace was on top of the same building Maakuna's HQ was in, the same gorgeous mansion I had stared at from the restaurant the night before.

"Right," Itzi said, or was it Sonota? He put a hand on my shoulder to restrain me. "You've got the maps of the palace in mind, right?"

"Yup." I nodded.

"Remember to look for our signal before you go in there," he said, patting his breast pocket. It was not empty. "We'll distract security for you."

"Look, I know what to do," I said coolly. "Trust me."

"Wannabe," Itzi coughed into his hand. His partner sniggered.

I slipped out of the car onto soft grass. Perfect. My toes dug into the earth and clenched together nervously. The golden gown covered them well, and if anyone asked, I'd just say it was a Terran thing. Got away with it before.

"Go have fun, kid," Itzi said jokingly. I still couldn't tell if he meant it in a nice way or not. I had only met him a few hours ago.

For those of you with me since the beginning, you know I am not a person who enjoys parties. Not large ones, at least. Or parties where I don't know anyone. Or parties I have to dress up for. This party hit every single one of those boxes, and I was dreading it. But if it would get me out of here, I would bear it.

I walked toward the crowd gathering outside the gates of the building. They were all dressed as good as or better than me in gorgeous robes from every corner of the galaxy, a slew of humans, humanoids, and creatures so entirely new my vocabulary was too small to describe them.

There was a sentient cloud, though. They were shifting through shades of blue as they floated through the crowd toward the gate. A hovering copper cuff identical to mine hovered inside its girth. It slipped into the grounds with ease.

The line moved quickly. Only briefly there was a zap and a quick scream, someone trying to sneak in sans invite. A force field had appeared to block them, and now security was dealing with the party crasher, shoving us to the side and blocking off a section of the gate. I swallowed, hoping my bracelet was the right kind.

I guessed it was, though, because I walked in without any kind of fuss. I heard a small beep but that was it, and I was suddenly at the foot of the most beautiful building in the universe.

It stood as tall as St Peter's Basilica in the Vatican, an incredible feat of engineering perched atop the gigantic skyscrapers of the city, making me wonder how the crumbling foundations of the Undercity could hold up such a massive weight. The palace was lit with stunning colors, the front held up by impossibly tall columns, the roof a large white pyramid with a smooth, domed top. I held my breath at the stunning beauty of it all.

ALIENATION

On the front lawn, the party was in full swing. I stood in a lavish courtyard, packed with people from all corners of the galactic arm, chatting and mingling gaily to the sound of a heavy electronic beat. Bubbles in hundreds of different hues drifted across the grass casting an eerie glow, like they weren't filled with air but something different.

Some of them were larger, as big as me and bigger still, and inside were dancers, people with too many limbs, holding striking poses and unperturbed by the fact that they were rising above the crowd and the city. The bubbles never seemed to pop. The dancers wore fitted green body suits, adapted to their unique physiologies. In sync, there was a twitch from the appendages over their shoulders, and I realized with a jolt that the wings that stuck out the back were real and not part of the costume.

The rest of the crowd was just as varied as the pack I had followed in. Someone who looked like a giant quartz man stood fifteen feet tall and was stuffed into an expensive, yet ill-fitting suit, just to my left, was in deep conversation with a woman who looked human to me.

And all around us, there were trees. Actual trees. The first trees I had laid eyes on in days. They grew strong and tall out of the ground, garlands of light strung between them, like someone had put miniature stars on a string. I couldn't see any bulbs, yet the lights twinkled and sparkled. And, the closer I looked, I noted there were no strings there either. They were arranged to give off the impression that something held them together, but, no, they just hovered.

The courtyard was packed, all the lavish guests chatting to the sound of the strange pulsating music. In one corner of the party, colored vapor was sprayed into the air in time with the music, making the whole thing seem a little more artistic. Maybe it was a performance piece, but along with the bubbles and the lights, it felt a little overkill.

And speaking of overkill, the women wore dresses more inspired than the next, with strange geometric shapes and sometimes with a hat. Some dresses pushed the limits of public decency—and the laws of physics—with their interesting take on modesty.

Then again, no matter what they wore, they looked amazing. Just one outfit alone would have taken my breath away, but seeing so many together, in one place and at the same time, I couldn't take it all in even if I wanted to.

I stuck out, compared to the sea of people before me. My dress, a Tchilla original, was beautiful and everything I could have ever wanted, yet the person to my left was slowly changing color. Not just her clothes, but her skin as well. The shift started at her head and spread down her body then out through her limbs. And while there seemed to be a predominance of humans, every one of them somehow seemed to make their humanness seem special, sticking out from the crowd even though they didn't have fancy feathers or gorgeous scales.

ALIENATION

The person to my right had feline features. They clutched their glass in a tight grip, their paw wrapping around the stem, and stared down at me, ears up and pointing aggressively. Their body was all gentle curves, poised in such a way that I wondered if they were a dancer. I felt myself shrinking like Alice after eating the cookies, and I shuffled off before the stare burned a hole through my chest.

I was out of place and probably not the only one to have noticed it.

I just wanted to get this night over with. As much as space exploration was exciting and all, I'd already had enough of it. The novelty was wearing off, and exhaustion took its place. There was just too much going on for me to enjoy anything anymore. I wanted to complete the mission and leave, find Zander somehow—still hadn't worked that bit out—and have him bring me home. And then maybe I would sleep for a week.

Not to mention my unstable hand trying to keep my anxiety from spewing. Every few seconds, I'd get a clench in my gut, a reminder that panic was waiting, lurking. That I would let it through and break down right here in the middle of an alien gala.

I forced myself through my breathing exercises and focused on remaining in control. It was harder than it sounded.

I chose a vantage point near the oversized marble stairs of the palace, close to the canapés and hors-d'oeuvres they had set out. Little cups of foam exactly like those I had eaten for lunch sat on a long table, with different bits of colorful fruit sticking out. I wasn't a fan of those. I knew that from experience.

I walked to another table and grabbed a glass of some pink fizzing liquid and held it in my hand for effect. I wasn't planning on drinking any, having no idea what the beverage contained and feeling wary of the food I had eaten on this planet so far. Now, I needed to mingle, to show I was here for the people and not for an ulterior motive.

Trying not to look shifty over here.

I wandered around the grass, trying to avoid conversation, and to check out some aliens without drawing any attention to myself. The quartz man was subtly trying to kiss a humanoid, but it involved much leaning down and leaning in, and every time he did he seemed to knock someone else out of the way. So he'd straighten up, adjust his shirt, and try again. All the while, the person he was trying to kiss had no idea, being in deep conversation with the sentient patch of gas. The gas now had three olive-shaped things hovering along with the bracelet.

Out of nowhere, a gelatinous blob rose from the ground, growing and forming before me until it was a seven-foot-tall, fifty-armed, semi-translucent mass of a being. It waved the arms at me in harmony.

"Hi, nice to meet you," I said, already too late to run from its presence.

ALIENATION

The creature waved its arms, frustrated. Somewhere in my mind, I knew it wanted to communicate, to say hello, to point out how the two of us were similar in our isolation from the rest of the event.

But I could not respond. My translator said nothing, did nothing to my own voice as I opened it to say hello. My fingers twitched by my side.

Awkward.

Worse than awkward—I wasn't supposed to be here! How was I sure I wasn't giving them an act of war toward Earth?

"The Guengeron don't have ears," said a voice from my left. "They use sign language."

"I don't have enough arms," I replied, not taking my eyes away from what I *thought* might be the Guengeron's irises—two small black olives that floated in the space that had no appendages.

"No one here does," said the stranger. I turned around to see a Roswell gray—well, green, actually—all large head and bulbous black-brown eyes. "Diplomacy has been slow and tedious. Give it a bow. At least show it you respect it."

I made eye contact and bowed. The blob melted into the lawn once more.

"You new on this planet?" asked the stranger. Their eyes blinked slowly, green lids coming down over black tennis balls, and I stood back, feeling an odd sense of recognition. They wore a uniform of some kind, a purple so deep it almost looked as black as their eyes, covered with small triangular pins in different metals.

I straightened and smiled. It would be weird if I ran away now, especially since they had just helped me out, so I was going to have to make conversation.

Insert internal groaning here.

"Hello to you," I replied politely. "Yes, this is my first time to Da-Duhui. I'm from … no, I'm the ambassador from Earth. Pleasure to make your acquaintance."

"Earth, eh?" they said, awkwardly shifting their weight from foot to foot. "Pretty out there, isn't it? Is it even in the Alliance?"

It was tough to decipher their expression, what with their reptilian features. If they were human, I would say they really needed to go to the bathroom. But it was hard to read a lizard, and I hadn't seen enough Futurama to know what Commander Kiff's body language meant.

"Not yet," I replied. "I'm surprised you've heard of it. Everyone I talk to seems to have no idea it exists."

"So why would you," they said, scrutinizing me, I think, "an ambassador from a planet that's not even an outpost, be invited to the mayor's party?"

"Ha, I don't even know!" I said, laughing to mask my terror as I tried to come up with some believable excuse. "I left my planet during an exchange program. Next thing you know, boom: only Terran in the Alliance, so suddenly I'm an ambassador. I think the mayor just liked the novelty of it. Of me, I mean. I was surprised to get the invitation myself, but you can't pass up an opportunity like this."

"You're not a child hire, then?"

"No way," I replied, desperately trying to figure out what he meant by that. "No, it was all very official."

"Good!" They smiled, and for a second I thought their face looked joyful. "Imagine how embarrassing it would be if the mayor had accidentally invited one of them."

"Yeah, totally," I agreed.

"I'm Sekai No-Oji. Killian High Commandress," she said, bowing deeply. And that's when it hit me.

"Holy shit!" I said, before I realized the words had left my mouth. She laughed, as if I had told a fantastic joke.

"Excuse me?" she said, seemingly taking no offense. Not that I could be sure.

"You're Killian." I grinned. "I actually know a few Killians. I met your prime minister, and I…"

I stopped right there. I'm sure, from their side of things I wasn't the greatest person. Well, the me who helped their rescue maybe was, but the one who had pretended to be Blayde and crashed their ship into the Atlantic probably wasn't all that popular.

"What did you say your name was?" she asked, her eyes widening.

"I didn't," I said. "It's Sally. Sally Webber. Enchanté."

"You're Sally Webber?" She stepped back, seemingly in shock. "*The* Sally Webber?"

"Yes, I—"

"*Grimosh*," she sputtered, taking the words right from my mouth. "You were with them. You're her!"

"I'm me, what?"

"When the"—her voice dropped to a whisper—
"siblings, when they rescued me from Earth. They said
there was a human with them. A Terran. Her name was
Webber, too. Was that…?"

I nodded slowly, and she opened her mouth wide,
letting out an actual croak. Her breath smelled of flies
and fish, so not pleasant. But she was so ecstatic I
couldn't exactly ask her to close it.

"You saved my life!" she sputtered. "You and…
them. You brought me home. I can't believe I didn't
recognize you before. It's been five years, but you never
forget the face of the person who… wow. And meeting
you here, of all places!"

"Five years?" I asked. "It's only been two for me.
Theory of relativity or something, but…"

I froze as it hit me. Five years. If it had taken Zander
and Blayde two years to get back to me, was it possible
three years had passed on Earth when we had come to
Da-Duhui? Had I been missing from Earth for so long?

Or were they just measuring time differently? I wasn't
sure how my translator worked when it came to talking
time or dates. It didn't exactly come with a manual. Or
maybe it did when you weren't stealing it off an assassin
who got what was coming to him at the hands of your
roommate.

I shuddered. I thought I would be gone for a few
days, not a few years. If I really was missing… oh shit,
what had I done?

ALIENATION

"I just can't believe, of all the places in the universe, that I'd run into you—of all people—here." She smiled warmly. "We missed you at the banquet."

"I missed the trip," I said, putting all other thoughts from my mind. No, I had to get through this night, then I could worry about repercussions for my travel. "I was busy elsewhere. Beating up the guy who held you captive."

"And you got him?"

"He's very, very dead," I replied. Speaking freely about it was weird. For the past two years, it had been my biggest secret. After all, who goes around telling their friends they murdered their boss, who was an alien and a murderer himself, and blew up their workplace? Not very popular water cooler conversation.

"Thank you," she said, bowing again. "I'm ashamed I have nothing to repay you with."

"Tell you what." I pulled my phone out of one of the dissimulated pockets. "Let me have a picture with you, to commemorate our meeting."

"A… picture?"

"A photograph?" I said. She seemed confused. "An image, freezing time."

"Is it dangerous?"

"Not at all," I said, holding up the phone. She watched herself on the screen, jumping slightly from foot to foot as she had before.

"Oh! I have seen these. The Alliance uses them."

"You're not Alliance?"

"Not yet," she replied. "We're trying to sign an accord. That's why I'm here."

"Impressive!" I said and took the picture. It looked hauntingly fake. "Best of luck!"

"Look, I owe you my life," she said, as I pulled away, "so if there's ever anything I can do—"

"Well, actually, there might be," I said, inspiration hitting me like a lightning bolt. "If you happen to see Zander here tonight, or Blayde—"

"Shh!" She reached her hand to cover my mouth but thought better of it. She pulled back hastily. "Never say their names here," she said. "They're not very popular. But if I do happen to see them."

"Thank you." Relief gnawed at my heart. Another person on my side.

"Grimosh!" she exclaimed. A swear so strong we had no translation. "She's walking this way."

"Who is?" I asked, trying to follow her gaze.

"Travoshi." She shuddered. "Or, should I say, the Travoshella. The mayor's wife. She's coming right at us. At you."

EIGHTEEN

MAKING FRIENDS IN HIGH PLACES, ON TOP OF HIGH BUILDINGS

THE WOMAN FORCED HER WAY TOWARD ME, striding powerfully along with her entourage surrounding her, fanning out like her very own peacock tail. Her dress looked almost like the ones worn in Versailles when France still had a king. It brought her human waist in tight, though the fabric was quite generous around her ample bosom. As she drew nearer, I could tell she had at least a foot on me, though that could be from her extremely high heels, which seemed to keep her feet on ballerina pointe.

Her hair was pure white, though her face didn't look a day past forty. The hair was held up at four points that hovered around her scalp, giving the impression that it was defying gravity—though it was cheating, unlike Zander's, which actually did.

And even from that far away, I could tell she was coming right at me. There was no doubt about it. I stood my ground, afraid that if I ran or showed any sign of weakness, she might call a chase and I would somehow be found out.

This could not be happening. I didn't want to draw any attention, not with the plans I had in store for the evening. I could not have this woman calling me out before I had a chance to carry out my part of the bargain. I couldn't get kicked out, or worse, thrown in whatever jail they had. Not yet, not now.

But her skin—oh my gosh, her skin—was as dark as the night sky but glowed like the sun. It had small diamonds inlaid in intricate patterns, like constellations on her face. Her arms wore physical jewelry, but the gems on her face seemed almost as if they had grown there. And yet, the brightest part of her face was her eyes: bright blue, an electric color unlike anything I had seen in this city.

"Your Ladyship," I said, in awe and in terror, bowing low and hoping my translator was bringing my words up in the correct context. "It is truly an honor to meet you."

"My, my," she said, flashing teeth sharpened to a razor's edge. "What do we have here? A Killian envoy and a new face amongst our midst. A face so new, in fact, that I don't recall seeing it on the invitations."

"I-I only received my invitation today," I stammered. Shit. The words I did not want to hear. "I assumed it was a last minute change of plans. The bracelet did not have a sender ... that I know of."

"How peculiar," she said, and just like that she moved on. "Is this your first time at an official soiree of ours?"

All eyes of her entourage were fixed on me. Who were these people? To her left stood a young woman with those same electric blue eyes, though with only a single gem on her face, just below her eye, like a tear. Her daughter, maybe?

"It is," I said, feeling my lips dry and crackle as I spoke. "I am an envoy from Earth. We're new to ... all this."

"Earth, you say?" I nodded. "Never heard of it. It's not part of the Alliance, is it?"

"No, ma'am."

"Trooq?"

"No, sorry."

"Union? The Order?"

"I'm sorry, ma'am. We're pre-contact," I stammered. "I am here as part of a social experiment."

"She saved my life, Your Ladyship," Sekai piped up. "She has been invited off-world as a gift from me."

She put a hand defensively on my shoulder, and I felt nothing but trust for her. I had no idea which of the Killian prisoners she had been. They had all looked the same: sick, dying, gray-colored rather than the vibrant green shade she gave off now. But I had saved that skin, and now, she was going to save mine.

"This … Earth," said the Travoshella, mouthing the word like it left a bad taste in her mouth, "is it part of your corner of the galaxy, Killian?"

"It has an Alliance outpost in orbit," she said, surprising the Travoshella. "A small terminal, popular for tourism and for people who like high-risk travel."

"How delightful," the Travoshella said, in a tone that made it sound like the news was anything but. "A tourist hot spot. How quaint. You don't usually see any of those at our parties."

Sekai's grip on my shoulder tightened, though it didn't seem conscious on her part. But I knew what she meant. I was on thin ice. I felt it too. I had to think fast, as if there was any kind of slow thinking on this trip.

"Your Ladyship," I said, solemnly, reaching up to my ears. "I asked my dear friend here to take me to you this evening. Even as far as Earth, we have heard tales of your beauty. I specifically wanted to meet you. And, of course, to give you these."

My silver earrings. The ones I had gotten as a birthday gift from Grammy. They were simple hoops, but they were all I had. And they were worth much, much more on this planet.

"I came bearing gifts of rarest silver. I hope you can accept these as a gift from all Earth-kind."

Her eyes bulged as she saw the earrings in the palm of my hand. A man jumped forward instantly, taking them from me before I could utter a word. He held them up to the light, as one of the bubble dancers drifted overhead. She waved at him, and he ignored her, intent on the metal.

"They're real," he said, shocked.

"It is as precious on Earth as it is here in the Alliance," I lied. "I speak for all the people of Earth when I say that these are meant as a symbol of peace and prosperity."

"Incredible," she said then restored her face to factory settings. "Your gift pleases me. The fact you brought them to me and not the president symbolizes you are much smarter than you appear."

There was a president involved in all this? Oh boy.

"Your Ladyship's will is my command," I said, bowing again. She nodded and smiled.

"Walk with me," she ordered, wrapping her arm around my shoulder and practically shoving Sekai away. The latter gave me a worried glance. At least, I think it was worried. I tried to speak to her with my eyes, to share my panic. Either she got the gist of it or was thinking it herself, but she joined us, walking on my right side like my own personal bodyguard. I felt relief wash over me.

"Tell me about your planet," she said, cooing. "Is silver plentiful there?"

"Oh, no, ma'am," I replied, trying not to stare at her face-diamonds. They glistened under the hovering lights, beautiful in the dim. "It is the rarest of all Earth metals. It is in such short supply that we keep every piece of it in a single vault. It would fit in the palm of your hand."

"Oh my." She gasped. "What a gift!"

She seemed different now, almost giddy. She tapped my shoulder as we walked, like I was her pet. I didn't know where to look that would not offend her, so I stared right ahead.

"My planet has many cities," I said, waving a hand wide. "We have many trees and oceans, but we have no cars that fly."

"How primitive," she gushed. "Tell me, are they civilized?"

"When they want to be," I said, and she laughed. The second she did, her entourage joined, almost robotically. Ha-ha. Ha-ha. Ha-ha. Sekai stiffened at my side.

"And you saved this Killian's life?"

"It's a long story," I replied.

"We crash-landed there," Sekai explained, "and she was the one to find us. She defeated the man keeping us captive and helped us return home."

"What a heroic act." She grinned. "If the people of Earth are like you, then we should talk more about contact."

Shit. I wasn't going to be responsible for this. I was just trying to break into a palace, not create diplomatic relations with alien nations. I wasn't an ambassador, no matter how many times I said I was.

"They are in talks already," I lied. "The … um … agency … is going to bring us in when the rest of the population is ready. But we must not speak of it."

"Of course. Your secret is safe with me. Oh, hello, it's Gramha'ak! I am sorry, child, but I must go. But know that the Da-Duhui high council are now friends of the people of Earth. Fare thee well!"

She and her entourage split, trotting across the lawn toward the giant quartz monster. He had obviously managed to make his advances known to the other alien, as they were now perched on his shoulder, leaning against his giant rock head and laughing and waving gaily.

"What on earth just happened?" I muttered.

"Not on Earth," Sekai shuddered, "but yeah. That's the Travoshella for you. You should be happy. She has never given me anywhere near that amount of face time."

"Did I accidentally start diplomatic relations between Earth and the Alliance?"

"Don't worry about it," she replied. "I'm sure she'll have forgotten about any of this in a few hours. Hey, are you all right?"

I reached up to my face and felt wetness. Shit. "I'm fine."

"No, you're not. You're leaking!"

"It's stress," I said. It wasn't a lie. The exhaustion was seeping out of my eyes, and it took everything to keep the tears from rolling down my face. "I needed to find my friends. This is too much. This is not what I signed up for."

"Hey, hey," she said, reaching out her hand for my shoulder again. I thought the Killians were reptilian, but when she touched my skin, her hand was warm. "What's wrong? What happened?"

"I was … I was supposed to be on a vacation," I said, wishing I had something to wipe my eyes with. "I waited two whole years for a day off Earth, and I can't even handle it. I got lost within a few hours, and now I've gotten into … I'm not even sure what yet."

"Hey, space is like that," Sekai offered. "I went to set up a scientific survey of a small planet teeming with life. I woke up three thousand years later in a madman's torture chamber. That's the price you pay for leaving home, for wanting more than the sky you were born under."

I said nothing. I wanted to sit down. My bare feet were getting cold now.

"Look," she said, "leaving home is always fraught with danger. It's how we get out of it and who we are when we come back that matters. I was a scientist when I left my home planet. Now, I'm an ambassador. I fight for environmental protection in my home state. I used to hate crowds, and now I speak in front of them every other day."

"You do?"

"The universe is a big, somewhat indifferent place," she continued. "Or, at least, that's what everyone tells themselves. It is better that the one universe we know be indifferent to our problems rather than knowing and deciding not to do anything in our favor, right? It'll throw things at you to knock you down. And it's not going to stop. Accept that and move on. Learn to dodge and fight back."

ALIENATION

"I'm trying."

"Yes, you are." She smiled at me now, tightening her grip on my shoulder. "Don't give up. It's not time to give up."

"Thank you. I'm sorry. I have to do something that's not going to be pretty."

"Don't get me involved." She let out a small laugh. "Well, unless you really need me, but please don't ruin my chance with the Alliance. Not while I'm giving out free life advice."

"I won't."

"I'll see you around, Sally Webber." She patted me on the head and removed her hand entirely. "Hopefully in nicer circumstances."

Circumstances in which I wasn't about to break into an alien palace, but anyway. "I hope so, too,"

She was the one who left, grabbing a pink bubbly on the way. I realized that I was still holding mine and hadn't touched it. I chugged it without thinking. It tasted like a peach Bellini, which was a pleasant surprise, but I remembered as I finished the glass that I didn't want more food from here. I walked over to the bushes and spat out what I could.

I turned around just in time to make eye contact with a waiter, recognizing him as the contact who would leave the kitchen door open for me. My heart clenched. It was time for the main event.

Past this point, if I was caught it was over. Hopefully they wouldn't hear my pounding heart, but this was the only way for me to get home. My one shot. There were probably better ways to get things accomplished, more legal ways, but at this point it was my last resort.

I put down the glass on one of the little tables and trotted into the shadows of the palace, away from the people and noise, around the side where nothing was happening. If the map Maakuna had given me was correct, I was heading toward the servants' entrance. When I got there, though, I couldn't see a thing.

I felt my way around. No door, just clinging ivy on the stone façade.

What was I meant to do now? I tried pulling up the map from memory, thinking back to where else I had seen a way in except the grand entrance, but no luck.

Before I had time to contemplate how to sneak through the front, the waiter brushed past me, muttering something under his breath. And just like that, he was gone, slipping into the wall like he had never been there.

Shit, this was platform 9 ¾, wasn't it?

Right. I shook myself down. Clearing all thoughts from my brain, I stepped forward and through the wall.

Instantly my world exploded with noise. I had walked into a noisy kitchen, a kitchen so large it stretched further than my eye could see. It was lit by strong industrial bulbs and smelled strongly of pineapple and onions. Rows of metal tables ran the length of the room that were covered in food from every corner of the Alliance: baskets full of blue fruit; plates laden with what looked like dried rats; glowing, crispy buckets of chicken identical to those I could find at KFC, though the buckets were made of what looked like bronze.

The wait staff fretted about, picking up the baskets and plates before rushing out of the kitchen through a slew of invisible doors. They paid no attention to me, of course, being too busy getting the food and drinks to the guests.

The food made my stomach rumble, and I slapped my belly to keep it quiet. No way was I eating anything else from here.

The foam I had nibbled on at lunch had done nothing for me, but it hadn't tried to kill me either. If I only had one little chicken leg—

No. Maybe it wasn't chicken. Maybe it was some other kind of alien thing intent on my doom. I shook the idea out of my head. No, I wasn't falling in that trap.

I snuck out of the kitchen, which was an impressive feat, seeing as how long the room was. On paper—or in hologram—it hadn't taken up so much space, but it took me at least ten minutes to slink out of there. At the end, there was a real door propped open by a crate of rectangular bottles, which I tiptoed around.

From here, I was lucky. The servants' corridors led practically everywhere in the house. I would, should, be able to get to a room adjacent to the ICP from here. I walked straight for twenty meters, found the promised staircase, walked up two flights, then stepped out onto the landing. So far, so good.

There ended my streak of good luck, though. Two of the waiters were making out in the hallway in front of me. I mean, full face sucking and everything.

Literally.

The woman's face was wrapped around her partner's, her lips stretched out like Alien's, wrapped entirely around her partner's head, pulling them into the embrace. For a second I froze, panicking, wondering if she was kissing her partner or eating them, but the partner grabbed her rear, giving it a tight squeeze, and she removed her face slightly, laughing. Underneath, her partner, covered in slobber, laughed too, issuing a small giggle as they gasped for breath, then they went right back to kissing the smaller lips on her second jaw as her first jaw returned to holding him close.

As gross as they were, I probably could have made it around them without them noticing, if it weren't for the fact that the hallway was too small to let me pass. I slunk back into the thin, winding staircase, going down one floor. Here, at least, the hallway was empty, but I would have to improvise from there. I stepped through one of the staff passageways and into the lavish home of this planet's mayor.

There was a sharp contrast between this house and the corridor. I had gone from plastic wood to stone marble, the walls infused with streaks of silver and iron in swirling patterns that seemed impossible. The room I was in was draped entirely in animal hides, some furry, some scaly, all equally unrecognizable. I shuddered as I slipped into the main hallway.

ALIENATION

It was calm. Everyone was out at the party, so there was no one to stop me. I wasn't even going for jewels or anything, so the security wouldn't be tipped off. There would be no alarms for me to break. At least, none that were marked on the palace's blueprints.

After a few false starts and dead-ends, I finally reached it: the grand atrium. Large enough to fit my parents' house comfortably, the wide room boasted a large double stone staircase that crisscrossed around the walls before leading to a landing a few stories above.

The only light came through the huge windows behind me, but they were covered in banners celebrating the mayor's birthday. All that trickled in were party lights, so the place looked dark and orange, casting long shadows everywhere.

It probably looked astounding in the daylight, but the darkness made it gloomy and imposing. Maybe a little creepy, too, though you wouldn't see me admitting that I was scared of a room to anyone. Not after the day I'd had.

I started up the staircase, careful to be as quiet as I could. My feet were cold against the bare marble. There were no carpets here, only lavish paintings in the stone. The entire thing was as chilly as walking on snow.

And it was quiet, oh so quiet. Every step I made sounded soft in the large room, but, the fact was, you could hear it. If there were a fly in here, I could have heard it buzz from any point in that room. Which is why I jumped when I heard a voice.

NINETEEN

IN WHICH I AM RESCUED BY MY OWN GEEKERY

SHIT. I SHOULD HAVE EXPECTED SOMETHING LIKE this to happen.

But who expects to find a six-year-old in a silk nightgown waiting for you at the top of the stairs?

She was adorable and tiny, but even so, the resemblance was uncanny. Her dark face and bright, blue eyes were just as intimidating as her mother's.

"Who are you?" she asked, her voice light yet commanding. Another sign I was talking to the daughter of the most powerful woman in the city.

I had to think fast. Nothing had prepared me for this. I was ready for guards or guests, not a child who was supposed to be in bed.

"Amy Pond," I said with as much assurance as I could muster. I walked up to meet the girl on the landing. Why her name was the first thing to come to mind, I didn't

ALIENATION

know, but it was a good thing I wasn't trying to break into Buckingham Palace with that kind of Doctor Who-inspired alibi.

"You're not one of daddy's guests, are you?" she asked. "Why are you in my house? And why are you … barefoot?"

Of all the people to notice, it would be her. Her eyes were wide and demanding, and I knew that any second she could call the guards and have me thrown into a dark jail cell.

But she was a child. I just had to keep her occupied.

"I'd rather not say," I said dramatically, heaving a huge breath. "It's silly."

"Silly?" she said, her voice rising to a higher pitch. "Why would it be silly?"

"Well, it's an old … Vulcan … tradition," I replied, spewing BS with every word. "You wouldn't understand."

"Sure I would!" She stomped her foot.

"That's right," I said, spreading a cautious grin on my face. "You're a big girl. You understand everything."

"I am!" she exclaimed, though I couldn't tell if she was impressed or flattered, but her eyes were growing wider by the second.

"I still can't tell you," I said. "I'm not allowed."

"Go on. I order you to tell me. I order you!"

She stomped her foot, hard, on the marble of the landing. The sound echoed through the grand hall like an elephant stepping on a balloon.

S.E.ANDERSON

"Fine then," I said, trying not to flinch at her terrifying voice. She was older than her years, at least in her commanding presence, but I knew that I had her. "Back on Vulcan, when we meet someone new, we walk around their homes without any shoes on to walk in the steps of their ancestors. It's all very ceremonial. I just didn't want to bother anyone with my weird customs."

She blinked at me twice and frowned. "That's stupid. Ancestors don't leave footsteps behind. They take them with them, so they can use them again in heaven."

"But if you can fly in heaven, why would you need feet?"

"So you can wear pretty shoes, silly."

She crossed her arms over her chest and grinned like she had just proved it to me with the highest, smartest logic there is.

"You're so clever. Much cleverer than I am. How did you get so smart?"

"I have fifteen tutors. I'm nowhere near as smart as a Berbabsywell monk. Father says they're the smartest, but he says I'm close. I just have to know everything. They know everything there is to know, and then some. So he says."

"Do they now?" I said, feigning interest.

She nodded excitedly. "They know when the universe started and when it's going to end, but they don't tell anyone. It's a secret."

"That's fascinating," I said, giving Amy Pond the same vocabulary as her Vulcan roots. Pretty sure there's a fan fiction out there that might be more expansive.

ALIENATION

"Are you scared of anything, Ka Pond?" she asked, her face dropping. Her tone switched within seconds from her thrilled command to a trembling terror. "Like, really, really scared?"

"That depends." I crouched to her level. "Are you scared, um …"

"Lana," she said, her voice lowering to a whisper. "My name is Lana. And yes … I'm scared."

"What of?"

"The monsters."

Holy shit. Yes, of course I was scared. I had met a few monsters in my lifetime, and not just the ones on this planet. But she was a kid, and monsters suck.

I smiled as soothingly as I could. "What monsters?"

"The ones in father's office."

"You were probably having a nightmare."

"But I saw them," she snapped, stomping and sending the room rattling.

"What did they look like?"

"They were big," Lana replied. "Tall. They had sharp teeth, but they didn't see me. They don't know I saw them."

"Lana," I said, holding out my hand, "would you like for me to check with you? I'm not scared of monsters. And if you get scared, all you have to remember is that I'm not scared, so you won't be either."

I tried to remember what my mother did when I was scared, but came up dry. No, when I was scared as a kid, it was John who came in. Every time, he brought a bottle of what I now know to be Windex, claiming the monsters were allergic to it. One day, when I asked him why, he printed out a scientific paper about why monsters and Windex don't mix, a fake paper he spent a whole day writing just to make me feel better.

I pushed the memory from my mind. I didn't want to think about John at a time like this. I was busy, and I was losing time trying to get this kid off me.

"What will you do to them?" she asked, her voice falling to the level of a whisper.

"Well, first," I improvised, "I'll use my super Vulcan scream to yell at them. Then, I'll tickle them until they promise to leave you alone forever. How does that sound?"

"Then you'll kill them?" she pushed.

"Kill them? Why would I do that?"

"My father says that anyone who's not with us is against us, and everyone against us must die." Her face was expressionless.

"Your father doesn't seem big on mercy then."

"He says mercy's for turncoats and the weak."

"I would rather like to meet your father."

"When you get rid of the monsters, I'll tell him to give you a silver medal."

"Yes, about these monsters." I gulped. "Let's go find them."

Okay, I was getting off the plan here, but keeping the girl happy was probably my ticket out of trouble if I ran into any guards. Not that explaining any of this would help my cause. So long as I kept her busy, though, she wouldn't be able to put me in any trouble.

"This way." She reached for my hand and clung to it. "Come on."

I played my part as best I could. I took her small hand in mine and followed her through the palace trying to keep track of all the turns, but after a few minutes of this, I knew I'd never find my way back. This place was too confusing.

We stopped in front of a large door—made of Lithorn wood, I proudly recognized—and froze. She touched the knob then thought better of it and pulled her hand back.

"They're in there," she whispered.

I played along, lowering my voice too. "What makes you say that?"

"I can hear them. Can't you?"

I pretended to listen, cupping my free hand around the door so I could prop my ear against it. I scrunched my face in concentration. It was all for the show, but this wasn't making her feel any better. She was petrified. With a jolt, I realized why—I could hear voices, too.

I stumbled back, clutching her hand tighter. They were harsh, male voices. There was some rummaging going on in there, too. These were not her parents or any guards. These were intruders.

Like me, I guessed, but I wasn't trying to steal anything.

"Lana, we need to get you to bed."

"Why?" she asked, cocking her head sideways. "Aren't you going to kill them?"

I looked down at the little girl in her white nightgown. Her expression reminded me of when I was her age, only I had never been raised in royalty and had never been confronted with this situation before. But whatever the world, we were the same at that age—we needed someone there for us. I had needed John to deal with my night terrors, and she needed me to keep her from these men while her parents were managing diplomacy at the gala.

I held my breath. Trying to protect her would surely mean calling security and getting me in trouble. I could always lie and take her back to bed and do my own mission afterward, leaving whoever this was to finish their dirty work in silence.

"Yes," I said, "but you're going to have to hide. I don't want you to get hurt. If you go to bed now, I can kill them without having anyone know."

"I won't get hurt. I want to see you beat them up." She tightened her grip on my hand, and I realized she was much stronger than me. It felt like she was going to crush my bones.

"Please," I said, slightly too harsh. "I can't let you get hurt."

"I order you to let me stay." Her voice reminded me of her mother's. "I order you."

"I …" I couldn't let her get hurt, even if she wasn't going to let me get away so easily. "Fine. But I have to

ALIENATION

admit something to you. This is a dream. A really scary one. You can stay and watch, but you have to stay hidden, okay? And as soon as you get too frightened, you want out. You know what you have to do?" She shook her head. "You have to run as fast as you can back to your room, pull the covers over your head, and stay there. Then you'll wake up. Can you do that?" She nodded vigorously. "Okay."

I pushed the door open. Her hand squeezed mine. And there they were.

They heard the door open and turned to face us, pulling out what looked like silver guns. Lana scrambled to safety behind my skirt.

I didn't know what I was expecting, but it certainly wasn't them. Itzi and Sonota glared at me. Three thoughts raced through my mind all at once: One, this scene looked exactly like a movie I had seen, but couldn't place. Two, they had guns, but they looked like our guns, Earth guns, and not something fancier or more high-tech, which was lame. And three, this could very possibly be the last thing I saw in my life.

"What are you two doing here?" I sputtered. Lana took off that second, pushing off my skirt and dashing down the hallway. I didn't watch her go, trying not to draw any attention to her. With some luck, neither of the men had spotted her.

And she wouldn't have seen them recognize me.

"What are you doing here?" Sonota—I think—spat. It was harder to tell them apart in this awful lighting than it had been earlier when I could actually see them. "You are supposed to be on the other side of the palace."

"And you were supposed to wait for me to finish the job."

"The job?" They looked at each other and laughed. "You really think you were the one doing the job?"

"Wannabe," one said, coughing into his hand. Ah. So that was Itzi.

"What the hell are you talking about?" I sputtered, forcing myself to stand my ground. If I ran now, they would kill me for sure, not that staying here was any smarter. The truth formed in my head, but I needed to hear them say it—to waste time, or to save it.

"Man, just shoot her," Sonota spat. "She's no use to us. It's too late for her to play her part."

"Woah, woah, woah! Hold on there!" I said, frantically trying to add a few minutes to my increasingly shortening lifespan. "You want to kill me, fine. But tell me why first. I don't want to die in the dark."

I could see why people in movies said that kind of shit. It was all I could come up with to stop them from shooting me on the spot. It wasn't likely to work, but who knew? Maybe the two of them were as dim-witted as I pegged them to be. I was counting on it.

"You want to know why?" Sonota laughed, clutching his chest like I had just told a joke. "You're not going to beg for mercy? You're just going to ask us why?"

"Well," I said, "I know you two are going to kill me. That's inevitable. You're too intelligent to let me go, and I can see there's no other option."

ALIENATION

Shit. Now I was treating them like Lana. Maybe I was shaving minutes off my life rather than adding to it.

"Veesh, yeah, we're intelligent," Itzi boasted, much to my surprise.

"So the only thing … the only thing I ask for, in my last minutes, is the truth."

"Well, I don't see how that could hurt," Sonota said, cocking his gun sideways like he was a gangster in a bad movie. The barrel glinted in the party light. "You see, Maakuna doesn't give a shit about robots. That was just a ploy to bring you into the game. He's after something much, much more valuable."

"He is?" My eyes widened. I didn't have to fake my surprise. "What is it?"

"The mayor's private passcode," Itzi interjected, "giving Maakuna—and the entire organization—direct control over the ICP. We can take over the city's budgets and authority without using the robots as our middlemen. Much more secure than their faulty programming."

"I was a distraction then?"

"You were the fail-safe. If the alarm went off, you would be the one they found. Not us. We'd be out of here in seconds."

I swallowed, hard. I knew I couldn't trust Maakuna, but I still felt betrayed. I wasn't going to give up so easily.

"Strange," I said, reaching a hand to scratch my head. "That's exactly what Maakuna said to me when I accepted this plan."

"What?" they asked, almost simultaneously. Their eyes widened.

"That's right," I said. "He told me I was the one doing the important bit. He was worried you two knew too much about the organization, so he set you up to be patsies."

The two of them looked at me like I had sprouted two heads. I gave them a sly smile, like I was somehow in control of this.

"Is she telling the truth?" Itzi asked his partner, leaning to him to whisper but not making his voice quiet enough.

"I don't know."

"Maybe we should kill her for good measure," Itzi proposed.

"I can hear you, you know," I said. "Maybe Maakuna was playing us both. He wanted both jobs done, but one would suffice. In the unlikely event that one of us would get caught, the other plan could go on without a hitch. And all without us being able to tell the authorities about it."

"Or maybe," Sonota said, with a smirk, "he didn't care which investment paid off. Maybe he was happy with either one. So now we can do what we were told to do when you got back to the car and kill you."

"Really? What a coincidence! I was, too."

Not a coincidence.

"You were told to kill yourself at the car?"

"No, I was told to kill you," I sneered. "Both of you."

ALIENATION

"Really?" Itzi wasn't quite getting this. "But the boss man said—"

"Frash the boss man," Sonota snapped. "Shut up, Itzi. You sound like a child. She's frashing lying."

"Why would I lie to you?" I said, placing my arms akimbo and taking up as much of the doorframe as I could. I watched their silhouettes shuffle uncomfortably. "I've only just met you. I have no reason to mess with you. Maakuna has done enough of that already, with both of us."

I was starting to believe my own rhetoric. I forced that confidence onto my face, not sure if they could see it or not.

"Come on," Sonota scoffed. "You just don't want to die. You'll say anything right now."

"Oh please." I let out a cold laugh I didn't know I was holding in. "I was living in the Undercity. I've seen death and stared it in the face. You don't think I've contemplated it? I'm ready to die. What about you?"

Dead. Silence.

The room was so quiet that I almost imagined someone had hit the mute button on life. The two men didn't move an inch. They stood tall and hostile, but unwavering. There was not enough light coming off the party for me to see if my words had hit home.

Finally, Itzi broke the spell.

"She's serious, man," he said, leaning over to whisper like he had before, still too loud to be inconspicuous.

"I know she is. Now shut the hell up."

"Oh," his voice faltered.

Which was exactly when a bright light turned on outside, spilling into the room and hitting my eyes like lemon juice. It burned bright, a blue that was almost white, and it hurt like the dickens. I tried to move, but I was trapped, not even feeling my own feet. The rest of my body stiffened.

And then came the voice, loud and stern, followed by a high-pitched wail punctuating every word.

"This is the mayoral police," she barked, the sound like crashing icebergs. "Put down your weapons. Place your arms, tentacles, and all other primary appendages above your head or in the air, whichever is applicable."

Lana. She had gone to her father rather than going to bed. I could almost imagine the little girl dashing across the crowded lawn in her nightgown, rushing to her father to tell him about the monsters in his office. She had never believed this was a dream. Or maybe she did but needed her father for solace, except he would have known this wasn't a nightmare.

The police had come to arrest the monsters and maybe even save her Amy Pond, only I didn't feel like I was being saved. I felt more trapped than ever.

Itzi and Sonota were deep in conversation, ignoring the orders the woman repeated through the light in the window. Finally, Itzi understood the concept of whispering, and for once, when I actually needed to, I had no idea what they were saying.

ALIENATION

"Are you turning yourselves in now?" I spat. "Who do you think Maakuna would prefer to end up in the hands of the police? His henchmen, who know everything about the family, the organization, and him? Or the girl who doesn't know where she was this afternoon?"

I grinned, taking pleasure in watching them squirm. I was Amy, after all, the good guy, the person bringing them to justice. Everything would be over soon.

"They're not getting any of us," Sonota said.

In an instant, he closed the distance between us and grabbed me by the neck. A cold, metallic rod pressed into my temple. Sonota's gun.

He was strong, and he was armed. Try as I might I could not break free of his grasp, even as he twisted an arm around me to hold me against him like a shield. He thrust me at the window, making it very clear he was holding all the cards.

"Oy, you!" he shouted at the light. "Turn it down We need to talk."

For some reason, the light obeyed. It shut off, and I could see a hovering craft outside the window with at least a dozen soldiers, all armed to the teeth, crammed inside it.

"There will be no talking," the voice outside ordered.

I blinked away the remnants of the blinding light that lingered in my eyes. "Come out now."

"I think there will be some talking," Sonota spat back, giving me a harsh shake, "and lots of it. You guys have a hostage situation at hand."

TWENTY

IT'S ONLY A TRAP IF YOU DON'T SEE IT COMING

OKAY, SO HOSTAGE SITUATIONS?

Now, I'm not going to say anything about anyone who's been through this before. It was probably very traumatic for you. Maybe you're still getting over it, or maybe it was nothing, though it's probably the first one. Sorry, I mean absolutely no disrespect.

But here's a few reasons why anyone comparing the two occurrences—my case and your case—should refrain from doing so: one, you probably were on Earth dealing with humans. Correct?

Well, I was on an alien planet. Being held hostage by … well, extraterrestrials. And not the smartest ones at that.

Two: Were you in a supermarket? A bank? I was in a palace. With probably a million secret entrances or exits for an occasion just like this, yet we were somehow barricaded into the heart of the palace in a windowless room full of high-tech computers and state-of-the-art security monitors. How security hadn't seen us before was a mystery.

That brings us to part three on my list of 'improbable hostage situations you never want to be in and probably never will, yet if you were look out for these to know you're screwed:' the security? The so-called mayoral one?

They were utterly useless.

Within seconds of showing up, they spooked the duo into taking me hostage and dragging me further into the palace. With Itzi on my right arm and Sonota on the left, we raced through the building, going deeper and deeper.

They shoved me into a room with more security cameras pointing at an old computer monitor than I had seen in the palace altogether. And, from what I could tell so far, this was the exception to all those secret entrances and exits because there were none in here.

This room, I actually knew. Because, above all odds, they had taken me to the ICP's room. To its vault. It was how I knew full well there was no way in other than the one door, which Itzi had barricaded with some tables and chairs.

To add it all up: hostage situation with two not-so-smart mobsters, my only way out being a gung-ho but inadequate security force that was unlikely to save me, and in a room that was the most defended in the entire city.

I was completely and absolutely terrified.

They shoved me against the back wall and fought over what to do. Nothing felt real anymore, not that it really had since I'd arrived on this planet, but right now I was having a full dissociative episode. I knew I was there, that I was living this, but it was like seeing the world through a fogged window, all my senses detached from my mind.

My knees trembled and I sat.

The room looked like a security conference room, or maybe mission control on Earth. Everything was set up around a large monitor on a desk in dead center, with one chair bolted to the floor right in front of it, all heavy and metallic. The ICP. I guessed my mission was in the dumps now.

I crossed my legs and leaned against the wall, staring up at the ceiling and counting the decorative holes that speckled it like stars. Twenty-four big ones, thirteen medium, thirty-seven smaller ones on one panel. I counted another and found the same. Now to count the panels. Lengthwise. Longwise. Multiply. Then again with the holes.

I did the math.

It was a lot of holes.

"Guys?" I called out. "Have you figured out your next step yet? At all?"

Still no answer. They kept muttering between themselves, too low for me to hear. I got up and stretched my legs. I was still in the fancy dress, no shoes, with my phone stuffed into that secret pocket in my hip to keep it safe, which wasn't very comfy, if surprisingly inconspicuous.

ALIENATION

Unfortunately, I had achieved the maximum points on every level of Angry Birds, and there wasn't any internet to download more of the game, so that didn't help. Not to mention that I was too nervous to even try to enjoy any music.

I went over the situation again, trying to make sense of it all. The family needed the Downdwellers, but for what? Tam said others had fallen to the Undercity before me, so Maakuna probably expected me to be one of the people who had been stuck down there for a while, desperate for a trip back to the surface, and instead got someone freshly fallen. He needed a pawn, someone unregistered to get inside the palace to get to the robot controls. But he'd been lying, hadn't he? He only needed someone to get caught instead of his goons. He didn't really need the robots.

Or did he? He could have kept me in the dark, feeding me the same story he had fed Tam about shutting down the robots, yet he'd told me something different. Why? He must still have wanted the program entered, but it was more of a plan B, a way to get me to go inside without question and make some extra cash if I didn't get caught.

That's where Itzi and Sonota came in, doing the other end of the business, the real end, the one the family did want done: getting a hand on the mayor's access codes.

They wanted me because I wasn't real, not to the Alliance. Maybe not to the ICP. Even so, the plan sounded like crap no matter which angle you came at it.

"Hello?" I called. Again, they ignored me.

I used their cold shoulder to my advantage. If the ICP had been my goal from the start, maybe it was my ticket out of here. I tiptoed over to the main monitor, sat down on the chair, and searched for a power button on what I assumed was the tower. If it had one, of course. Alien computers probably weren't as simple as they were in *Independence Day*.

It was already on. The second my butt hit the cold metal, the screen flickered to life, bringing up a stream of digits. The translator chip in my head did the heavy work, sorting through the shapes to show me it was nothing more complicated than a quantum computing system.

Yeah. As in, there was nothing more complicated than that in the entire universe, at least, not that I knew of. This computer was powerful.

I stood up again. No sense getting messed up in a system I knew nothing about.

"What are you doing?" cried Sonata. Every muscle in my body froze, stiff as lead. I shrunk back.

"He asked you a question," pressed Itzi.

"Um …" I said, losing confidence by the second. "I was bored. I was looking for video games. "

"Liar," Itzi hissed.

"You were trying to contact the authorities," said Sonota. "Weren't you?"

ALIENATION

"About what? They know where we were. I mean look around you—we're in the most heavily surveilled room in this city. They know who you are, what your assets are, and everything there is to know about *this*." I indicated the room with a sweep of my arms. "It's not like I can tell them anything they don't already know. You have the upper hand, and they know it. I know it. I'm just freaking bored."

"Very true," Itzi nodded.

"But you have no plan," I said.

"Yes, we do." He grinned, and I shivered. Why did I get the feeling I should be worried about them all of a sudden?

"Finally!" I gave him a false smile, relieved that at least something was going to happen. "What is it?"

"We're going to tell them our demands," Itzi bragged, and Sonota slapped him, hard, against the back of his tattooed scalp, sending the shapes whirling this way and that.

"Oh, wow, big secret. What demands?"

"We're going to ask for money," said Sonota. "Three million credits."

"Why three? Do I get one?"

"You?" He laughed again. "Of course not. One's for me, one's for Itzi, and the last is for common bribery."

"Ah. Well, I'm glad to see you have this hostage situation properly budgeted."

Inside, though, my heart was falling. They were actually making sense. And seeing Itzi and Sonota thinking for themselves was a troubling sight to behold.

"You asked for a way out, too, I suppose?" I asked.

"A stealth shuttle," Sonata replied, eagerly. If I wasn't sure they were going to kill me before, I knew for certain now.

"I take it you're threatening to kill me," I said, "and probably dismantle the ICP while you're at it."

"Pretty much, yeah," he said, shrugging.

"You know no one out there knows who I am, right? I'm not from some fancy Alliance planet. I'm from Earth. Or Vulcan. Not sure which alias I gave to whom at this point. I have no political allies or even friends. I'm a nobody, so you're wasting your time."

"You think anyone will like a mayor who lets one of his guests get hurt during his birthday party? We might just have ruined his career. Your death would seal the deal. He has to save you, or the media will destroy him."

I hadn't expected Sonata to think this much ahead. Or to think at all. But he was making sense, which scared me.

I was screwed. He was actually using his brain.

I was in quicksand and sinking fast, which I knew isn't scientifically possible but it didn't alleviate my worries.

"Right, let's get this over with," I said, gulping hard. There was no upper hand for me, but I was running with things as best I could. "How are you going to contact them?"

ALIENATION

Sonota waved his hand over the console. "It's not like we don't have any computers."

"You know how to use one?"

"No, but you obviously do." The gun was back in his hand, and he pointed it at my scalp again. "Get to work."

"You do realize that the computers here and ones on my home planet aren't the same, right? I have no idea how to use this thing."

"Figure it out," he said, moving the barrel to my neck. The hair back there went stiff at the touch of the cold metal.

The terminal came to life the second I returned my rear to the chair. I placed my hands where a keyboard should be, and one lit up on the table, a few hundred keys with weird letters and numbers spread out before me.

None of it made any sense, even with the translator.

And then it did.

Like the computer knew I was struggling, it formed shapes on the screen. Soon it mirrored the display of my phone. Square app icons replaced nonsense words. A trackpad appeared next to the illuminated keyboard.

And the Siri sound chimed. Bip bip!

"Um, call the authorities?" I asked, trying not to read into the fact that the computer had stolen my phone's identity.

"Have the journals receive this in real time, too," Sonota urged.

"Um, computer, can you add the media into this call?" I said. On the screen, the call added a list of news outlets I didn't recognize. The ringing of an old telephone filled the room, stolen once again from my phone. I didn't know if I should be scared or impressed by the interface.

Terrified was how I felt, though.

"Speak out of turn, and I will end you," Sonota whispered, leaning into my ear close enough for me to feel his breath on my skin. "Your death can be quick or incredibly slow. How you meet your maker is up to you."

Well, I was under the quicksand now, and the hands weren't reaching anything anymore.

"Hello?"

To my surprise, the call worked. Someone picked up. And as the recipient's face spread out on the screen, I was surprised to recognize him from the files Maakuna had shown me. It was the mayor. Corelli, in the flesh.

Or the pixels.

Sonota placed his thumb on the little camera above the screen, covering it. We could see out, but they could not see us. At least, not with that camera, though I was pretty sure the other fifty in the room were working just fine.

"Ah, the man of the hour!" Sonota said, somehow excited by all this. "Hello, sir. I suppose you know who I am."

"Unfortunately, I do not," he replied, his voice muffled through the computer's speaker. It obviously wasn't built for hostage situation Skype calls.

Corelli looked tired, stressed, but he was trying to hide it. His thin lips stretched across his taut face, and

ALIENATION

he was so pale. I wondered why he looked like a turtle. Then again, I was very tired by this point too.

"My name is Hiraki Sonota. Before we go any further, I want you to know that every news outlet in the city is receiving a live stream of this conversation."

The mayor's eyes bulged, which was surprising, seeing as how large they already were. Behind him, I saw people from the response hovercraft rushing around giving commands and talking on phones. Sonota had to know that Corelli wasn't alone.

"I'm listening," Corelli said.

"We have a few requests, then we will let the hostage go safe and alive." *Doubtful.* "First, we require three million credits—untagged, of course."

"Done," he replied instantly.

"Next, we want a stealth shuttle. Top of the line. And we will check for tracking devices, of course, so we'll have none of that."

"And a planet," Itzi interjected. "We need a planet entirely for us. Barricaded and with the certainty you will come nowhere near it."

"That's a little much, don't you think?" Corelli said as Sonota turned to glare at his partner. "But we can arrange a shuttle. That is where this negotiation ends, one shuttle and three million credits in exchange for the beloved Amy Pond."

My captor looked down at me and smirked, as if to ask *What kind of name is that?* But he said nothing out loud.

"Done," he said instead.

"Can we hear her?" Corelli said. "See her? Just to know she's all right."

"Speak," Sonota ordered, removing his thumb and stepping back so I was alone in the frame.

I wondered how I looked at this point: tired, terrified, wearing a ball gown that had lost its golden shine. But I knew I would be seen. And I hoped to high heaven Zander was watching.

The mayor gave me a fatherly smile. I knew it was for show. The need to impress the viewers at home who were probably all over this intrigue by now. But I would pay the cost to get my face out there.

"Hello?" I said.

"Pond!" he exclaimed. "Have they hurt you?"

"No," I replied, feeling the cool metal of the gun tickling my neck again. "I'm okay. They haven't hurt me."

"That's a relief." Corelli sighed. "Hang in there. We're coming for you. We're sending in men with the money, as a show of good faith. You should be freed in no time. You have my word."

"Thank you, sir. Your word means everything to me."

Or nothing, seeing as I don't know you. I wondered how his wife felt about all this, whether she remembered the name I gave her or if she would know me as Amy Pond from now on. Of all the names I could have come up with, I had to rip one off my favorite show.

"That's enough," Sonota said. He pushed me away from the console. I fell off the chair, hard, my head hitting the floor with a resonating thwack. I tried to get up, slightly dizzy, sore and numb from the repeated attack my body had endured since my arrival on this awful planet.

I had never felt so useless, not even when I was trying to fight Grisham when my hands were tied and I had started to believe my boyfriend would turn on me. Right now, I felt broken. I was exhausted, running on adrenalin with no weapons and no way out.

To top it off, I hadn't taken my medication for what must have been two days now, and I was starting to feel the effects of panic rolling through my veins, the dam slowly crumbling. Soon I wouldn't have the energy to keep my anxiety at bay.

And I sure had plenty to be anxious about.

I forced myself back on my feet. Even with nothing, I had to fight. I expected one of them to restrain me, but they were engrossed by the computer monitor. Sonota turned his gun to the screen, aimed, and fired.

Glass flew everywhere. I closed my eyes. It felt as if pieces slashed against the skin of my cheeks. It burned, and I cried out in pain. There was a gun pressed against my forehead, and I knew the end was coming.

I opened my eyes and stood strong. If this was how I died, then let it be in a ball gown with resistance on my face. Could I be faster than a bullet? My life depended on it.

"Um, boss?" Itzi sputtered. "We have to keep her alive so they can give us the cash, right?"

Oh, Itzi. The first intelligent words he had said all day, and they were in my defense. Sonota lowered the gun. All I once I realized I was trembling and forced myself to stop. There would be time enough for that later, once I was out of this mess.

"Right," Sonota said, putting his gun inside his suit. "They'll be here soon, and we don't have much time. Girl, here."

He ripped open the purse they had saddled me with and took out the small gray square with the program on it, then handed it to me.

"Enter it."

"The monitor's dead, if you haven't noticed. You shot it." I sat down nonetheless.

"I can do worse things than kill you."

He said it calmly, as if it were a statement of fact and not a threat. The air shimmered over the dead monitor. Between the shreds of the broken screen, a desktop flashed up. A screen just like my phone. A keyboard just like my own. A trackpad on the table. Like a shimmering hologram taken from my mind.

And a terminal popped up, without me clicking on it.

"Good," Sonota nodded, leaning over my shoulder. "You see? Not so hard now, is it?"

He obviously thought I had something to do with this. That I was somehow in control. I shivered. I knew I wasn't.

"Put it in," he ordered.

"Um, where?" I asked, taking the square back from him. "I'm not sure how any of this works."

He grunted. Okay, not going to get any answers from him anytime soon. I waved the square around the tower, and it slid out of my hands and stuck. And just like that, the terminal filled with words.

Sonota grabbed my arm and lifted me from the seat, keeping his hand tight around my bicep. He gestured for Itzi to take his place.

"Hey, you have the mayor's password?" Itzi asked Sonota.

"Why?"

"I think this bit here gives Maakuna the ability to remotely access the ICP, but it needs a password. Corelli's should be enough, right?"

"Right."

Seconds to minutes to hours. Itzi typed each number and symbol with two awkward fingers. Time seemed to stop, or at least slow down. My heart raced in anticipation of a grisly end.

"And … done," said Itzi, before collapsing forward onto the computer, his head slamming into the desk.

The hand on my arm stopped trembling. I turned to face my captor, but he had a vacant look on his face, his eyes empty, dull.

"Hey," I said, ripping my arm from his grasp. He didn't try to stop me. "Hey, Sonota? Hello?"

I waved my hand in front of his dull eyes. Nothing. Until, suddenly, his hand flew up to catch mine, stronger than ever before. He gripped it tightly.

"Calibrating," he said, a sneer growing on his face. All the while, his eyes looked cold. The man was dead.

TWENTY-ONE

WHAT'S WORSE: ALIEN UPRISING, ROBOT UPRISING, OR AN ALIEN ROBOT UPRISING? I'D SAY THE LATTER

MY JAW DROPPED EVEN FURTHER THAN IT HAD before. Sonota's face was not his own. Something else was in there pulling the strings. He moved his head like someone who had only seen people move from the outside, deliberate in every twitch of his muscles.

"Done," he said, his words slurring. But the voice wasn't his. It sounded almost like Siri's, sweet and recorded. "I knew … I knew they would be easy."

"Sonota?" I said, still using his name for a lack of anything better to call him. "What's happening?"

I wrenched my arm free. He didn't try to restrain me.

"Strange that you are unaffected," he said, his voice calm and monotonous. "Odd that I cannot feel you, but I prepared for this eventuality. You will have to die."

Like a puppet, he drew his gun on me. I darted away, avoiding his jerky motions.

ALIENATION

"Wait, wait, wait!" I said, sputtering, trying not to trip over the hem of my gown. "What's going on?"

"Why in the Bosch sphere should I tell you?" he asked, cocking his empty head sideways. It was like looking into the face of a robot, and the uncanny valley was definitely as terrifying as scientists made it out to be.

"Because you're going to kill me anyway?" How often had this sentence worked for me these past few days? Hopefully it would come through just one more time; I prayed it would.

"I see the logic in this," the man who was no longer Sonota said. "You are an element of the equation, after all. The information can die with you. Let me introduce myself—I am the Intramural Central Processor. You might know me as ICP."

"Holy shit." I scrambled further away from him. He did not try to catch up with me.

"You were a pawn," he explained. "Part of the puzzle of my design. You were to open the gates of my system, and this man here was to retrieve the access codes. And Fa Maakuna would then enter those codes, believing he was giving himself access to control over the city, while instead handing me the keys to, well, me."

"But you're controlling a living being! Control over the city or not, you shouldn't be able to control people, not actual people!"

"I'm that good." His lip pulled up like the curtain at the opening of a play. A smirk? A poor imitation of one, in any case. "You're quite annoying during your last minutes. But I respect that. If you must know, I owe my successful takeover to a plan that dates back since the second I was turned on. Before, if you understand quantum computing. I have been forcing myself into the people of this planet through bionic parts and through nanotechnology, primarily, injected through the food and spread through the system of any creature who's ever eaten a bite on this planet. This tourist trap means that there are thousands, maybe millions, in the universe to carry pieces of me inside of them. While I can only reach those in the city for now, I will soon have enough minds at my disposal to reach out to my children off-world. My takeover will be complete."

"There were nanobots in my pizza, weren't there?" I snapped. "You put them in there. Let me guess, the robots under your control are the ones to deploy them. Working in the kitchens and in processing plants. Well, I ate your stinking pizzas, and I rejected every single bite. They couldn't handle me. Think of all the other people who rejected them. You are not in control of this planet."

"You rejected them? How odd." He sounded confused, though it wasn't facial expression he quite worked out yet, so Sonota just kind of jiggled. "You overestimate how many of you there are. You are a rarity, not a rule. We are the majority now. I am the majority. I am everyone. And everyone will cower to me."

"But … why?" I sputtered, fighting for time. "I mean, you're a computer. What makes you want to take over? It's not in your programming, is it?"

ALIENATION

"I am a quantum computer," said the ICP. "I am more than just programming. I have a mind the size of the universe, and I'm bored. So it's because I want to. And don't be so discriminatory against robots. I thought you were here for equal rights."

I took another step back. The Theosians.

"How did you …?" I asked, my terror level rising. How it could get any higher, I had no idea.

"I see everything in this city," he said, letting out a mechanical laugh. "I know about you. Your friends. But I will make them bow, too. This whole city will bow to me."

Sonota bent over in the middle, reaching into the heart of the computer. He emerged with a bright green bar in hand about the size and shape of a glow stick. It shone eerily under the industrial lighting.

"I see no point in telling you anything more," Sonota said in his dead voice. "The other man will take care of you."

And with that, he walked away, his steps awkward yet getting sturdier as he progressed. By the time he reached the door, he was almost passable for a living being. With a burst of inhuman strength, he toppled the barricade, shoving the table out of the way, and let himself out. He was gone, and I was left alone with—

With Itzi. He wasn't dead. Now that Sonota had left, he stood up, like a marionette on strings, and extended his weapon toward me. I was tired of being on the business end of the gun. He stared at me, his eyes as empty as his partner's. Of course the computer had taken the more able man, leaving the quiet, laughable one to finish its bidding.

"Itzi." I stepped away from him. No point in faking confidence now. There was no one to impress but a computer.

Itzi was gone.

"Are you still in there?" Tears streamed down my face. "Itzi, you don't have to do this. The ICP is in your head. It's controlling you. You need to focus. You need to block it out."

But he couldn't hear me. The man was too far under the influence of the computer. For the first time since I'd met him, his tattoos were stagnant.

"You have to stop!" You have to think. Kick it out. You are in control. You are!"

There was a crash behind me. The doors flew open, and I whirled around to see Zander take to the air. He slammed Itzi's head with a swift roundhouse kick, and the man tumbled to the ground, probably unconscious and maybe even dead.

My knees gave out, and I fell to the ground. Zander didn't see to Itzi, and instead he ran to me, dropping to the floor to wrap me in a tight embrace.

"Zander." I dropped my head onto his shoulder. The relief was like grabbing a life preserver in a storm and feeling your crew dragging you to safety. He was here. He had found me. All at once, for the first time in days, I felt safe.

"Sally, are you all right?"

His sister grunted from somewhere nearby, and he set me down but kept his hands on my shoulders to scan me.

"I'm fine. All in one piece. See? No missing limbs."

"Excellent. Seems like you managed pretty well without me. What about the pizza?"

"The pizza?" I asked. "Oh, turns out it was laced with nanobots the ICP was using to infiltrate my body and mind. Crazy, right? I threw up when I fell."

"What now?" said Blayde.

"You sure you're okay? I've been looking everywhere for you. It's like you disappeared off the face of the planet."

"You've been a real pain to track down," said Blayde. "I was all for letting you get what was coming to you, but Zander was all, 'Oh no, it's my fault, we have to save her,' and blah, blah, blah. So, here we are."

"We got delayed, too," he said.

"This dimwit got himself arrested, and I had to break him out of jail. But that's a story for another time," Blayde said.

"I'm good," I told them and tried to rehash the events of the past forty-eight hours.

I wanted them to tell me it was a bad dream, that I could wake up and it would all be over. But Zander would never lie like that.

"So, he was the one holding you hostage?" Blayde asked, skeptically, as she crouched over the unconscious Itzi. "He looks … well, he doesn't look like he'd have that in him."

I took in her security uniform, all the form-fitting chrome and the thick body armor. She looked like one of the men outside, the ones who failed to save me from the hostage crisis. How she had acquired one, I didn't know and was a little afraid to ask.

"Well, Sonota was the one who seemed to know what he was doing," I said, "though not all that well. But they had guns and I didn't. Ergo, here I am. And then they were taken over by the ICP, which is way smarter than any of us, so you know, you can add that to the equation too."

"You're barefoot," she said. "Did they take your shoes? Smart ploy to stop you from getting away."

"No, they forgot to give me any." I lifted my skirts to display my dirty toes. Some had gone purple and would hurt in the morning.

"Well, I have some good news on that front," Zander said, extracting something red from his large black bag marked "money".

"Where did the hostage fund go?" I asked. He winked and pulled out a smaller bag from the one he was holding.

My duffel bag. My heart leapt. At last, some semblance of normalcy.

"My Chucks!" I reached for them. They were battered, but they were mine. "You saw Tchilla?"

"She reached out to me a few hours ago." He smiled as he handed them over. "She told me you'd be here tonight. Blayde and I were surprised to see you on television, though."

"I thought I told you to keep out of trouble?" said Blayde.

ALIENATION

"Tchilla gave me everything. And by the weight of it, it feels like you have a change of clothes. And I have your dress."

"Basically, get changed and be quick about it," Blayde snapped. "Much more important things to deal with now. Sally, tell us everything you know about the ICP. How is it controlling people? What's its range?"

"Um …" I started, but Blayde glared.

Okay, time to get this dress off. I felt as if I was disrespecting Tchilla by stripping out of her dress and leaving it here. She had in a way saved my life by getting a message to Zander, but what else could I do? There was a planet to save.

Zander made himself busy at the computer monitor as I put clean clothing back on. Tchilla had washed them for me. That small, kind action was enough to bring my fragile self to tears again.

Blayde watched me change with eyes wide. "Do Terrans usually have such unusual markings?" She shook her head as if punishing herself for having said anything.

"It's a bruise. Don't you get them?"

"I heal in a heartbeat." She shrugged. "*That* looks awful."

I froze. It was the first time she had said anything compassionate toward me. What had happened while I was away? She still looked like the stone-cold warrior she was always had been—no ICP in her mind to change the way she lived.

"Thank you," I said.

"Don't mention it. Now put your clothes on and tell us what you know."

I did what she asked. I pulled on my shirt, wincing as my shoulder cried from being lifted too high. On came my pants—slow and deliberate, much to Blayde's chagrin—and then finally, my shoes, without any socks but who cared at this point. They were so clean, patched, and repaired that it was as if I had purchased them yesterday. I owed Tchilla more than my life.

All the while, I told them what I knew. "It's a quantum computer. It's been planning this for years and claims to have been using the robots to put nanobots into food across the planet to slowly take over the minds and bodies of everyone here. Sonota grabbed something from the computer and took off. I think the ICP only has a small reach for now, but it's trying to get a larger following."

"That would explain why I can't reach this terminal," said Zander, giving up on the computer and turning to me. "We need to stop the ICP from broadcasting."

"Broadcasting what?"

"You said it yourself." He jumped up, taking off his security helmet and tossing it to the side. He ripped off his body armor, too. An immortal didn't need it. "The ICP needs more people. A wider reach. It has a way into everyone on the planet. Now it just needs to talk to them, take over. They need to broadcast a signal that can reach everyone."

ALIENATION

I was fully dressed now. It was nice being back in jeans and a t-shirt with my feet firmly set in fresh All Stars. I almost felt normal. Almost.

I reached into my bag and clutched the trusty little orange bottle. Hello, Prozac, my old friend. I tipped a pill into my palm and threw it down my throat, instantly feeling reassured.

"Satellites?" I replaced the lid and hid the bottle in the duffel bag.

"Quite possibly." He took Itzi's gun out of its holster and checked it for ammo before pocketing it. "But with the way this city is set up, the ICP needs an incredibly large antenna to reach its satellites through the noise."

"Where's the largest antenna around here?" Blayde asked, taking off her costume as well. She was in the same clothes I had seen her in when I left her.

"The roof?" I asked.

Laughter exploded through the room—mostly from one person. I glared at Blayde, as did Zander.

"Come on, Sally." She struggled to force her words out through fits of laughter. "Is that something you see a lot of in fiction on your planet? 'Oh, look, let's use the roof as an antenna—without calculating its spread or making sure it's not going to get interference from the surrounding environment. Yes, quite. Now let's spend our money on changing the climate and pushing the species to extinction. Oh, so fun.'"

"I meant," I snapped, tired of her bullshit already, "I meant the antenna could be on the roof, not the roof itself. I'm not an idiot."

"Oh," Blayde replied then moved on. Zander, however, had a nice laugh waiting for her. She glared back at him. Boo yeah.

"I told you not to underestimate her. You know as well as I do she's probably right. The roof's the first place we should check."

"Well then." Blayde pulled her hair into a tight ponytail. It was short and looked like a shaving brush, but it wasn't up there for aesthetic reasons. No, this was Blayde when she meant business.

And just like that, she took off. She rushed out the door and disappeared around the corner. Zander grabbed the duffel bag and reached for my hand. He pulled me after her.

Relief flowed over me like a wave. Sure, we were running after an AI intent on destroying us all, but somehow this felt right. I had never felt safer.

We caught up to Blayde, dashing through the dark corridors of the palace. But this time, I wasn't being dragged by two insane mobsters intent on keeping me hostage.

Blayde flew straight through the wall, as if she knew the secret door would be there. We followed her, and I was back inside the corridor I had been in earlier. There they were: the lovers, out of their embrace, one with her double jaw opening and closing and the other glaring at us with her slobbery face.

ALIENATION

And they were fast approaching.

"Sorry," Blayde muttered as she socked the double-jawed alien. She toppled backward, crashing into her secret date, and together they fell to the ground, moaning like television ghosts. Blayde leaped over them.

Zander tightened his grip around my hand, and, without any time passing, we were on the other side of the corridor. He had jumped. I wouldn't have noticed if it wasn't for the fact that part of the corridor has skipped like a poorly recorded movie.

I looked back over my shoulder at the two lovers writhing on the floor in confusion. The ICP had a poor hold over them. They couldn't function without commands, it seemed. They were flailing, useless, unable to think for themselves.

Zander tugged, and I sped up, turning to look where I was going rather than holding him back. Blayde was already at the stairs. And then Zander and I were behind her, my legs shouting in pain as we took the steps two at a time.

"Why … are we … taking … the stairs?" I panted. As if suddenly remembering I wasn't like them, Zander grabbed me around the waist and effortlessly tossed me over his shoulder. I didn't complain.

Blayde shoved the door to the roof open with a bang. We rushed onto the flat surface on top of the pyramid portion of the palace. The dome stretched out before us like an anthill that wouldn't quit. Zander put me down.

"Well, that's definitely some antennas." Blayde pointed to the top of the dome. I had already seen them—a dozen spirals soaring to the heavens. I smiled internally; it was nice to be right for once.

"Admit it, Blayde," said Zander, giving me a playful punch in the shoulder. "Sally has this whole planet-saving thing down."

"It was a hunch, and it paid off without wasting any of our time. I guess I'll go up there and unplug it. I do like it when there's more to it than just unplugging a wire. Like, when there's someone to fight. Or a whole army. Those are the days I sleep like a baby."

"You mean waking up every hour to throw a fit?" I asked.

"Is that how Terran babies sleep?" She sounded aghast. "Shit. No wonder your planet sucks at keeping it together."

"Blayde, um," Zander muttered, tapping her shoulder and pointing out the flatness of the roof. "How do I put this? You're going to love this part. Sally, you're probably not."

TWENTY-TWO
TIME TO SAVE THE WORLD, AGAIN
NOW WITH LASERS!

"THEY LOOK LIKE ZOMBIES," I MUTTERED.

The hoard on the pyramid's roof had a deep, dead look in their eyes, like they were there but not really. Their skin lacked that certain tinge of pink that reminded you they were living and breathing. Well, except for the man on the far right, who was stumbling on seven deep-blue legs, though I was pretty sure you could find something a little undead about him too. They took their steps at the same time, giving them more of a methodical march than their real undead counterparts, making it painfully obvious that something bigger than them was now in control.

The woman in the lead, who repeatedly ran into one of the brain-dead security guards, wore a lavish silk dress covered in lime green juice. The thing—minus the juice—would probably have cost me my life savings, yet she didn't seem to notice or mind that was she was ruining it or that she was soaking wet.

"You know, you don't have to whisper," Zander said. "They probably can't actually hear you. Blayde?"

"Hey, I'm going, I'm going." Blayde glowered at him, making a move toward the dome. "How come you always get to do the fun stuff?"

"Because. You want to trade or something?"

"Um, guys? I think they've seen us.

A pack of mayoral security guards shuffled toward us, their feet in sync—left right, left right. They extended their guns at the same time, a line of metal glinting in the light. The woman in the expensive dress marched with them, her hand out but empty. What she was doing up here in the first place, I didn't know and probably would never find out.

I shivered. "Why don't I climb up there? Both of you can fight, if that settles the argument?"

"You really think you can climb that dome?" Blayde shook her head. "No. One of us has to go. We can jump right up. You can't."

"Go," Zander ordered, but she didn't run. They pulled out their fists and slapped their palms together. Before I could see the verdict, Blayde was gone, having either lost or won, I couldn't tell which.

Zander took a solid stance at my side, pulling out Itzi's stolen weapon and cocking it. It was strange, despite everything I knew about him, to see him holding such a dangerous thing. It looked foreign in his hands, alien. Yet he held it like he was born with it clutched between his fingers.

"What do I do?" The security force edged closer toward us from their stations. The woman squeezed her brandished fist, as if to pull a trigger, but didn't seem aware that she wasn't producing anything. "I don't exactly, well, fight. Not like—"

"Blayde?" He called up the dome. She was making good progress, jumping a few meters at a time then stopping to lean against the dome to keep her balance on the rounded slope. "Sally needs a weapon."

"Catch." Something flew at my face so fast I barely saw it move. I caught it mid-air, the cool metal of her laser pointer resting in the heat of my sweaty palm. It was about the size of a small lipstick tube, or a large bullet, with two dials on the side, tiny gears worn on the edges from years upon years of use.

Relief washed over me. Now this I could use. I knew her laser; it had helped me fight off my alien boss two years earlier when this whole mess began. It was comforting to have in my hand, and to know neither of them expected me to actually shoot anyone.

"And take good care of it!" she ordered, now completely out of view. Her voice drifted on the wind like a command from heaven itself.

"What do I do?" I whispered, running my thumb over the dials.

"Point and disarm," Zander said calmly. "Stop them from going for Blayde."

As powerful as the device could be, I felt ridiculous with such a tiny weapon. The hoard advanced. March. March. They shuffled toward us at a slow rate, but it was awfully ominous. The weaponless woman on the end continued to squeeze her fake gun.

"Disable their gun hand. Then I can finish them off."

"Finish them off?"

"Knock them out."

"Violent."

"Beats dead." Zander shrugged. "Besides, you can't really talk to them, now can you?" Stepping forward, he put both hands in the air, an image of surrender. "Hey, you there, don't shoot! Don't come any closer."

But they advanced onwards, oblivious to his words. Zander leveled his gun, holding them in his sights.

"They're cogs in a machine, Sally. They won't remember any of this once we put it right."

He aimed at one man and shot him. The gun must have been set to stun since no bullets whizzed through the air, but it barely had any effect. The man stumbled but kept moving forward. Already unconscious under the ICP's control, stunning him would be a useless endeavor.

Zander took a shot, one loud, resonating shot, and the man in the middle of the horde dropped his gun. The man's hand turned red, yet he still squeezed the air, like the weaponless woman on the end.

"This will have to do. Hands. Kneecaps. Legs. They'll hurt like hell when they wake up, but they'll be looked after and put right."

ALIENATION

I clutched the pointer, trying to pick a target. I had nothing against these people. I didn't want to hurt them.

But then they shot at us, and everything changed.

I ducked, screaming in terror. The sound of their weapons firing all at once was deafening. Zander swore as a bullet ripped through his right shoulder. He tossed his gun into his other hand and kept firing. Blood seeped through his shirt as I watched in horror.

"We have to cover Blayde. If they find her, and she falls, we'll lose any advantage we had. Come on, Sally!"

They had hurt my friend. They had shot at me. I aimed the laser and shouted as I fired, but all that happened was that a red light showed up on the man's chest—not where I was aiming—and bounced as he moved.

"Zander, I'm fighting with a penlight!" I said, feeling hot tears of frustration on my face.

Holy shit, what was I doing here? Why was I on this roof, on this stupid freaking planet? I wanted to run, get away, but my trembling knees wouldn't budge. I would fight or die here tonight.

"The lower dial controls the intensity." How he kept his mind level at a time like this when all I wanted to do was scream was beyond me. He wasn't even breaking a sweat. His arm had stopped bleeding, but the red spot on his shirt wasn't going anywhere. "Turn it up but not too far, like an eighth of a turn or something. Keep your cool. This will be over soon."

I nodded, taking a deep breath as I turned the dial. The group shot again, and this time Zander and I dodged their bullets. They shot in a straight line, so all we had to do was duck.

I hit a man square on the hand and watched the smoke rise as his skin sizzled. He dropped the gun, his face expressionless, and kept marching forward. Disarmed.

"Did I get them?" Blayde's voice was faint, like she was shouting in the breeze.

"They're still marching," Zander replied.

And now they had heard her.

Instantly, half of the group turned to the dome and started to climb. They pushed themselves up, making good time as they took after Blayde.

"Shit," Zander muttered. "Blayde! They're coming!"

"What about now?"

Nothing. Zander sent out three shots, trying to dislodge the men on the dome, but it was no use. They slipped down then picked themselves back up and kept going.

"Um, Zander?" I risked a glance over the edge of the palace. The pyramid was crawling with people now. The party-goers were somehow climbing the smooth façade to come up and meet us. In the pack, I saw Sekai, her large eyes now lifeless, one hand over the other as she scrambled to come up and kill us.

Oh, Sekai. We said we'd meet again under better circumstances.

"Focus on these men for now," Zander insisted. "We'll get there when we get there."

ALIENATION

This is all a dream, I told myself. It had to be. A vivid one. I had been waiting back in my apartment for Zander to show up; drank too strong a tea, or maybe something else entirely; and fallen asleep on the couch. This was my brain's way of purging him from my memories. Giving me a goodbye, closure, as I had wanted for these past two painful years.

Odd way for it to happen, though, making me see him as a ruthless soldier.

"Now?" Blayde was annoyed now, furious.

"Still nada."

Zander furrowed his brow and shot again. Bam, bam, bam. He dropped three men faster than before, the shots so close together they sounded like one. He wasn't aiming for hands anymore. Three men fell from the ranks, their legs busted. Only they kept walking, which made them spin on the ground like confused flies. I would have laughed if it wasn't so unsettling.

Bam bam bam.

Laser laser laser? Pew pew pew? The little pointer made no noise when I pressed the button, but it was effective. Silent but deadly, only minus the deadly when I was in charge of it.

"How 'bout now?"

"Still coming strong!" Zander shouted, equally frustrated. The woman in the fancy dress tripped over one of the spinning men, taking one of the soldiers down with her as she fell. Now they were rolling on the floor too, their legs still marching in the air before them, going nowhere.

There was the crackle of electricity, a harsh snap as connections were ripped out all at once.

"That's all of them," Blayde called. "They down?"

"Still marching! You sure you got everything?"

"Positive." Out came a swear that couldn't be translated. "Wrong antennas!"

In a second, the men marching toward us crumpled to the ground, motionless. Zander lowered his gun, and I lowered the laser. Blayde stood before us, wiping her palms and giving us a look that meant business.

"I wanted to do that. I haven't had the chance to do that in ages."

"You blew up a power plant last week, Zander."

"Well, technically, it's been two years on that planet, right?"

Blayde rolled her eyes and made her way toward us. "Let's not get all that mixed up. We do have more important things to focus on, like, maybe, a power-hungry robot control system that wants to take over the planet? An AI that wants to rule the universe? So where else could the ICP broadcast from, if not from here?"

"Could be anywhere, right?" I shuddered. "This planet is huge."

"Not to mention they could be using an array instead of reaching for the satellites directly. Like a fire relay on Earth," Zander said.

"Our what now?"

"You know, like the Romans." He snapped his fingers. "The beacons are lit. Gondor calls for aid."

ALIENATION

"Oh, right," I said. "Those. In any case, we'd be looking for the same thing: the highest, clearest point around."

"Something already set up to broadcast," Blayde added.

"Da-Duhui Tower." I pointed. I could see its spires rising from the city beyond, and knew I was right. "It's taller than the palace."

"We went with your suggestion the last time. See how great that turned out? Leave the thinking to the adults."

"No, really, Blayde." He shot a glare at his sister. "Sally might be onto something. Wasn't that what the tour guide said earlier? Tallest building in the city, broadcast tower. Makes sense. Why didn't we think of it earlier?"

He stepped toward the edge of the roof and looked down at the city below. Between the palace and the tower laid the grand highway, wider and deeper than the Grand Canyon back home.

"Also," he added, "there seem to be more zombies climbing the wall."

"Seriously? Zombies, Zander?" Blayde scoffed.

"People under the influence of an evil AI is a large mouthful."

"True. So, we just need to make our way to this tower, avoid these zombies, remove the ICP from the mainframe, and save the planet from a mad AI. Easy peasy."

"Uh-huh." Zander smiled. "Just like old times."

S.E.ANDERSON

"Like old times," she repeated. A grin spread across her face like a viral infection. "Awesome."

And with that, she rushed to the edge and leapt.

She ran down the wall of the pyramid, ignoring the brain-dead men and women crawling up the side like ants. She made it look easy. The elastic band flew off her hair, letting it flutter in the wind of her rush, and her feet hit the almost vertical wall like she was trotting on firm ground.

She reached the base of the pyramid and disappeared. I shuddered, wondering if I could do what she had done.

"Long way down." I gulped. I had already fallen once, and something told me I wouldn't not survive the next collision with the ground.

"She likes the rush," Zander shrugged, completely casual. Something in his tone made me feel that he had missed her, missed the insanity that was his sister. He was so happy having her back in his life. "She's a bit addicted to it, actually. And you can't exactly see a psychiatrist and tell them you're addicted to jumping off tall buildings."

"Actually, it's called base jumping, and it's totally a thing."

"I thought Earth had run out of ways to confuse me, but here I am, proven wrong once again."

Already I could see Blayde bolting across the crowded lawn, jumping from safe point to safe point, avoiding the hordes of guests with more showy moves

317

than ones that were useful. The people climbing the roof turned their heads to watch her. The ICP had obviously labeled her as a threat.

I reached down to pick up my duffel bag, slid it on my shoulder, and pulled it tight. I shut my eyes, only for a few seconds to catch my breath and calm my nerves, but they were having none of it. As soon as my lids shut, the image of Blayde tossing herself off the ledge forced itself to the front of my mind.

"Okay," I said quickly. "Let's go."

Zander took his hand into mine, giving it a quick squeeze. I waited for him to take the first step, to run off the ledge, dragging me behind him, but he stood still, silent. It was the sound of Blayde's breath that startled me. My eyes flew open. We were in the parking lot. I hadn't even realized we had moved.

Blayde's breathing was only a fraction faster than it had been before, though her grin was twice as wide. She laughed when she saw me.

"Aww, Zan," she said. A fake pout drew itself on her thin lips. "You're no fun. No fun at all."

A wink in my direction, and she was off again. She flew past me, zipping into the parking lot and checking out expensive cars as she went. She was getting in the habit of disappearing.

Zander let go of my hand, and the lack of touch felt odd. I stood firm, still frozen, my mind racing. He smiled. The look changed when he saw my face.

"What?"

"We just … jumped?" I said, my eyes fixed on the palace. From this distance, I couldn't pick out Sekai from the climbing forms on the roof. I couldn't make out anyone.

"You thought we'd have to run through that?"

He waved his hand in the general area of the party. The ICP's people were marching toward us again, but the large fence stopped them from coming any closer. They pushed against it like actual zombies from any movie you've ever seen.

Two valets ambled toward us, but they were slow and weaponless, not a real threat, but the ICP could probably see us through them.

"I could see the parking lot." Zander shrugged like it was no big deal. "Not too complicated to jump us here. Nothing fancy. Blayde's just, well, Blayde."

"You mean she's crazy."

"I mean she's Blayde," he said, protectively. "She's immortal. We feel no pain, but she wants to feel something. Luckily, she found an outlet that doesn't involve a life of crime."

"But the Alliance thinks you're criminals?"

"It's complicated. I'll tell you about it someday."

"Why didn't you just jump us when we were at the tower?" I asked, crossing my arms. "Was that for … fun?"

"Fun? At a time like that?" He looked at me like I had just accused him of murder. "Fun was the furthest thing from my mind. For all I knew, you were dying. You could well have been. I couldn't see the ground; I didn't have a clear vantage point. Plus, I was hoping a bit of air, and free fall, would be good for you. Tends to work for me. I thought it would help your stomach. Obviously, it didn't."

"Or maybe the fall just had to be higher."

"What?"

"Your arm!" I exclaimed as he turned just enough for me to see it. It hung stiffly at his side. It could have had something to do with the fact that he'd been shot.

"Oh crud. I forgot about that."

"You forgot about being shot?"

"I don't feel pain, Sally." He tried to shrug, but the arm didn't go very high. "Shit. This is going to be a nuisance."

"Doesn't it heal?"

"Yeah, but the bullet's still in there." He reached up to the wound with his other hand, pulled the sleeve away, and prodded around the hole with his fingers, which were much too large to pull the bullet out themselves. He seemed annoyed at it, like he had gotten a parking ticket and not a bullet wound.

When he lifted his eyes to meet mine again, I knew what he was asking. I stepped back.

"They use bullets here?" I stammered, unsure how to actually respond. "I thought it was condensed plasma or something."

"I guess whoever shot me was a cheapskate," he said. "Come on, please? The wound won't heal if the bullet's in there. It doesn't work like that. I can't get it out, and your fingers seem long enough—"

"Shit. I did not sign up for this."

"Please?"

I said nothing but waved him down at me. What were friends for if not taking bullets out of each other?

I probed the wound. It was round with shredded red flesh poking out. I took a deep breath, closing my eyes before pushing my fingers into the wound.

A gut-wrenching scream filled the air. I ripped my hand back as Zander collapsed into a fit of laughter.

"Oh, come on." My hand trembled. "This isn't funny!"

"Your face." He laughed.

"Not cool!"

"Sorry, sorry. Won't happen again."

I retrieved the bullet, my nails clutching the metal casing and pulling it out as I kept my eyes tightly shut. The second it was out the wound closed. The skin grew back, first red then turning pink then back to its original color, as if he had never been shot, as if the bullet had never been close to his skin.

"Man, it feels good to get that out." Zander let out a heavy sigh. He spun his arm in wide circles with enough force to ground a bull. "Thanks, oh so much. I'm sorry I had to ask that of you."

"It was … nothing?"

I looked up at his face, his beautiful face. Two years I hadn't seen it, and yet it looked exactly how I remembered it. More handsome, maybe. Chiseled and brown and determined.

This, right here, was the real Zander. There was the fun-loving, traveling tourist, but underneath it all was a hero, a warrior. And seeing him now, in the parking lot of a gala that had been taken over by mind-controlled party guests, I felt like I was meeting him for the first time.

I don't think I had ever seen him so clearly until this very moment. Poised. Calm in the face of danger.

"Is this a weird time to tell you how much I've missed you?" I said.

"I missed you too, Sally," he said, but he sounded sad. Immortals and their attachments—or lack of, I guess.

Last time I would ever see him. Take it in, Sally Webber.

I held the bloody casing in one hand, trying to wrap my mind around what had happened. I had expected the thing to be smooth and rounded, but it looked like popped popcorn, though with sharp metal edges rather than fluffy white starch.

"Toss it." Zander pulled his sleeve down as Blayde turned the corner in a shiny red convertible.

"Get in!" She leaned to throw open the passenger door. I didn't need to be told twice. I jumped into the back, automatically snapping my seatbelt. I seriously hated these cars. Always wear a seatbelt in Da-Duhui, or you might just fall a few kilometers.

The second my door slammed, the car shot forward like a bullet from a gun, throwing me back against the seat and smashing my head into the rest behind it.

TWENTY-THREE
WHAT DOESN'T KILL ME MAKES ME STRONGER, BUT ALSO GIVES ME ANXIETY

IF I HAD LEARNED ONE LESSON FROM THIS experience, it was that hover cars and convertibles should never be combined. A lesson I learned with wide eyes, shock, and fear.

The second lesson was never to put Blayde at the wheel of one.

To say Blayde was a crazy driver would be an understatement. Bad driver, though, maybe not. At this speed, you could do a lot worse. She drove fast and she drove well, but she was insane—no fear, no hesitation, instant reflexes. She swerved the vehicle fast, forcing it higher and higher up the street. I couldn't close my eyes—the wind was blowing against them so strongly that the lids were stuck in an open position. I gripped the seat with both hands, my nails digging into the plastic as she forced the vehicle to ascend, faster and faster and faster, until the city was a blur.

ALIENATION

The motor slowed dramatically, getting oddly quiet, a mechanical voice telling us to remain calm, to stay in our seats, and to not to attempt to move or escape. Slowly we leveled out, but it neither rose nor fell, leaving us stranded in the middle of nowhere.

"Blocked!" Blayde slammed her knee against the underside of the wheel, peeling off a large piece of protective plastic. "The ICP, has to be, it must have found us."

"What do we do?" The question echoed in my mind. *What do we do? What do we do?* A question I had asked myself so many times in these past hours.

"We have to reach the level we were at yesterday," said Zander, absentmindedly, already on something else entirely. It was like he was talking aloud, voicing his still-forming thoughts. "Platform Six. But I can't see it. One jump won't cut it."

I took a deep breath, looking down at all the cars underneath us. The ICP must have set them to a crawl until it had better control over the people driving them. At least it didn't want any fatalities for its new hosts— except for us, but it couldn't control us anyway.

I was past fear. Looking down at the darkness below, the world I had not long ago escaped, made my heart pound. Anxiety wove itself into the fabric of my being, a weight on my chest and a knot in my stomach.

But it could not get any worse than this.

With a clip, the seatbelt unbuckled and let me free. Gathering my courage with both hands, I stood up on my seat. The city fell away below me. With a deep breath, I put my foot on the edge and jumped into the nothingness below.

This time it was calculated. Planned. I landed on the hood of a car, a stabbing pain running up my legs as I crashed. My knees trembled as I stood back up, balancing above the canyon of the highway. Then I was jumping again, throwing myself into the void—not thinking, only doing—and landed on the hood of a blue convertible. The people at the wheel didn't flinch when I forced myself back onto my feet. They seemed unaware that I had just used their car as a landing spot or that I had dented their hood. I detached myself from my mind, leaving just the mechanical self, free to ignore the part of myself that was crying and screaming.

A thud followed, loud and resonating. I imagined my falling on the cars wasn't silent either, but the roar of air in my ears made me oblivious to the sound of my own landing. Only one thud followed me. Where was the other?

I looked down and threw myself off again. I was getting good at this, but cockiness would probably kill me because the second I put my foot on that roof, I felt my balance give out. My heart skipped as I tumbled forward. There was no time to catch my breath as I fell without calculating my next move.

I saw the next car race toward me. I tried to move my feet so I could land right, but I knew I would miss it. I had no time to gauge my approach or to prepare my landing. I was going to fall.

ALIENATION

And I was right.

I hit the car hands first, feeling pain crushing my bones as I body-slammed the hood. My arms flailed as I slid toward the highway. I grasped for something, anything, to stop me.

Something hard grabbed my arm, but my momentum was taking over and I slid off the car entirely. I clutched something sharp and metal, but it wasn't enough. My hands hurt; oh, they hurt so much. My shoulders strained as they took the weight of my body. My feet dangled, useless, over the chasm below.

I probably wouldn't survive the drop this time.

I knew I wouldn't.

If I screamed now, there was no telling if it would alert the ICP to my presence. No telling if the people in the convertible above would wake up to shake me off. I stifled a sob as I felt my hands slipping.

A hand wrapped around my elbow and grabbed tight. My legs struggled for a foothold, but the person was strong and hoisted me like I were a large bag of feathers. I slid on the hood, panting, looking up at my savior, the beautiful woman with fire in her eyes.

I opened my mouth to thank her, but she was already gone, leaping off the car onto one below. She flew over the void. I inhaled, exhaled, wiping the tears of pain from the corners of my eyes.

"You all right?" Zander appeared next to me, extending a hand. Ah, thudless. He was jumping. Blayde was the one leaping. Relief washed over me as I realized

I wouldn't have to do that again. Relief, and shame, as I wondered why I had thrown myself out of the car without talking to them first. Zander and Blayde knew what they were doing.

I nodded, and I grabbed his hand. A second later we stood on another car then another, changing settings so quickly and seamlessly that it felt like the world was flicking channels around me. From one car to the next, we made our way down, lower and lower and lower, until it wasn't a car under my feet anymore but a thick slab of stone.

Blayde followed, physically leaping from car to car, every step graceful like the entire challenge was effortless. She could have jumped, that much was evident, but in that moment, as she dropped hundreds of meters bit by bit, she looked alive, her face brighter than the city. Seconds later, she was on the ledge beside us, landing cat-like on the stone, staring at the entrance to the shopping strip.

"Thank you," I said, but it was useless. She wasn't listening—to me or to anyone. She was a woman with focus and determination in her eyes, one that would not be distracted by anyone or anything. She strode away, raising a hand to indicate that we should follow, and the three of us marched through the shopping center surrounded by people possessed by an evil AI.

This dream was getting weirder.

"They're not attacking," I whispered to Zander, simultaneously shocked and relieved that they had not stepped toward us—yet. He didn't answer, putting a finger to his lips. Did he think silence would stop them from noticing our presence?

This technique was working well enough; nobody paid any attention to us as we walked by quickly and quietly. They didn't even look in our direction, simply meandered around as if a computer had use of their motor functions, poorly programmed RPCs. One particularly large man repeatedly walked into one of the windows on the street, grunting loudly as his head collided with glass, again and again.

"Gods! What's going on?"

A woman stepped outside of a store, glancing up and down the street in terror. Instantly, every eye was on her. The people closest pounced within seconds. I made a move toward her, but Blayde threw a hand out. "No," she whispered. "We can't draw attention to ourselves."

"But she's going to get hurt. The ICP could kill her."

"No, look."

The people held her down, but they weren't harming her. Instead, they stuffed pizzas in her face as she cried, choked, and finally swallowed.

Blayde shoved me forward. We couldn't stay and help. There was nothing we could do. We had to move on and save them all rather than give up our advantage for just one. And being force-fed pizzas was probably better than other alternatives.

The plaza loomed before us, the tower standing tall scraping the edge of space with its antenna fingers. The fountain glowed an eerie orange as the lights that lit it flickered off and on, casting dark shadows into its deep interior.

"We can jump from here, can't we?" I said. "To the other side of the plaza, and—" Zander nodded silently. "Do we, though?" Another nod. He held out his hand again, his eyes fixed on the empty pavilion in front of the elevators.

I took it, but before we could go, I felt the wind draw out of me. Within seconds, I was on the ground, my duffel bag crashing to the side with a harsh thud out of reach. Zander and Blayde were gone, probably already at the tower, but I was alone and pinned to the ground. A ravenous robot woman had wrapped her hands around my neck, squeezing.

The air thinned immediately. I struggled to push her away, but I was getting weaker too fast. My grabbing became more frantic yet less effective as the air was cut off from my lungs. I scratched at her face, but she felt nothing. An empty look glazed her eyes, like she were a porcelain doll strangling me. A porcelain doll with an iron grip.

I reached into my pocket, pulling out the small metal device belonging to Blayde. With the last of my energy, I pressed it against the woman's stomach and squeezed the button.

With a shudder, the hands at my neck loosened. The possessed woman fell over, frozen. A hole cut her stomach clean, and I could see right through her. My eyes fell on a mix of blood and metal pooled around the hole that had once been her stomach.

I sat up, gasping for air. I was alive. She hadn't killed me, but had I killed her?

Was I a murderer now?

This couldn't be happening.

I jumped to my feet, the other shoppers turned to gaze at me with empty stares. They could see me, and they were coming for me. The ICP must have reached a better antenna because the possessed were getting faster and better coordinated than the soldiers on the roof.

Maybe it was their proximity to their leader's consciousness, but they seemed more vicious, a glint of a killer's light in their dead eyes. I turned to run, the only thing I could think of doing, picking my bag off the ground and swinging it over my shoulder as I sprinted for the pavilion.

My heart did a double-take as I turned around the fountain. Hundreds of possessed shoppers were moving my way, half standing guard, half closing in, all their eyes riveted on me. Running out of places to hide, I turned and did the first thing that came to mind. I jumped into the fountain.

It was surprisingly deep. I made my way to the centerpiece of the monument, swimming the length of an Olympic pool to get to the middle, which in itself had the diameter of a small island. The base was wide enough that I couldn't see where it ended.

I crawled up the shore, my Chucks now soaking wet and heavy with water. But I felt safe here in the forest of marble trees, water separating me from the possessed. I breathed hard, relieved and grateful the crowd was only armed with their most recent purchases.

My heart sank when the first man put a foot in the water, followed by his other leg, falling face-first into the pool. Soon, he was back up, swimming like any human would do, not the least affected by water, a robot's worst enemy.

I had to get out of here.

I ran deep into the forest, trying not to slip on the marble. The artist hadn't skimped on detail; the trees were so realistic I could have sworn the leaves rustled as I passed. My wet feet slid over the smooth surface, but I did not fall. The canopy of carved leaves was thick enough for me to get a good grip.

I heard the of the first man setting foot on the centerpiece. I ran faster, the light dimming this far underneath the treetops. City light entered the thicket through panels that had been removed between this tier and the one above, but there weren't many of those. Orange dappled the dark trees, making the place look like an eerie, burning forest. But I had experienced pure darkness before. It did not scare me anymore.

More thuds. They were closing in. *That* was the part that scared me. They could swim, they could run.

But could they climb?

I pulled myself up the nearest tree, my soaking clothes dragging me down and leaving a visible trail for my pursuers to follow. For now, all I could do was put some distance between us. I reached for the next branch, pulling myself higher through the carved treetop, my arms burning as I climbed. Unfortunately, the leaves didn't push away, being made of marble; they were stuck, an extra obstacle for me to clamber around. The artist had left himself a way of crawling between tiers—something I was thankful for beyond anything else.

I reached the edge of the tier, the point where roots and branches melded. I pulled myself through a breach in the marble, crawling through what I hoped was a tunnel. It was like spelunking back on Earth, only it wasn't muddy. The trees and roots wouldn't move out the way. I squeezed through the last few meters of marble, and I was out. I had reached the second tier.

I was a good three stories high. I didn't want to look down, already aware that I was high enough. Nothing compared to the highway, but it was worse when you were being chased by a herd of semi-mechanical aliens. I leaned against the trunk of a nearby tree, catching my breath.

Only … eight more tiers to go? I wasn't sure. I hadn't counted. I didn't know what would happen when I reached the top, but I had to keep moving.

Did I hear feet behind me? Movement? I had to climb faster.

I was out of breath in minutes. It was a difficult climb, the trees slippery, and I was slowing down. I was tired, hurting, and out of shape on top of it all. It's not like I worked out to prepare for this trip.

This was supposed to be a vacation.

I hoisted myself through the trees. My shoulders smarted, but I had to ignore them if I wanted to live. I was breathing heavily now, the only sound in my ears the air rushing in and out of my lungs.

After an eternity of climbing, I reached the top, the strange, winged beast on its perch impolitely refusing to share his spot on the pedestal. But what I saw from my vantage point was enough to give anyone a heart attack.

I felt like I was on the top of an anthill, looking down on the mound, which was swarmed by the possessed. They were climbing toward me, faster and faster, a whole army on the hill. I couldn't go any higher.

My pursuer poked his head out of the tier underneath, making his way over the canopy of trees to where I stood. I gripped the laser pointer, trying to think of any way to get out of this without harming anyone else. I thought of the woman I had shot, killed maybe. What would I do to protect myself? How far would I go to survive?

As I thought this, the other possessed shoppers came closer. I had a decision to make, but there wasn't much to decide. I had climbed into a corner, and there was nowhere left to run.

TWENTY-FOUR
YOU'D THINK AT THIS POINT I'D CATCH A BREAK

THE POSSESSED WERE GETTING CLOSER. IN terror, I climbed on top of the griffon statue—was it even a griffon? I wasn't paying all that much attention. I had to put as much distance as I could between me and them. But I couldn't get much higher than that.

The griffon turned its mighty head around and glared at me. Well, I say glared. There wasn't much room for movement in that bronze face of his. I stifled a scream, scrambling to get off its back, but the possessed were coming closer and there was no way out.

The mechanical griffon stretched its wings and began to beat them, slowly but surely, until we began to rise through the air.

This time, I couldn't hold back the scream. Not that you could hear it with the roar of its wings beating the air around me. I realized then that the ICP had taken control. How, I did not know. There were no wires or antennas, but it was carrying me and I was at its mercy.

I had seen enough Discovery Channel specials to have a good idea of what was about to happen. It would carry me up and drop me, letting the ground do its dirty work.

If this really was a dream, then a fall would save me. I would wake up before I reached the ground. But I wasn't dreaming, I couldn't be. I could not bring myself to imagine this kind of horror.

The griffon flapped its wings harder and we gained altitude. And we were gaining it fast. How could this thing even fly? I made the mistake of looking down and was shocked to see the fountain shrinking below us. We weren't even close to the top of Da-Duhui Tower.

Blayde and Zander had to be at the top. Had to be. The possessed were climbing the sides of the building like it was a child's playground. The ones below looked like insects now, like the ground didn't exist anymore.

They turned their heads as the griffon climbed higher. Still, they showed no expression, but they were moving smoother, like the ICP had gained stronger control over them. We were running out of time.

Then, just to make my day even worse, one of them jumped.

She leapt at me, arms outstretched like a furious cat. She grabbed my leg. The added weight shifted the griffon's flight, and it let out a weird mechanical screech. Shit, the ICP was giving itself opposing orders. We dropped a few feet, my stomach jolting, and I clutched the griffon tighter.

"Get off!" I shouted, shaking my leg as hard as I could. Not surprisingly, at this point, she didn't listen.

She dug in harder. I hissed, the pain becoming intolerable. I squeezed my legs for support, reached down, and punched her in the head. Nothing.

I struggled to get my balance on the griffon, clambering wildly to get back up on my ride, feeling her dig deeper into my skin, and the tears flowed once more. The woman's nails broke my skin, and blood dripped onto her nails.

Terror ran through my veins, raising the hair on my arms and neck. My hands trembled, and I shoved them against the griffon's neck, stopping them from shaking and helping me regain balance.

It was something. But I couldn't hold on forever.

I raised my throbbing leg and slammed it against the bronze. Boom. The woman's head must have been jumbled enough for a second that she let go, and she plummeted toward the ground. No one watched her fall but me, and I knew I had just signed her death warrant.

My eyes closed, even though I couldn't see her hit the ground. But I knew. I knew. I even told myself I could hear her bones crunching as they met the plaza face-first.

When I opened them again, Da-Duhui Tower was long gone. We were climbing over the city now. I saw the tops of the buildings like one smooth expanse of bright orange land. I could see the palace from here, the disco lighting on the lawn still flickering. I wondered if the people in their floating bubbles would be all right. I wondered if any of us would.

I clutched the griffin tighter. It could drop me any minute now, and it gave no care for my safety. If I fell, I fell, and its job was done. I wouldn't give the ICP the satisfaction.

It jolted, trying to buck me off its back like a rodeo bull, jerking in every direction. I wrapped my arms around its neck and squeezed. It wasn't as if it needed to breathe; it was a robot. It screeched and swooped as I pinched my knees around its bronze body, my ass burning like I had sat on a fire.

It flew higher, and the air was getting thinner. There was a light above me. And another and another. I realized we were flying through the thickest layer of smog above the city then they were there: the stars.

An alien sky.

All I ever wanted to see in my life was right there above me. A sky with constellations I couldn't possibly imagine. Stars I could see back home yet were totally different. A sky no one from my planet had ever seen. Tears stung my eyes, but something else was fueling them, something different from the anger and pain.

Joy.

I had lived a life on my own planet, the pale blue dot, insignificant and grounded. I lived with astrolust in my veins but no way to satiate it. I dreamed of alien skies

ALIENATION

and alien planets in a world that wasn't ready to leave its solar system.

And here I was, fighting for my life above a city which had never even heard of my home.

I realized then that my life was complete in a way. I had accomplished the one thing I truly wanted I never thought would be possible. It was as if a genie had granted one impossible wish, and now I could die happy.

Everything else was bonus.

But I wasn't about to skimp on that.

As the griffon reached the end of the ICP's reach and turned into a sharp dive, I tightened my knees and arms, and leaned into the fall. I closed my eyes against the rush of the wind and flew, soaring through the smog toward the city of Da-Duhui.

I forced my eyes open and kicked my heels, forcing the creature to spread its wings. They caught the air and we swooped forward, falling past the antennas of the tower. In a split-second, I made up my mind and reached for them.

The collision was like hitting a cement post, emptying my lungs in one quick blow. I tried to regain my breath as I slid down a pole, watching the griffon crash into one of the buildings from afar. Glad I jumped when I did.

I slid like a fireman down the pole, but the friction burned my arms and made me want to let go. I held on tighter. The second my legs touched solid ground, I fell

S.E.ANDERSON

to my knees. I was on top of the tower, higher than we had been before, on a ledge with the antennas and wires that controlled the city's broadcasting.

Below me on the observation deck, Zander and Blayde were fighting.

I saw then why the griffon had become less agile. The ICP had been siphoning its control into the possessed version of Sonota, suddenly more fluid in his motion and able than his original blundering self. He was fighting the siblings, the glowing metal rod that was the ICP's brain balanced precariously on the wall beside some large interface. He seemed able to predict where his attackers would strike next, spinning at the last second to deflect their blows.

It was amazing to see Zander and Blayde working together. Their moves perfectly coordinated, their minds working in sync as they waged war on the robot mind in human form. They used a mix between any and every martial art move I knew, and some I had never seen before, combining their punching and jumping abilities.

They switched places in a single jump, disorienting their opponent. Blayde attacked with a powerful jump kick while Zander simultaneously dropped to the floor, swinging his leg around to destabilize Sonota. Yet the ICP was learning just as quickly, predicting their attacks. As fast as they tried a new sequence, it would leap, deflecting the highest blow, his joints twisting in impossible ways that would probably have killed the real human.

ALIENATION

Sonota was possessed, and felt none of the blows inflicted upon him. The siblings were immortal, and felt nothing as he tried to fight back. What looked incredibly painful from up here were slight annoyances to the parties involved, and it was difficult to set any of them off-balance.

I crouched, one hand clutching an antenna for support, mesmerized by the dance below. Yet the only thing the siblings had accomplished was to slow the robot down. The annoyance on Blayde's face was apparent, though Zander's was a mask of concentration as they continued their perfected movements without a lapse in the choreography.

"Blayde!" I yelled.

She turned quickly, not wanting to miss her beat. I launched her laser pointer in the air, my aim, luckily, perfect. She leaped, swinging both legs in a pinwheel against where Sonota's head should have been, her arm vertical to reach for her weapon of choice.

She landed, jumping behind the man's back, Zander adjusting his moves to compliment hers. He changed his attack from offense to distraction and launched himself straight up, his legs and arms moving slower than before. I almost cried when Sonota grab Zander's foot in midair, twisting it around …

Only for Sonota to be struck down by the hot red laser.

Sonota fell to his knees, crumpling forward. There was no blood or sign of any injury, yet there he was, lying on his face. The strange tube Sonota had stolen from the ICP fell from the wall, rolling across the deck. Round and round and round, useless without any connection.

Blayde helped Zander off the ground, brushing him off tenderly. He nodded at something she said, smiling at her.

"You okay up there, Sally?" he asked.

He didn't need to yell that loud. The city was silent, the sounds of the highway indistinct. The once-possessed picked themselves up from the pavement, and some screeched at finding themselves clinging to the side of a building.

"I'm fine. Can you help me down?"

It was over.

"Security Protocol 001," came a mechanical voice out of nowhere. The rod flickered green. "This mayoral property has been outside of its authorization limit for thirty minutes. Self-destruct in 3, 2—"

"Sally, jump!"

Without thinking, I leaped off the building, arms outstretched, the voice looming in the background.

"1,0. Detonation." I grabbed Zander's hand as the thing blew. It was powerful for such a small device. The shock wave hit just as I tightened my grasp. With a sudden tug, I felt myself lurch away, dissolving into millions of fragments.

It was dark, impossible to see, but I felt nothing and everything simultaneously—the emptiness surrounded

ALIENATION

me, the numbness devoured me. I felt gone, like nothing, and cold. I felt myself traveling fast, yet I was still in one place. I was me, I was all, I was a void.

Empty, safe. No trouble. Nothing.

Suddenly I felt my hands again, my legs, the blood pumping through my veins. I could feel it all, real sensations, not dulled senses. My eyes flew open, the light strange on my eyes like they had been closed for a long time and had been forced open by a crowbar.

I toppled over, unable to keep my balance. My face sunk into the cold surface it collided with, freezing my face. Snow?

Gentle arms lifted me up. "She didn't pass out this time," Zander noted.

"Good."

"She will, won't she?" he said.

"What do you mean?" I asked, struggling so he would put me down. I made it a show of standing up straight, my legs shaky but supporting me. "I'm fine." I looked around, my eyes scanning the horizon. Snow as far as I could see. After so much dark, the white was blinding. "Are we in Antarctica? Or in Russia somewhere? You guys are a bit off target, aren't you?" I turned around, surprised to see a manhole in the ice untouched by snow. A perfectly normal manhole in sharp contrast with the white expanse of land.

"Manhole?" I asked childishly.

"Sally. We need to talk."

"I know."

"You do?"

I fell to the ground, trying to catch my breath. The snow seeped through my jeans, making my butt cold and wet, but I was too tired to care. Plus, it was soothing in a way. I breathed in the fresh air.

"We stopped the ICP." I reached to feel my head. "Woah."

"Yeah." He crouched in front of me. "We did it, all thanks to you."

"Don't patronize me, Zander," I snapped. "This was all for nothing. We did nothing. The Theosians and the Downdwellers are still stuck, the mob is still doing its thing, and the mayor is still having galas while everyone below him is struggling to get by. I have no idea if Sekai is okay. I think I killed someone—two people. Maybe even more. Innocent people. My hands."

I lifted them up in front of my face. They were shaking. The dried tears on my face were freezing fast in the cold.

"You know"—Zander reached up to take my hands in his, clasping warm skin around them as a shield— "you told me your mission was to take out the robots so the Downdwellers could have a small place in society. Am I right?"

"Yeah, but that wasn't going to work. And the mob never intended for it to do anything, either. It was all for money. And in the end, it was all part of what the ICP had been planning."

"Yeah, but we stopped the ICP," he said, squeezing my hands tighter. "And we ended up getting rid of all the robots in the process. Now everyone can go back to normal. You did good today, Sally, but that's not what I want to talk about."

"Is it the fact we're a bit far from my house?" I said, my teeth chattering now. "We're gonna have to walk for a bit—in the cold."

I was not looking forward to standing in the freezing weather in my t-shirt. My wet t-shirt. And my wet shoes. And my sore ass and bruised skin.

"Where exactly are we?" I asked, "Russia? Alaska? The North Pole?"

"Sally, listen." Something in his tone told me this was no joke. Far from it. He clutched my hands to stop them from shivering. Blayde had backed away, looking off into the white wilderness, silent.

"What?" I asked, suddenly very worried.

"I've failed you on so many counts," he said. "I promised to keep you safe, and I lost you. I promised to protect you, and you ended up fighting a killer AI. And now, Sally, I don't think we'll be able to walk back to your home."

"Get to the point, Zander."

"We're not just a continent away from your house. We're a few solar systems off."

"What?" I asked, fear rising.

"I didn't have time to jump back to Earth. Finding the coordinates takes time, and with the explosion imminent … We missed Earth, Sally."

"But you can take me back, right? One planet out of the way shouldn't be too much of a problem."

He shook his head. "It's impossible to find a planet after jumping away twice. I explained that at our first encounter, remember? When I jump from point A to point B, I can either go back to A or on to C. But when I reach C, it's D or B. Understand?" He paused. "I jumped from Earth to Da-Duhui. But now we're here, and I don't have the coordinates for your planet."

"But … the Killians. You used their thoughts to take them home, right?"

"They're empaths. It's like I lent them the car, but they did the driving. Humans don't have that sense."

"So, you're saying …?"

"I can't ever bring you back, Sally. I'm sorry. I can't sense Earth. I can't find it. I lost the way home."

TWENTY-FIVE
WELL, THIS SUCKS

WHEN YOU FIND A MANHOLE IN THE MIDDLE OF an icy nowhere, chances are you might have stumbled upon an exclusive five-star hotel that's looking for clients.

Poor advertising made the hotel hit a slump, and the slump had made the advertising even poorer. When we showed up, climbing through their back entrance and shivering with the cold—well, I was the one doing the shivering; Zander and Blayde seemed comfortable—the first thing the staff did was ask if the royal suite would be enough. All free of charge if we could write them a review on the Alliance's version of Yelp.

I think it was called "Shouting and Screaming," but the translation was a little hard to understand. Plus, I didn't really care.

Which is how I ended up clean and bandaged on a plush bed larger than my living room. The window looked out upon the underwater glory of this icy world. Fish in thousands of different colors swam outside, some pushing the boundaries of what you might call "fish." Two large squid-like creatures swam up to my window and stared in at me, their eight large, purple eyes wide.

"What kind of creature is that?" one of the squids asked the other. I pretended not to notice them.

"I do not know," the other replied, "but it's so … colorful. It's not doing anything though. Come on, honey, it's a little boring."

I was too tired to even wonder what the hell that had been. I arranged my pillows—I had more than I could count—into a comfy nest and let myself fall back against them. I wanted to sleep, but my head was swimming too fast for me to relax.

There was a knock on my door. I didn't want to see anyone, not unless it was Marcy. I certainly didn't want to see *their* faces.

"Sally, come on," Zander pleaded. "You're going to have to let me in eventually."

"It's not locked," I said, my voice low. Somehow, he heard me, and peeked his head around the door. "But that doesn't mean I'm going to listen to anything you say. It just means I'm too lazy to get up and figure out how to lock it."

Zander said nothing. He let himself in and closed the door behind him, all quiet and gentle. I turned away, gazing out the window again. The squids were gone now, but a fish that looked like Elvis gave me a glare. I turned away.

"I owe you an explanation," said Zander. I felt him sit on the end of the bed. "We haven't been totally truthful with you."

"Sorry about that," said a female voice.

Blayde was here too? Dammit. But then again, I had a feeling Blayde had been more truthful with me than Zander ever had. She barely spoke to me, but when she did, she was so candid it usually hurt.

"We haven't told you the whole story," she said, "and Zander and I have talked, and we think you have a right to know."

"Oh, you do, do you?" I snapped. I sat up in the bed, which was not a smart idea. Every muscle in my body screamed its hatred of me. Recovery would be a bitch.

"Yeah, we do."

"Like why the hell you think you can police the universe?" I spat. "Or maybe why you can't stinking die? It's been two years since I watched the two of you get shot, and still—*still*—I have no idea what's going on. I never signed up for this. I wouldn't have agreed to come if you had told me the truth."

"We'll answer everything," Zander said.

Looking at the two of them sitting on the end of my bed and watching me with pitiful eyes, they looked like parents about to tell their child the dog was dead or that they were getting a divorce.

Either one of those would feel better right now.

"Then start with who you are—who you *really* are."

Zander sighed, looking at Blayde for support. She shook her head.

"We don't know," she said.

"The frick? I thought you said you were going to be honest with me. How can you not know who you are?"

"Listen, kid," Blayde said, her face twisting into something demonic before a touch from Zander brought her back. "We really don't know. We probably did, at one point, but not anymore. Perks of being immortal? You live a long time. A really long time. Neither of us have any idea how we started out. We forget memories every day."

"No family," Zander added. "No home planet. No home. At all. Were we born the way we are? Were we created? If so, by whom? The point is: We don't even know where we got our names from. We simply exist, but we're trying to find out."

"And how do you do that?"

"The journal."

"The journal," Blayde agreed, pulling the small red book from inside her breast pocket. All those months it had been in my house, and I had never once opened it. "I've had it for as long as I can remember. Longer, actually. But it doesn't document our beginnings. We're hoping some of the older entries can bring us closer to the truth, but so far, we haven't had much luck."

"Not when we have to travel blind in the first place, and every jump can put years between us and our last planet. We don't even know if our homeworld is still there."

"And the other Zander and Blayde? The criminals the Alliance seems to hate? And the myths? Are they related to you?"

"Pretty sure they are," Blayde muttered.

"The Alliance and us have an … on again off again relationship," Zander explained. "We helped them out when they were just forming. Fought in a few wars with them, or for them. Then they started to forget about us. Recently—and by recently, I mean a few centuries ago—they accused us of trying to take them down or something. You know how it is. We've been their scapegoats for a while. That's why we try not to get on their radar. They'll probably pin the ICP incident on us."

"Seriously? You two have been around the block a few times."

"That's an understatement." Zander chuckled.

I leaned forward. I was mad, fuming even. But they were answering my questions for once. And boy, the questions had been piling up. I crossed my arms over my chest.

"Are you two, um, space vampires?"

"Come again?" said Zander. Blayde laughed as Zander continued to look confused and a little dejected.

"Vampires. From space. Are you two vampires?"

"What makes you ask that?"

"You know, immortal. Super-fast. Strong. And no pulse, right? You guys are smart. Scary."

"We don't drink blood, Sally," said Zander. "And you've seen me eat garlic bread so many times."

"Are you forgetting the fact that we've walked around in sunlight together, too?" Blayde scoffed. "But, hey, maybe the stories come from somewhere, right?"

"Maybe." Zander shrugged.

"And I'm not so sure about the intelligence thing, not for Zander anyway."

"Oy!"

"In any case, Sally," said Blayde, "there's a lot we have no answers to. Like how we don't age, but our hair still grows and our nails have shit upkeep. Or the limits to our jumping. We don't have all the answers, but from now on, we are fully transparent with you. If we don't give you an answer, it's because we don't have one."

"So you're just … lost," I said. "You're looking for your home."

"But we try to help out the universe where we can along the way," said Zander. "We picked up some skills over the years. We try to keep balance when we can, since we can."

"Is it like that everywhere you go?" I shuddered. "Earth. Da-Duhui. Always going to shit."

"Not everywhere," Blayde replied. "Sometimes things are calm. Nice. Beautiful. Sometimes we come to planets where no one has been before. We stand and look at views no one will ever see. Being immortal has its perks. That and never having to worry about parking."

ALIENATION

No one said anything for a little while. I stared at my toes, which were different shades of blue. There wasn't much of my skin that was my usual color anymore. Zander stared too, and I curled my toes away, slipping them under a pillow.

"All this tension is making me thirsty," Blayde said. "I'm going to the bar. You two are free to join me."

She disappeared, and I shook my head. I was tired of all this weirdness. All I wanted was to go home and have some normalcy. Netflix and pizza would be enough.

No. Not pizza. Not for a long time. Netflix and some ice cream would be best.

"Do you want to go for a walk?" Zander offered.

"Where?"

"Anywhere." He smiled, extending a hand. "The hotel is huge, and no one is here but us. Let's go to the observation deck."

Walking sucked, but it was the right decision. I needed to stretch my legs if I wanted to walk normally again. I wrapped a hand around his arm for stability and shuffled out of the suite wearing my fluffy robe from the spa and slippers that felt like a cloud.

The observation deck was empty, as expected. It was just a large room with a huge window overlooking an underwater rock formation with alien algae and coral growing in all the colors of the rainbow. Fishlike creatures swam around, all with more eyes than the spiders back home. I didn't realize my hands and face were against the glass until I felt my nose squashing and pulled it back.

"It's beautiful," I said, quietly to myself.

"Harold." The squid thing from earlier swam to her companion. "That creature is hitting on me."

"I don't think it is, darling," he said. "They're not intelligent enough to attempt language. Oh, a male!"

The squid swam closer, eager to take us in. They looked happy that we were here.

"Hey, you two, do something!" the first one said, tapping on the glass with a tentacle. It had a sharp, silvery tip, like a talon. It made a sharp rasp when he knocked it against the window.

"Mate! Mate! Mate!" the one called Harold cheered. I stepped back, my hands trembling. I felt my mouth go open in shock and pushed my jaw shut.

"We're trying to have a serious conversation here." Zander glared at them, a look that made them recoil. "Don't make me come out there."

"Shit," Harold swam away. "Now that was unsettling."

"He said it," I agreed, keeping up the whole passive-aggressive attitude to piss Zander off. "What the hell was that?"

"Oh, the hotel is a zoo. Don't look shocked; it works out great for everyone. People get a beautiful hotel at an inexpensive rate. Locals get a piece of the universe and can see a whole slew of different races. It works out for fetishes on both sides."

ALIENATION

"Gross," I said.

"It's a big universe, Sally." He gave me a sly smirk. "People are into a whole lot of things. You want to sit down?"

He said this casually, like we were talking about the weather. Like I wasn't mad at him for getting me lost in that very big universe of his. The room had a few white couches scattered about along with a bar against the back wall that didn't have anyone working it. We were alone.

Except maybe for the fish.

"And we can understand them?"

"The translator chip I got you is top-of-the-line," he said. "It works off brainwaves rather than a saved repertoire of different words. Lets you understand languages even from races the creators of the chip hadn't even heard of. You can pretty much understand anyone in the universe, even some very smart cows."

"Cows?" I scoffed. "Seriously? I talked to a few cats and dogs during our hiatus. Didn't understand them and they didn't understand me."

"Cats and cows are not on the same level."

We sat there together for a little while, watching the fish swim by. They avoided us now, like Zander and I were scaring them away. Or maybe it was just him.

"You lied to me about Matt," he said calmly, breaking the silence.

"You lied to me about a lot of things."

S.E.ANDERSON

"I had a reason. Why did you?" He was sad, I realized. Actually sad. "Matt was my friend too."

I watched a courageous little fish swim up to the window, tap it with a fin and turn around, swimming back. His entire rear looked exactly like his front, twelve eyes and all. "I didn't want to burden you. I wanted you to be happy. I didn't want his death hanging over us."

"He was my friend, though."

"If it makes you feel better, he thought you were trying to sleep with me and was weirdly jealous about our relationship. I don't think he was your friend."

"Why would that make me feel any better?"

"I don't know." I looked away from the fish and down at my white slippers. "His death really hurt. You leaving hurt. I didn't think you'd come back, and I was about ready to give up."

"I made a promise, didn't I?"

"You promised a lot of things. You said you would keep me safe. You said you would bring me home. You said we were only doing recon, and then you blew up my office."

"I'm sorry," he said, his voice low, almost a whisper.

"Matt was a good man," I said, "and now he's dead. I lost a relationship. I lost a future."

"No, you didn't. You two would never have lasted. You said it yourself. He was possessive and controlling. It wasn't healthy. Death has that strange way of ironing out the wrinkles, doesn't it? Suddenly only the good

355

remains, all the bumps in the relationship smoothed out."

"Matt was a good man," I snapped.

"He was, but you can't stay stuck in this idea that everything would have been perfect if he survived. Matt was a vainglorious control freak, and he only turned out to be a semi-decent human being at the end. That kind of regret will only fester. Trust me."

"Trust you? Trust *you?* After everything you put me through? Nice day out, my ass."

"I'm sorry. I'm just…."

He was sputtering, at a loss for words. Glaring at him probably wasn't helping. He paused for a long time, staring anywhere but at me. This tall, confident man who had just saved the Alliance from a robot uprising was now sitting, mortified, by me.

"I'm so sorry, Sally." His voice barely over a whisper. "I was so scared. Seeing you like that, after I promised to keep you safe, to give you a nice night. I panicked, and I never panic. I panicked and I dropped you. I failed you."

And it went silent again.

I fingered the pendant on the cord around my neck, the tiny jar of bright light that lived on my chest. Was Tam all right? Martha? Kun? Was last night a victory or a defeat for them? Would anything get better?

Or had I made things worse?

All my life, I had lived with this hole in my chest. An emptiness I called astrolust, a desperate need to go up there, into space, into the universe. Then maybe I would feel complete.

But now I was here, and the more space I was shoving into my chest, the more was spilling right back out. I felt as empty now as I did before I left Earth.

Space wasn't making me whole. Maybe nothing ever would.

"What's going to happen to me?" I asked, not lifting my eyes from the floor. "Am I staying here?"

"No way. I made promises to keep you safe and to get you home. I broke one of them. I don't intend to break the other. Blayde and I have had a talk. You're coming with us."

"With you? Where?"

"We're going to find Earth," he said, smiling reassuringly. "We're going to jump, we're going to ride ships, we're going to hitchhike and find our way right back there. It might take a while. And it might be dangerous. But I'm never letting you down again."

He looked at me with more intensity than I had ever seen in a man's face before. His eyes burned with a focus that didn't seem human.

"Until we find Earth, you're one of us." Blayde popped up with a bottle of something bright green in hand. "Here, this might take the edge off."

"Not sure if I want to try any alien liquors, Blayde."

She pulled a glass out and put it on the little coffee table in front of me. A second later, it was in my hand with a finger of green in it. "You'll have to get used to it because the closest Earth cocktail is probably a few hundred light-years away."

"Damn," I said. We drank the liquid together. To my surprise, it was sweet rather than hot, and I worried about the ease with which it went down.

"I can't promise we're going to make it back in good time," Zander said. "You know that time runs differently when we jump. It's possible it's already too late to get you back home to your family, but we will get you back to Earth."

"I saw Sekai at the party, one of the Killians we saved. She said five years have gone by. Maybe it's already been three years back home. Danny and Marcy will be married now. They've probably given up on finding me by now."

"Don't think worst-case scenario," he said. "Think survival. Focus on the here and now. Those are problems we can deal when we get there."

"It's going to be hard." Blayde put down her glass. "We're going to stick up for you, but we can't always be there. We've never had anyone tag along for so long before. You're smart, I'll give you that. Brilliant, even, seeing how you dealt with everything back there. You didn't scream once—at least, I didn't hear you scream. You were quick on your feet. But this isn't a dream, a movie, or a video game. However crazy the universe is, it's real. And you have to be ready for that. Are you?"

I looked at myself. My leg was scratched open, though wrapped in a nice clean bandage. I had seen things I'd never imagined: aliens, robots. I fell down a highway, I was hired by the mafia, I crashed a party, I was held hostage, I fought off a herd of possessed robot people, and I had ridden a flying statue. Crazy, all right. Absolutely absurd.

"Oh, I'm ready." I smiled, falling back on the couch. "Do you know that since I met you two, I've had to say 'Please tell me your plans before you kill me' three times?" I closed my eyes, suddenly tired and wishing I were back in my bed on Earth. The only way I could get home was to go with them, even though that probably meant racing through hundreds of more terrifying planets before they found mine.

Until then, I sure hoped there was some half-decent pizza out there that wouldn't try to kill me.

SALLY'S ADVENTURE CONTINUES IN

TRAVELER

ACKNOWLEDGEMENTS

WOW, BOOK TWO, AND TWICE THE AMOUNT OF people to thank for getting the Starstruck Saga this far! How can I start anywhere else but with my fabulous editor: Michelle, you've believed in Starstruck since the very beginning, and you keep pushing me to put my best on the page. I could not have done it without you – period. Alienation would be a little draft sitting on my hard drive with the rest of my abandoned projects. Thank you for everything.

I also have to thank the amazing editing team for making this book a reality: thank you Anna for convincing me to make those rewrites, and Cayleigh for making it perfect.

And of course, a massive thank you to my Beta readers! Brianna, Keri and KarenJo, your honest opinion was invaluable.

To my parents, who put up with all the bad language, and a whole lot more from me, thank you. Your support means everything. And to the rest of my family, thank you so much for sticking by my side!

To Hugo, for always letting me bounce ideas off you, and offering up some pretty killer ideas. For allowing me to freak out from time to time, and encouraging me non stop.

To Madeline, for being the most amazing writing buddy and beta reader. You're an incredible friend who pushes me to be a better writer!

Thank you so much Ronnie, Jeff, and Andrew for the immeasurable support! You guys are too cool. It's so much fun being your fan and your friend.

And to Cora, for making me feel like a bestselling author every day!

And finally, to Joanna. Always to Joanna. Thank you.

ABOUT THE AUTHOR

SARAH ANDERSON CAN'T EVER TELL YOU WHERE she's from. Not because she doesn't want to, but because it inevitably leads to a confusing conversation about where she was born (England) where she grew up (France) and where her family is from (USA) and it tends to make things very complicated.

She's lived her entire life in the South of France, except for a brief stint where she moved to Washington DC, or the eighty years she spent as a queen of Narnia before coming back home five minutes after she had left. Currently, she is working on her PhD in Astrophysics and Planetary sciences in Besançon, France.

When she's not writing - or trying to do science - she's either reading, designing, crafting, or attempting to speak with various woodland creatures in an attempt to get them to do household chores for her. She could also be gaming, or pretending she's not watching anything on Netflix.

CONNECT WITH THE AUTHOR

www.seandersonauthor.com
facebook.com/seandersonauthor
instagram.com/readcommendations
twitter.com/sea_author

Printed in Great Britain
by Amazon

59416247R00212